UNEXPECTED
STORM

Dedication

This book is dedicated to my new friends at the Clockwork Bar book club, in Catterall, Lancashire who read Just Breathe and Forever Hold Your Peace and gave me necessary feedback.

As a book club, we haven't known each other long, but I love the group and I know that we will be friends for a long time.

I'd particularly like to thank Andrea, who helped me with my editing and badgered me for a sequel to Just Breathe. So here it is! Just for you.

I'd also like to thank my friend, Eleanor, who eagerly awaited chapters as I wrote them and has encouraged my writing journey from the very start , and of course my husband, Darrell, who helped me with the editing.

Other Books by Caroline Blake

Just Breathe

Forever Hold Your Peace

The Brief

Introduction

It's frustrating when you read a sequel to a book and you can't remember the first one isn't it? I hope this recap, followed by an extract from the last chapter of Just Breathe, helps to refresh your memory.

Caroline x

Charlotte, a successful lawyer from London, fell out of love with her stressful job and made the decision to move to Warkworth, a village on the Northumbrian coast. The beautiful beach, the independent shops and cafes and the peaceful lifestyle lured her. Her decision may also have been influenced a little by a man called Liam, whom she met in The Bridge End Cafe.

One day, as she was walking down the hill to the village centre, she came across Linda, who was being harassed by a local policeman, PC Dave Benson. He was trying to get her into a police car, to take her to the station and Linda was telling him that she didn't want to go. The policeman threatened to arrest her and as Linda's friend Ava, and Linda, a meek fifty-five year old, didn't appear to be the type of people who would generally find themselves on the other side of the law, Charlotte stepped in and asked them if everything was alright. Charlotte put the horrible policeman in his place. He then got a call on his radio and drove off, saying that he would speak to Linda another time.

As a thank you, Linda and Ava invited Charlotte to join them for coffee at The Bridge End Cafe.

At the cafe, Linda told Charlotte the story of her husband going missing. The horrible policeman was investigating and was convinced that Linda was hiding something, which she was, as she had told the police that her despicable husband, Phil, was watching the snooker when she had left for work a few days ago, and when she got home from work, he had gone. She admitted to Charlotte and Ava that in fact she and Phil had had an argument, a common occurrence in her household, and after shouting at her at the top of the stairs, Phil had stepped back and had fallen down the stairs and knocked himself unconscious. Rather than helping him, Linda had stepped over him and had gone to work. Maybe she was hoping he would be dead by the time she returned.

Phil wasn't dead, of course, as he had managed to get up and walk away. He had just gone missing for a short time, probably to punish Linda, who he had been bullying and beating for many years.

Just as Linda was beginning to enjoy her quiet life without Phil, reading her books and pottering around the garden, the police arrived at the door to tell her that a dead body has been found and she was required to go to the hospital mortuary to identify it, as it might be her husband.

However, it wasn't Phil. On the way back home, Linda grappled with herself and wasn't sure whether she missed and loved her husband or not.

When she arrived home, Phil opened the door, large as life and just as cruel. He told her that he had been watching her and had fun seeing her being spoken to by the police. He had also been watching her with her new friend, Charlotte.

After being initially angry with him, Linda settled back into her life with Phil and over the next couple of months, she lost touch with Charlotte. Phil didn't like her going out and having friends and it was easier for her to bend to his wishes, rather than face his wrath.

Finally, she could endure him no longer and she felt brave enough to leave him. She walked to Charlotte's house and was offered a sanctuary in her spare bedroom.

At this time it was winter and one morning when Charlotte was moaning about how cold the weather was in Northumberland, Liam persuaded her to go back to London for the weekend, to see her friend and do some shopping for a new coat. While she was there, she bumped into her ex-boyfriend, Miles, who had cheated on her. After too much to drink, she again fell for his charms and ended up in his bed.

In the morning, she regretted that she would hurt Liam, but she told herself that it was inevitable, as she believed that she and Miles were meant to be. Liam would be sad for a while, but he would easily move on, she told herself. After all, they had only been together a matter of months. She quickly got dressed and went out for coffee while Miles was still sleeping. When she returned to his flat, she heard a text arrive on his phone from someone called Zara, saying that she was looking forward to seeing him. She confronted Miles, who, baffled by her angry and confused reaction, told her that he hadn't made any promises to her and he thought that Charlotte was a one-night stand - exes getting back together for one last night. That's normal, isn't it?

She left in tears, after throwing the coffee all over his cream sofa.

Back in Warkworth, against the advice of Linda, she confessed to Liam about spending the night with Miles. She hoped it would make them closer; she planned to explain it away by saying that they hadn't had the conversation about being exclusive, but now she wanted to be. She thought that Liam would be pleased that she now wanted them to be a couple, officially. But Liam didn't see it like that and dumped her immediately, leaving her alone on the beach. They didn't speak for weeks.

In the meantime, Linda was going through a difficult time of her own. Her father, who had spent many years in a care home, had just died. He left her a large sum of money, which she intended to keep for herself, rather than share with Phil. She filed divorce proceedings and Charlotte acted as her solicitor.

On a visit to the estate agent, looking for a new house for herself, she saw Liam there. He admitted that he missed Charlotte and Linda arranged to take her into the Masons Arms that night, where Liam would also happen to be.

"Linda went home, after making an appointment to meet the estate agent the following day. She wanted to make sure that Charlotte looked her best tonight – not that Liam wouldn't love her anyway, but to give her some confidence, which she had been very much lacking lately.

Two hours later, they sat in a quiet corner of the pub. Charlotte was looking radiant in a tight fitting black linen dress and boots. Linda had suggested to her that they dress up for the occasion and Charlotte had agreed. They ordered a bottle of wine from the bar while they looked through the menu. Charlotte was facing towards the wall, with her back to the front door, so she didn't see Liam as he walked towards them. Linda mouthed at him to *wait there* and told Charlotte that she was going to the toilet and would be back in a few minutes.

Linda got up and nodded to Liam that he was free to approach Charlotte. She stood and watched, as Liam gently tapped her on the shoulder. Charlotte turned around and when she saw who it was, stood up and the two of them clung to each other, like their lives depended on it. When she saw them kissing, Linda knew that they had forgiven each other – he had forgiven her for cheating and she had forgiven him for ignoring her apologies.

When they finally pulled apart and Liam sat down in Linda's seat, she went over to them and explained that she was going to leave them to it, as they had a lot to talk about. Charlotte asked her to stay but she said she wouldn't dream of third wheeling, if that was the phrase that young people used nowadays. She left a hundred pound on the table and insisted that she wanted to pay for their meal.

She walked back to Oriel House, stopping for a few minutes to look at the houses for sale in the estate agent's window. She was now free to make her own decisions; she had money and she could live wherever she wanted.

For once in her life, she was looking forward to the future."

Chapter One

On the first day of her long-awaited early retirement, Linda stood in her kitchen, leaning against the countertop with a mug of hot tea in her hands, watching the rain pounding against the window and bouncing off the window sill. Even the sparrows, forsaking their premium organic wild bird seed that had been scattered on the bird table in the back garden, were sheltering in the hedge. Today wasn't a day to venture out, she decided. Even though summer had officially begun, England was experiencing the coldest and wettest June for a long time.

She wandered into the living room of her small but perfectly formed bungalow, where her book was waiting for her on the sofa. She settled down with her back resting on one end of her leather Chesterfield sofa and her feet resting on the other end and beckoned her young ginger tabby cat, Nutmeg, to join her. Nutmeg jumped up and settled next to her, making herself comfortable on one of Linda's plush cushions, allowing Linda to rest her hand on her head and gently tickle her behind her ears.

With her cherished pet at her side, a hot drink on the coffee table, and a new book in her hand, Linda had never been more content. She couldn't imagine a better start to her retirement.

She finally had her own home and she had made the decision to divorce Phil, her cruel and abusive husband whom she had endured for the last thirty-five years. She hadn't heard from him for months and she was happy to keep it that way. Her personal cloud of crisis and drama had finally lifted. As far as she was concerned, they now lived separate lives and she didn't want to give him another thought. Their divorce was almost final and his new lady friend was very welcome to him. Linda had her own bright future to look forward to.

She put her book down, ignoring the disdainful look from Nutmeg for disturbing her after she had only just settled down, and grabbed her mobile phone from the coffee table next to the sofa and sent a text to her close friend, Charlotte.

I'm on the sofa, reading! Thinking about my holiday. I need another suitcase just for all my books :) x

Charlotte replied, *I've been cleaning skirting boards on my hands and knees:). Living my best life x*

Linda knew from the smiley face emoji that Charlotte really was living her best life. She had been living her best life since she had left the London law firm where she had worked as a matrimonial lawyer and moved to Warkworth last year. After many months of not working, while she tried to figure out what she wanted to do, Charlotte had finally made the decision that she wanted to continue being a lawyer and she was in the process of opening her own high street law firm in the centre of Warkworth.

The office had once been an old terraced house, whose front door opened onto Bridge Street, directly opposite The Warkworth House Hotel, but had been converted into an office in the nineteen-eighties. Previously occupied by a chartered surveyor, it was dull and dreary. Whitewashed walls, bleached plastic Venetian blinds, and dark grey industrial strength carpets did not lend a welcoming ambience. Morose grey filing cabinets occupied each of the rooms, bearing down on the cheap pseudo-wooden desks that divided the professionals from their clients.

But it was in a perfect location and had rooms upstairs to expand into if she needed to take on some staff in the future. She had picked up the keys from the estate agent a couple of weeks ago, stripped the rooms of the old neglected furniture and was getting the office ready to welcome her first clients, whenever anyone needed her. Cosy armchairs, bright cushions, oak desks and lush plants had been ordered to fill the space.

Linda, too, was determined to live her best life, at last. She had sailed the stormy sea of an abusive marriage into the quiet calm of her semi-detached haven, where the television was no longer constantly blaring out football commentary or Formula One track noise. She was free to have peace and quiet in the house, or to listen to the afternoon play on Radio Four, the type of entertainment that Phil had told her was only for 'toffs'.

She could hear Phil's voice in her head now, "Who do you think you are, listening to that hoity-toity crap?"

Well, now she could listen to whatever she liked, without being called names. The house could be as silent or as noisy as she liked. She would make that decision for herself. If she needed background noise while she read a book, she could play music or open a window or sit in the garden and listen to the birds singing. It was her choice.

Charlotte was handling her divorce. The matrimonial home had already been sold, the money in the joint bank account had been divided equally between her and Phil and they had gone their separate ways. In a week or so, the divorce would be final and she didn't ever have to see him or speak to him again.

Throughout the negotiations, which had been conducted entirely through their solicitors, he had failed to show any concern for her financial status and whether she would be able to afford to pay rent and bills on her small wage from the care home, where she had worked part-time. Consequently, she had failed to tell him that she had inherited almost four hundred thousand pounds following her father's death, which had enabled her to buy the beautiful bungalow overlooking the river, with plenty of money to spare. She had also failed to tell him that she had given up her job at the care home and was now a lady of leisure. Well, what he doesn't know won't kill him.

When her offer on the bungalow had been accepted, she had confessed to Charlotte about the money left to her by her father, which she should have, strictly speaking, shared with Phil, as they were still married at the time. She told her that she didn't want Phil to have a penny of it and Charlotte had put her fingers into her ears and began singing 'la, la, la', had told her that she had gone temporarily deaf. They never spoke about it again.

The ringing of the doorbell followed immediately by heavy knocking startled Linda and she jumped up quickly, brushing her cat to the floor, who miaowed her objection. She hadn't ordered anything to be delivered and she wasn't expecting any visitors. She smiled to herself as she made her way to the front door, imagining Charlotte, ready for a break, a cup of tea and a chat; anything to take her away from her last-minute cleaning duties before she welcomed her first client. She had offered to help her, but Charlotte wouldn't hear of it.

"You're not spending the first day of your retirement scrubbing a dirty office," she had said. "It's only small, it won't take me long."

She had promised to let her know when she had finished, later in the afternoon, and Linda could walk round to the office and they'd go to the Bridge End Cafe for cake and coffee. Linda had told her that she'd look forward to it.

"Oh it's you," she said, as she opened the door.

"Are you expecting someone else?" It was PC David Benson, the dreadful misogynistic policeman who was convinced that Linda had been responsible for Phil's disappearance last year, when in fact he had simply left her for a few days; whether to punish her or simply for his own amusement, Linda never found out. PC Benson seemed to have been of the preposterous view that she had murdered her husband, cut his body into tiny pieces, and buried him in the back garden, even though there wasn't a scrap of evidence to suggest such a thing.

Linda felt like telling him to mind his own business. What had it got to do with him whether she was expecting someone or not? "I just thought it might be the children from next door," she said, as politely as she could. "Their ball keeps coming over the back fence into the garden." She had no idea why she had just said that. There weren't any children living next door, but for some reason, she didn't want to tell him that she thought it might be a friend, calling to collect her for a coffee. Her social life had nothing whatsoever to do with him. "What can I do for you?" she said.

"I have some news about your husband," he said. When Linda didn't reply, he continued, "It's quite upsetting, I'm afraid." He examined his huge black boots, head down. When

Linda hesitated, he looked up and continued, "Can I come in or do you want to discuss this on your doorstep? I'm sure you wouldn't want all and sundry listening?" He looked over his shoulder at a man walking past with an old dog and scowled at him, as though the man had shown the slightest sign that he wanted to stop and listen, when in fact he had done nothing of the sort and had walked on, seemingly oblivious to the conversation on her doorstep.

Linda's thoughts whirred, baffled as to why he was talking to her that way. Why did he have to be so hostile? Was she imagining it, or did he have an ugly sneer at the corner of his mouth? She wished she could slap it away. Why was he trying to make her believe that he wanted their conversation to be private, as though he had her best interests at heart? Since when had he ever cared? He knocks on my door, mentions upsetting news, and then manages to make me angry with just a few words, she thought. Evidently, it isn't only Phil who has the power to do that. It seems that he and this policeman are cut from the same cloth.

Reluctantly, she agreed that he could step inside, but she remained in the hall, rather than leading him into the kitchen and making him tea, like she did the last time he was in her home, the day that he had accused her of telling lies to the police and she had heard him call her a 'manipulative bitch' to his colleague, PC Fielding, as they were leaving when he believed that she was hiding something and not telling them the whole truth. She wanted him to say what he had to say and leave as quickly as possible. So far, her lovely new home had not been sullied by aggressive male behaviour and she had every intention of keeping it that way.

"What news do you have?" she asked, wanting him to get to the point. She crossed her arms, feeling a sudden chill in the air.

"I'm afraid your husband…"

"Soon-to-be ex-husband, thank goodness," she interrupted.

"I'm sorry?"

"I said soon-to-be ex-husband," said Linda slowly and a little more loudly, as though he had failed to understand her the first time. "We no longer live together. The divorce will be finalised next month." She felt it was important for him to know that she had finally extricated herself from Phil's grasp. She wanted to tell him that Phil was a cheat, a liar, a bully and a downright thug and that she had finally seen sense and left him months ago, but as his personality seemed to mirror PC Benson's, she didn't see the point.

"Oh," said the policeman. He fiddled in his jacket pocket and brought out a notepad, as though the answers to any questions he may have about Linda and Phil's relationship would be in there. He flicked it open and squinted at one of the pages. "I did go to your previous address, but the new occupants said that you had moved. Luckily, they had your new address."

Here he was again, just like the last time he had interrogated her in her kitchen, making statements without asking questions. This time, Linda didn't want to play verbal games with him; she just wanted him out of her house as quickly as possible.

"Yes, this is my new address. I do live here," she said with all the patience she could muster, "But Phil doesn't and he never has. Did they tell you that he did?"

"Who?"

"The new owners of our old house," said Linda with a sigh.

"No, no, but I assumed that he did because you did," he said. "I didn't check on the electoral roll, you know, with you not being here that long. Look, I'm sorry, there's been a mix-up about the addresses but if you wouldn't mind giving me your husband's address while I'm here, I'd be grateful." Linda thought she saw a flash of humanity across his face. There one second, gone the next. She wondered what Phil had done and why the police were looking for him. He had never been arrested before, as far as she knew. He didn't have any criminal convictions or anything like that, although, if they hadn't lived in a quiet village where seeing a police officer on patrol was a rare occurrence, he most certainly would have been arrested for being drunk and disorderly on quite a few occasions. Maybe his new girlfriend had made a complaint against him. Good for her. That would make sense. That's why the policeman thought the news would be upsetting. After all, telling a wife that her husband is wanted for beating up his girlfriend would be a shock to most people. Thankfully, Linda didn't care what he had done.

However, she was curious.

"He lives in Amble, at number 2 Acresfield Close," said Linda. "What has he done? I know there's privacy laws and all that, so you might not be able to tell me all the details about his arrest, but you said that you had some news."

PC Benson looked confused for a moment until it dawned on him what Linda was thinking. "Yes, yes, I do have news, of course. Not about his arrest though. I'm really sorry to tell you that Mr. Matthews is dead."

Chapter Two

"Dead? What do you mean? How?" asked Linda.

"There was a fight outside the pub, quite a brawl in actual fact, and I'm afraid that Mr. Matthews was involved in it. He was pronounced dead at the scene."

How ironic, thought Linda, that only a few months ago, this man thought she had killed her husband and now here he was, standing in her hallway, telling her that someone else had killed him. "Killed in a fight? You mean he was murdered?" she asked.

"I wouldn't class it as a murder, no," said the policeman. The way he frowned, rubbed his chin, and looked upwards, suggested that he was racking his brain for the legal definition of murder.

He had probably been to police college many years ago, Linda thought, but not being the brightest bulb in the box, he had more than likely forgotten most of what he had been taught.

"It might be manslaughter, but knowing juries nowadays, they will probably put it down to it being a tragic accident. Misadventure they call it, in an inquest. Just a bunch of drunken men having a disagreement." He shrugged, as though this type of event was normal, men killing each other in street brawls. This was Warkworth, not the Wild West. "It seems from witnesses that we've spoken to so far," he continued, "that Mr. Matthews took quite a few punches and then turned his back and walked away from the fracas. He said he had had enough and was going home." He peered down at his notebook again. "Someone then saw him grasping at his chest, a Mr. Frank Cooper, and then apparently he fell down. Just collapsed. Mr. Cooper went to help him and the landlord of the pub called an ambulance but he died instantly at the scene. Possibly a heart attack, although the post-mortem will have to confirm it. You'll be glad to know that he didn't suffer. It all seemed to be very quick. I hope that gives you some level of comfort." PC Benson snapped his notebook shut and nodded, pleased with himself for a job well done.

Comfort? It's been many years since Linda had any kind of comfort from Phil. As the policeman's words took their time to sink in, Linda wondered whether she was glad to know that he didn't suffer. A loving wife would be glad to know that, of course, she would, but Linda hadn't been a loving wife for a very long time. Right at this moment, she didn't feel anything at all, which she found odd. If someone had told her on her wedding day, as she stood side by side with her new husband, smiling at the many cameras that were being pointed at them to capture such a precious moment, that she wouldn't be upset when she heard the news that the love of her life was dead, she wouldn't have believed it for a minute. All those years ago, she couldn't have contemplated life without him and she would have been shocked and appalled at such a thought. Yet here she was today, thirty-five years later, feeling nothing.

He had been violent all his life, both towards her and

towards various men that he had taken a dislike to, in bars and at work, and his last moments on earth had been violent. If you live by the sword, you die by the sword.

"Hang on a minute," said Linda. "You said it was a heart attack?"

"More than likely, yes. Of course…"

"So he wasn't killed by someone else?" PC Benson stared at her, as though he was struggling to comprehend the question. He didn't really want to spend more time here than was necessary. It was almost time for his break and he was anxious to get back to the station. "You said that he was killed in a fight…"

"I don't think I said that exactly."

"You said there was a fight and then he died and that it might be manslaughter, but then you said it was a heart attack," said Linda. "I'm confused."

"At this stage of the inquiry…"

"Has someone been arrested or not?" Linda interrupted sharply, raising her voice.

"Quite a few of them have been arrested, yes," said the policeman. "Half a dozen blokes were brawling in the street. They'll all be facing charges for something or other."

"For Phil's murder?"

"Well…"

"Has anyone been arrested for Phil's murder?" Linda could feel herself becoming more and more angry. She had never met anyone as incompetent as this man. Why couldn't they have sent the nice policewoman, instead of this blundering idiot? Anyone else, except him.

"Well, I'm not entirely sure what the original arrests were for and what the ultimate charges will be, but it appears that fight led directly to the heart attack, so I'd say that could be manslaughter, but…"

"Oh for goodness sake!" shouted Linda. "You're making it up, again, aren't you?"

"What?"

"Making the circumstances fit your agenda. Someone had a fight and someone had a heart attack and here you are, distorting the facts and calling it murder, just so you can arrest someone for it. Is that what you want? Is that your career goal, to arrest a murderer?"

"I never said murder, Mrs. Matthews and it's not my arrest, so…"

"Manslaughter then. I don't care. Whatever you said, I don't want to hear any more from you."

Linda pushed past him and opened the front door, indicating that it was time for him to leave. She could tell from the look on his face that he was completely flummoxed. He clearly had no idea what he had said wrong, but he didn't put up a fight now that his exit had been shown to him.

When relaying the tale later to his colleagues in the police station canteen, he would more than likely tell them that the new widow acted very strangely because she was overcome with grief and was in shock. He did his best to give her the awful news in a gentle and sympathetic manner, he would tell them. But no one can predict the way a woman will react, especially with hormones and all that. Someone should make her some hot sweet tea. That would do the job. Although it wasn't something that he would volunteer for himself. The sooner he was out of here, the better.

"I'd like you to go now," said Linda. "Thank you for notifying me."

"Is there anyone that you'd like me to contact for you?"

Was he joking? He was standing in her hallway, taking

up far too much room, getting in her way and spoiling her carpet with his huge dirty boots and asking whether she needed him to contact somebody. That was the kind of thing that a normal person did for someone who had just received some bad news. For a start, it wasn't necessarily bad news and this man was certainly not a normal person, in her eyes. She wanted him out of her house. Now.

"I'm quite capable of contacting people myself, thank you," she said. "Like I said, 2 Acresfield Close, that's his address now. You'll need to go there and contact his new partner. She's called Dorothy Abbott."

"Yes, of course."

There it was again, that tiny flash of humanity. But Linda wasn't interested in seeing it. She ushered the policeman out of her house and closed the door behind him quickly. She listened to his heavy footsteps retreating down the path and it was only when she heard the police car drive away that she realised that she had no idea what to do next. He hadn't even told her where Phil's body was or what the next steps were. Presumably, someone would need to identify the body and register the death. And the funeral! There would need to be a funeral. Had the policeman mentioned a post-mortem? She couldn't remember him doing so, but there would have to be one, presumably. She wondered how long that would take.

For fuck's sake! Phil had done it again. He was ruining her day. Just as her peaceful retirement was about to start and she was enjoying her life without him, here he was, throwing a grenade into the centre of her plans and smashing her day to pieces.

When her father had died in January, only a few weeks after she had left Phil, and while she was still staying with

23

Charlotte, in her spare bedroom, she had felt so lost and alone. She found herself suddenly an orphan and missed her parents so much. She would never again feel that unconditional love that her parents had always given to her. With no brothers or sisters, and only one distant cousin whom she rarely spoke to, it had felt natural to turn to Phil for comfort and she had temporarily considered going back to him. He had hugged her and she had wept on his shoulder, as the shock of her father's death sunk in. They had clung to each other in the hallway of the house that they had shared together for a large part of her life and it was then that a fraction of doubt had crept in and she wondered whether she was doing the right thing in leaving him. It would have been so easy to move back home; better the devil you know, and all that. They had been together for so long that she honestly felt as though she couldn't manage without him. He was her other half.

But she had cast off her hesitancy like an old coat when she had gone upstairs to the bathroom and discovered that he had thrown out her mum's leather reading chair; the only thing that she had treasured more than her books and had left behind in the house when she had moved out. He knew how much she had loved that chair and how it reminded her of her mum. It had fit perfectly into the corner of the spare bedroom and Linda had spent hours and hours up there, escaping into her books. The chair wasn't in his way and the only reason that he threw it out was to hurt her. He knew how upset she would be to lose it.

When he nonchalantly told her that he had 'tipped it', that's when the penny dropped. She knew that Phil would never change and she made her mind up there and then that she never wanted to see him ever again.

Looking back, she knew that she should have left him much sooner, years ago in fact. She should have left him the first time that he hit her, the first time that his great big fists left bruises on her delicate skin. She had heard about women staying with abusive partners for years and she had never understood it; until she became one of those women. The control had crept into their marriage so slowly and insidiously that she had not noticed it: or if she had, she had not allowed herself to acknowledge it. Even before he was aggressive and violent, in the early days when he was still a young man, the red flags were flying high. Love is blind, don't they say?

But now Phil wouldn't be able to hurt or control anyone else. Ever again. He was dead!

She kept saying those words over and over in her head, but they didn't seem to be sinking in. You really do need to live each day to the fullest, she thought. She was now fifty-five. Middle age had grasped her and she needed to get on with things before old age replaced it, bringing with it aches, pains, and ailments. For the time being, hopefully, she had plenty of life left in her and she was determined to live it to the full.

Right now, her passport was safely tucked away in the top drawer of her sideboard in the living room, next to a large shiny cruise brochure that she regularly sat down with, flicking through the colourful pages, stopping to admire the elegant lady in her long dress on the cover, posing for photographs on the curved staircase in the middle of the ship with her handsome partner in his black dinner suit and crisp white shirt, on their way for dinner in the huge dining room. Maybe they had been invited to dine at the captain's table.

They looked like that kind of couple.

She was counting down the days to her first-ever foreign holiday, a Mediterranean cruise. Her ship was due to sail from Portsmouth at the beginning of November and would be stopping at all the beautiful cities that she had longed to visit - Lisbon, Valencia, Barcelona, Nice, Mahon on Menorca, Palma on Majorca and then Gibraltar on the way back.

As she sat back down on the sofa, stroking Nutmeg slowly, to try and calm her racing heartbeat, her mind wandered and she imagined herself floating about the cruise ship, going from one activity to the next, from the bar to the dining room, from the swimming pool to the spa, from the games room to the library. She couldn't believe her luck.

In the days when the ship was at sea, she would sit elegantly at a table on the main deck in the afternoon, wearing one of her new dresses, next to one of those round windows, staring wistfully into the horizon, watching the sea spray splashing onto the glass, as she sipped her Long Island Iced Tea. (Charlotte had given her a run-down of some cocktails that she might like and Linda was looking forward to making her way through the list). As evening approached, she would shower in her cabin, smother her skin with the complimentary, luxury body cream, and glide down to the dining room to meet her fellow passengers. She had booked herself on a large table for eight people. She would be quite happy to spend the days on her own, she thought, but it would be nice to have some company in the evenings.

She didn't care that some people on the ship would be married and would look like the couple in the brochure, sophisticated and in love. She knew that some of the passengers would also be single travellers. She was looking forward to making some new friends, whether they were married or not.

She had thought about asking Charlotte to go with her, but she was too busy with work and she probably wouldn't want to go away without her boyfriend, Liam. She thought about asking Ava, her old next-door neighbour who had recently tried to mend the burnt bridges between them, but their relationship was beyond repair. Ava hadn't supported her when she needed her, and although she may still be clinging to Linda's Christmas card list for dear life, she would never again be able to call herself a friend. When one burns one's bridges, what a very nice fire it makes, she thought.

So, after thirty-five years of marriage, of having to dance to someone else's tune, she had decided to go on the cruise alone. She had treated herself to a double cabin with a balcony, right in the middle of the ship, which she had read was the best position for those who may be seasick. She didn't know whether she would be seasick or not, having never been on a boat before, let alone a ship as large as a village, but she didn't want to take any chances. Half a dozen new books were already waiting for her to enjoy, next to the suitcase in the corner of her bedroom, and now that Phil was out of her life forever, she couldn't wait.

She opened her book, took a deep breath and tried to concentrate on the words on the page, but flashbacks of her life with Phil interrupted her reading. The shouting, the door slamming, the insults. The times he ignored her, the times he interrogated her, the times he hurt her. Plates being hurled at the wall, the meals she had lovingly cooked for him cascading to the floor. She threw down her book, got up, grabbed her coat from the hook next to the front door and, picking up the front door keys from the small table, she left the house. She needed to see Charlotte.

Chapter Three

The following morning, Linda was settling down in Bridge End Cafe with Charlotte when she heard her phone ping with an incoming text. She ignored it. They had ordered two of Amy's beautiful croissants and two cappuccinos. She needed an injection of caffeine, after a fitful night's sleep last night. A combination of too much wine (Charlotte had said it was the only remedy and they had shared two bottles of dry white at her house) and the shocking news about Phil meant that she hadn't slept for more than a couple of hours.

"I'm so hungry this morning," said Linda. "I don't know whether one croissant will be enough to fill me up. I couldn't eat anything yesterday after the news about Phil."

"Yes, I'm not surprised," said Charlotte. "That must have been a huge shock. I can't believe it myself. It just shows that you need to live your life to the full. Because you never know..."

"I know," said Linda, "I think you've hit the nail on the head. I'm not upset about Phil as such. I really don't care that I'll never see him again. I just feel shaken, I don't know why. Maybe it's just a hangover."

"It's because you're human, that's why," said Charlotte. "Anyone's death is a shock, even if it was someone that you didn't like."

"Such a waste," said Linda.

"I know. I mean, he wasn't even that old."

"I don't mean a waste of his life. I mean a waste of mine. Do you know how many years I spent being his dogsbody? I'm pretty bloody angry, to be honest."

"I'm angry at him too. He was a vile man. God rest his soul." Charlotte looked up at the ceiling, as though talking directly to God, and made the sign of the cross on her chest. "You shouldn't speak ill of the dead, should you?"

Linda laughed, "I don't think it matters. God won't be dealing with his soul. Saint Peter wouldn't have let him through the Pearly Gates, not in a month of Sundays."

Amy delivered their warm croissants and coffee to the table and Linda took a large bite immediately. "Amy, you're a genius, thank you," she said, with a mouthful of flaky pastry.

"You're welcome," said Amy, touching Linda's shoulder. "Let me know if you need anything else."

"No, I'm not angry at him; I'm angry at myself," continued Linda. "I feel so old and I feel like I've wasted the best years of my life with him." She stirred a spoonful of sugar into her coffee. Sweet sustenance was needed today.

"Linda, you're not old at all. A woman in her fifties is still in her prime these days," said Charlotte.

Linda raised her eyebrows to show that she didn't believe that at all, but she was grateful that Charlotte was trying to make her feel better by saying the right thing.

"I've had dozens of women clients a lot older than you who have split from their husbands and then started a whole new life. One woman opened a boutique in Clapham with her divorce settlement and she was nearly sixty. She said she couldn't find any nice clothes for a woman her age, so she opened her own shop. She invited me to the opening night, it was wonderful. I got very drunk!"

"Yes, that is wonderful," said Linda, "but I don't want to do anything as ambitious as that. I'm happily retired, for now at least. If I find myself getting bored in the winter, I might get a little part-time job, but the garden will keep me occupied all summer." She took another bite of her croissant. "I actually love the fact that I can do this kind of thing, you know, sitting in a cafe with a friend instead of having to go to work."

Charlotte was about to say that she was very lucky, but she stopped herself. Losing your parents was a high price to pay for the inheritance that allowed you to take early retirement, no matter how welcome the retirement may have been.

"It isn't the future that I'm angry about, it's the past. Like I said, I just feel like I've wasted my life."

Charlotte nodded. "Hindsight is a stick that we use to beat ourselves with too often. You can't change anything now, just be thankful that he's left this mortal coil for good."

"Oh, I am glad, believe me."

"Who will be paying for his funeral, do you know? Have you told his sister yet?"

"Yes, I spoke to her yesterday on the walk round to yours. She was upset, it was awful to hear her cry. She only saw the good side of him, so she will actually miss him, I think. As for the funeral, I don't know who's paying for it, to be honest. I suppose it will have to be me. We're not quite divorced yet, so technically I'm still his next of kin."

"I know, I'm sorry for the delay," said Charlotte. "I thought you would have been divorced by now."

"It's not your fault. You're the best divorce lawyer in town." Linda raised her cappuccino to Charlotte and they clicked their cups together.

"I'm the only divorce lawyer in town, but I will take the best title as well."

Linda's phone pinged again, a reminder that she hadn't opened the text message that arrived a few minutes ago. She reached into her bag and put the phone on the table.

"Phil! It says 'Phil'. Why am I getting a text from Phil?" she said, pushing the phone across the table for Charlotte to see. "Did that policeman lie to me? He wouldn't do that, surely? Do you think there's been a mistake?" Linda's face drained of colour and she felt a little dizzy, despite the sugar and the caffeine she had just consumed.

"What the fuck? Let me see," said Charlotte. She took the phone, opened the text, and read it quickly. "It's from someone called Dorothy. Not from Phil himself. Is that his girlfriend?"

Linda nodded and took a deep breath. She held her hand to her beating chest. After coming to terms with the fact that Phil was dead, and quite enjoying the idea of a future where he no longer existed, the last thing Linda wanted was for it all to be a hoax.

Charlotte read the text out to Linda.

Hi, it's Dorothy here. I found your number in Phil's phone. I hope you don't mind me messaging you, but I have his will and I think we need to talk. Please call me when you can. Thank you.

"You don't think he found out about the inheritance from my dad, do you? Do you think that's what's in his will, that he's claiming half my money and leaving it to Dorothy?"

"No, he can't do that, and I certainly didn't tell him

about your money," said Charlotte. "I haven't had any correspondence from his solicitor to indicate that he knows anything. I suppose he could have found out from the care home, but he wouldn't have gone snooping, would he?" Charlotte did a quick silent prayer that he hadn't found out. Her solicitor's practising certificate would be taken off her immediately if she was found to have misled the court by not declaring a matrimonial asset as large as four hundred thousand pounds.

"Who knows? If he thought I was hiding something from him, then yes, I wouldn't put it past him."

"Well, you'd better give her a ring then and find out, before I have a bloody heart attack," said Charlotte. She took a deep breath and held it in while she silently counted to three, held it for a count of four, and breathed out slowly to the count of five, as Doctor Singh in London had taught her. She thought she had left all her stress behind with her old job, but Warkworth certainly knew how to dish it out to her.

***

An hour later, Linda knocked on Dorothy's front door, which was something she would never have done if Phil was still alive. She knew his address, but she had never seen the house and had no desire to see it. The thought of him setting up a home with another woman, choosing furniture and soft furnishings together, and eating together at the kitchen table wasn't the thing that disturbed her. She just didn't want to give him any head space. Her mind was a Phil-free zone. But he always had his way and here she was, thinking about him

33

again and giving up her time because of him.

"Thank you for coming round," said Dorothy, opening the door and ushering her in. "I'm glad you came. I think that it's always best to discuss things in person, don't you? I'm not a fan of the telephone, never have been. We didn't even have one at home until I was a teenager. Even then, I didn't like it."

She was wittering, in the way that nervous people do before a job interview or when they're waiting for an operation. Linda instantly warmed to her, even though she hadn't planned to. She was a good-looking woman, small with light brown hair that curled as it reached her shoulders. Her kind eyes were friendly and welcoming.

"Come through to the kitchen," she said. "Would you like a drink, tea or coffee?"

"No thanks," said Linda. "I've just had breakfast with my friend. Cappuccino and a croissant."

"Oh how lovely," said Dorothy. "Anywhere nice?"

"The Bridge End Cafe in Warkworth. The lady who owns it, Amy, makes her own croissants. They really are the best in the world. There's a sign in the window saying that." I can't believe we're making small talk, thought Linda. This petite woman, who looks just like I used to, with her practical, unfashionable clothes is actually making small talk with me about breakfast items. What a bizarre situation we are both in.

"Please sit down," said Dorothy, pulling out one of the wooden chairs from the dining table in the middle of the large square kitchen.

"This is a nice house, I like it," said Linda. "The patio doors give a lovely view into your garden. I would have liked those, but Phil wouldn't…" She stopped herself.

Dorothy smiled. "It's okay, I know what you were about to say, he wouldn't spend any money upgrading the house."

Linda nodded.

"These were already here when I bought the house many years ago with my husband. He died five years ago now. Cancer."

"I'm sorry to hear that," said Linda, surprised to find that she was genuinely sorry that this woman had lost two of her partners. Even so, she wasn't here to make a new friend, she told herself. "So, Phil's will? You said you wanted to talk about it."

"Yes, of course, I'll get it for you."

She got up and walked over to one of the kitchen cabinets, where she opened the door and reached up to the top shelf. Linda was engrossed in watching a dozen sparrows fighting over the seed on the bird table in the garden and if she hadn't turned around at that precise moment, she wouldn't have seen Dorothy's t-shirt ride up, exposing the purple bruise on her back. It looked to be three or four days old, as the outer edges were beginning to fade into the horrible yellow that Linda had seen so many times on her own skin.

"Did he hit you too?" she asked.

Dorothy winced and pulled her t-shirt down quickly. She stood with her back to Linda, her hands resting on the countertop, as though she was ashamed to face her adversary.

"How did he do that? Was it a kick?" persisted Linda. "It seems too big to be a punch but how did he get his foot up there? Surely it wasn't a karate kick? He was never that agile."

"Please, Linda, please, keep your voice down!" Dorothy's words came out much louder than she intended, as she turned to Linda. She didn't want to be rude, but after what she had seen in the will, she was at the end of her tether. The sooner this episode of her life was over, the better. "I'm sorry," she said. "That was rude of me, but I don't want the neighbours to hear anything. I think they've heard enough from this house recently. The walls are paper thin, I'm afraid."

Linda nodded. She understood. She knew only too well. Her married life, too, had been made public because of Phil's angry temper. She looked out of the window and admired Dorothy's beautiful garden which was filled with colourful summer flowers, some of which had been brought in and carefully arranged in a small vase in the middle of the table. Feminine pink and white cosmos and white roses. Three votive candles surrounded the base of the vase. Linda could smell their gentle vanilla fragrance, even though they weren't lit.

The room spoke of warmth and love, of comfort and home-baking. It was a beautiful house. It was criminal the way Phil would have ruined it with his angry words and belligerence. She wondered how often it was that the outside of a property hid the truth of the inside.

She turned back to Dorothy, who had seated herself at the table. "I know Phil caused that bruise, you don't need to tell me. He did it to me too. I should have known that a leopard wouldn't have changed its spots." Dorothy didn't confirm or deny, but her nervous fingers, twisting the envelope in her hand over and over, told Linda that she wasn't comfortable. "Do you mind me asking how it happened?" she asked.

"It's nothing, really." Dorothy tugged at the bottom of her t-shirt, pulling it down, even though the bruise was no longer visible.

"Surely he didn't kick you when you were on the floor?" asked Linda. She wasn't sure why she was persisting. Maybe knowing that Phil was cruel to someone other than her would make her feel better.

Dorothy nodded. "Yes, he did," she said. Her eyes were full of tears and sadness. Her beautiful hazel eyes that probably once sparkled with the wonderment of life, just like hers used to, years ago before Phil entered her life, were now filled with tremendous sorrow.

"That's just a new level of depravity." Linda shook her head, unable to believe that her ex-husband would have stooped so low. "Why did you let him stay after he had done that? Why didn't you hit him back, or throw him out, or at the very least change the locks when he was out at the pub?" She knew the answer, even as she asked the questions. She knew what Dorothy was about to say. It was what she would have said if anyone had asked her the same questions in the early years. She loved him.

Dorothy's reply was almost a whisper. "I was lonely." She looked down at the envelope in her hands; Phil's last will and testament. "When he was nice, he was really nice. It was just an odd time when he was grumpy or when he was tired. And then…"

"He was a nasty evil twat who couldn't keep his fists to himself."

Dorothy looked up suddenly; whether she was astounded at Linda's bad language or shocked at the truth of her situation, Linda couldn't tell, but she felt immediately guilty for bringing such words into this poor woman's consciousness. Who was she to judge? She hadn't ever hit Phil back or thrown him out, or changed the locks, so why had she expected Dorothy to stand up to him? For thirty-five years he had demanded everything of her to the point where she was a shadow of her former self by the time they finally split. She had told herself that she couldn't leave him because they were married and her parents wouldn't approve of divorce. But if they had known the true extent of Phil's violent outbursts, then of course they would have supported her. Even her mum, with her "you've made your bed, you have to lie in it" attitude would never have expected her to lie in an unsafe bed. Linda couldn't understand why she had stayed with him for so long. Maybe a psychologist could answer the question for her. But that wasn't something she wanted to explore.

Right at this moment, she was too busy exploring Dorothy's situation from the moral high ground she had reached. It had been an extremely difficult climb for her and she felt as though she deserved her position there. But not at the detriment of Dorothy's memory of Phil. If she loved him and wanted to remember his good points, which over the years had been erased from Linda's memory with each slap, punch and harsh word, but may still be evident in Dorothy's mind, then who was she to ruin that for her?

"I'm sorry," said Linda. She walked over to the sink, pulled a section of kitchen roll from the roll next to the washing-up liquid, and passed it to Dorothy, who dabbed at her eyes. Linda took her seat again at the table opposite Dorothy and gave her a weak smile. "I'm sorry for your loss and I'm sorry for upsetting you."

She wanted to add, "I'm sorry I spent the best years of my life at his beck and call. I'm sorry that I haven't ever lived the life that I thought I would, with children and foreign holidays and the freedom to say whatever I wanted to say in my own home. I'm sorry that I was mesmerized by his charms all those years ago, so much so that I didn't see the warning signs when they were right there in front of me. I'm sorry I walked down the aisle and promised God that I would love, honour and obey him until death do us do part. I'm sorry our paths crossed that day back in nineteen eighty-one when Prince Charles married Princess Diana, when I was so enthralled by the romance of the royal wedding that I would probably have been charmed by the devil himself." But she kept those words to herself.

Dorothy put the envelope on the table. "You can read it while I put the kettle on. I need some tea." She got up and carried the kettle to the sink and filled it with water. Phil would have something to say about the amount of water gushing into it, Linda thought. She had always been careful to only fill her kettle with the amount she needed. "It's a waste of electricity, pure and simple. Why would you want to cost me more money than necessary? Do you want to pay next door's bill as well? You might as well, the way you throw money away." She could hear him, as clear as though he was in the room with them right now, stomping about, his angry words flying around the kitchen for Linda to dodge. It was his favourite game. Linda wondered whether Dorothy would have filled the kettle so much if he was here, or had he given up playing that particular game?

She wondered what had caused him to beat and kick Dorothy. What had caused him to lift his size eleven foot and slam it down on a delicate woman's back while she lay on the floor? She hoped that he was explaining himself to the Devil right now, as he was welcoming him into his fiery furnace of Hell.

"Is this for real?" asked Linda, after a few moments,

when she had read the will. " 'All my real and personal property I devise and bequeath to Linda Matthews'. Seriously?"

"Yes, it is real. He wanted to leave everything to you."

"What, even after the divorce? But why?" asked Linda. "Because he felt guilty?"

"Maybe," said Dorothy. "I don't know, it wasn't something we discussed. I mean, I knew the will existed, but we didn't discuss the content. We just printed a couple of forms from the internet and filled them in and then our neighbours witnessed them both for us. I'm leaving all my things to my daughter, so I don't blame him for not leaving anything to me. Maybe, if we'd been together longer, things might be different." She took a cup from the draining board and placed it next to the kettle. "Are you sure you don't want some tea?"

"I think I will have one please," said Linda.

Dorothy got another cup from the cupboard and added a teabag to each one. She poured milk into a small white jug and placed it in the middle of the table. She thought that Linda looked like the type of person who would be particular about her tea, as she was.

"What exactly is his real and personal property?" asked Linda. "He doesn't own half of this house, does he?"

"No. The house is mine," said Dorothy.

Linda sighed in relief.

"As far as I know, it will be all the money in his bank account, which is half of the sale of your house," she said. She poured boiling water into the cups, carried them to the table, and sat back down. "I don't know how much that is, but he didn't give me anything when he moved in here, and I don't think he has spent much in the last few months. Beer money, that's all."

"Well I don't want it," said Linda firmly, folding the will in half and pushing it up the table away from her. "You lived with him, you can have it."

Dorothy laughed suddenly. Not the polite laugh of a well-mannered stranger, but a loud belly laugh that one would share with a friend. "I don't want it either," she said. "Imagine how furious he would be if you gave it to the cat's home."

Linda laughed, "Oh my God, he would go berserk. He would be incandescent with rage. Now that I would pay money to see."

If anyone had looked into the kitchen at that moment, they would have seen two women laughing together like close friends do, sharing a private joke. Neither of them had the look of a grieving widow.

Chapter Four

Liam's text told Charlotte that he had just left work, so she knew that she had five minutes before he got to her house. He had got into the habit of leaving his car at home and walking up the hill to her house, so he could relax with a glass of wine or a beer. Most of the time, he stayed overnight, but if he was on an early shift at the hotel, he would walk the few minutes back home, so he didn't disturb Charlotte at stupid o'clock in the morning.

She flicked the gas on under the frying pan and sprayed it with a little oil. When it was hot, she carefully placed the extortionately expensive fillet steaks in the pan. If her timings were correct, they would be cooked and on the plates just as he walked through the door. The salad was ready in the fridge, the wine was already poured and her neck was freshly perfumed. She was slowly but surely perfecting the art of being an exemplary girlfriend. Or at least trying to.

She had previously lived by the mantra of 'take me as you find me', and 'if you don't like it, jog on,' which was all well and good, but being moody, flaky and self-centered had not served her relationships well in the past. She was a million light years away from trying to be a nineteen-fifties subservient housewife, but she was aware that relationships needed attention and a little effort here and there was all it took to keep a man happy. Liam was well worth the trouble.

"He's a keeper," her friend Hannah had told her when she had been introduced to him a few months ago. She had travelled up from London with her husband, Tom, and baby Ethan to stay at Charlotte's for the weekend and after a couple of hours in Liam's company, she could see why Charlotte was so smitten.

"I know," Charlotte had said. "I'm so lucky. He's not just a really lovely person, but have you seen that tight little arse of his?"

"Yeah, yeah, his arse is great," said Hannah, laughing. "Seriously though, don't fuck it up this time."

"I won't," said Charlotte. They were standing in her kitchen, both gazing out into the tiny garden where Liam and Tom were bonding over beers and barbequed burgers. Charlotte had taken a sip of her wine and bent down to talk to the baby, who was balanced on Hannah's hip. Ethan grabbed at her hair and giggled as she tickled him. "Hang on a minute," she said, standing up suddenly. "What do you mean don't fuck it up? I didn't fuck it up with Miles. He was the one who did the dirty on me, remember?"

"I know. Miles is a complete snake, but you didn't exactly invest in that relationship, did you?" Hannah had said, earnestly. "The writing had been on the wall for a long time."

"Hannah!" Charlotte felt her heartbeat quicken and couldn't quite believe what her friend was saying. The fact that Miles was a cheating, lying scumbag wasn't her fault. He could never keep his eyes to himself; every time they went out, he ogled other women, whether it was a waitress, a woman on the Tube, a bartender or someone at another table in a restaurant. Even the fact that the other woman may have been sitting with a man didn't stop him. He was hard-wired to be unfaithful and there was nothing she could have done about it. "I don't know what you're trying to say exactly. What writing on what wall?"

"Nothing, nothing. I'm just saying, look after your relationship with Liam. He's worth keeping." Hannah smiled at Ethan and blew kisses on his neck, while Charlotte reeled from what she had just said.

"I'm worth keeping too," said Charlotte, a little louder than she had intended. Tom and Liam looked round at her sudden outburst, but she just raised her glass and forced a smile, hoping that they hadn't actually heard her words through the closed French windows. "He's a lucky man, you know. I'm quite a catch." She smiled at Hannah and tried to appear light-hearted, but Hannah's implication that she was to blame for Miles straying was hurtful, there was no denying it. She used to love Hannah's forthright personality and her no-nonsense way of speaking, but not today. Her words were harsh and cutting and Charlotte wasn't sure what she meant by them. She wanted to challenge her but also wanted to change the subject and talk about dresses and shoes or the latest television drama instead. Anything to stop the tears that she could feel developing in the back of her eyes.

"Come here," said Hannah, pulling her into a hug, which made the urge to cry irresistible. "I'm sorry, I can tell you're upset. I shouldn't have said anything. I just want you to be happy and not make the same mistakes as before. Don't let history repeat itself."

Charlotte wiped away the stray tears quickly before Liam noticed that anything was wrong and began asking questions. The last thing she needed was for Hannah to tell him that they were talking about Miles and for him to think that she was still upset about him.

"I've never been happier," she said. "I don't..."

"Exactly," said Hannah, interrupting. "That's why I don't want you to sabotage it."

Charlotte kept a lid on her anger, not wanting to spoil the lovely weekend they were having and tried to change the subject, but Hannah was determined to say her piece. She told Charlotte that, in her experience, men only gravitated towards other women when they weren't a hundred percent happy with what they had. She said they were like toddlers and were extremely selfish, which wasn't fair, but it was a fact. "They want what they want and if they feel lacking in any aspect of their relationship, they'll look for it elsewhere. If someone doesn't give them enough attention, they don't like it."

Charlotte thought that Miles had had more than enough attention. Sometimes, it was draining. He was in the legal profession too, so he knew that the working days were long and sometimes urgent cases came in that forced you to work late and he, more than anyone else, should have understood when she couldn't always keep to prior commitments and she had to cancel dates at the last minute. It should have meant that he stayed at home and watched some telly or played on his Xbox; it should have meant that he was proud of her for being conscientious and ambitious at work. It wasn't an open invitation for him to go out and start chatting up someone else. Of course, when Charlotte explained her side, Hannah had said that she agreed with her. It wasn't all Charlotte's fault, she had said, at which point Charlotte had to bite down hard on her tongue to stop herself from saying something she would regret. But when the cancellations became more often than not, Hannah went on, then it would grate on anyone's nerves. The strongest of relationships would find it hard to survive neglect. Charlotte had taken a large gulp of wine while she allowed her friend's words to sink in.

Hannah knew her better than anyone and neither of them had to mention the times when Charlotte had cancelled dates, not because she had an urgent new case and was being conscientious, but because she couldn't be bothered having a shower and going out, especially after a long and stressful day at work. After she had told Miles that she was drowning under the pressure of her workload, she wouldn't get her laptop out and burn the midnight oil on behalf of a new client, which is what she led him to believe. She would run herself a bath, put on a fluffy dressing gown, and have an early night. Most of the time, she didn't even bother to call him to tell him to cancel the restaurant reservation. Text messages were quicker and easier.

After a while, Miles' invitations to dinner during the week became less frequent. They still saw each other on a Saturday night, sometimes with Hannah and Tom and sometimes alone. Saturday night was exclusively date night. Most of the time. But as Charlotte's workload increased, her desire to walk around London in high heels on a Saturday evening, going from one over-heated and crowded bar to another, rarely getting the chance to sit down, slowly decreased. She began suggesting 'quiet nights in'. That's what proper couples do, isn't it? They sit comfortably side by side on the sofa. Netflix and chill. Only Miles wasn't quite ready for that and she knew, deep down, that that's when he began to get itchy feet and wandering eyes.

When Liam and Tom called her and Hannah into the garden, telling them that the burgers were ready, she forced herself to smile and laugh and overall, she enjoyed the rest of the weekend, even though Hannah's words continued to reverberate around her head.

By Sunday evening, when her guests had left and Liam had gone home, she was beginning to think that Hannah had a point. She knew that her friend was looking out for her and often the truth hurts, and although she would never believe that it was her fault that Miles was such a prick, she was determined to put more effort into her relationship with Liam. This time, she had no demanding boss breathing down her neck; no court deadlines that she struggled to meet; no junior lawyers snapping at her heels to take her place at the first sign of an early finish. She now worked for herself and, although she would never let her clients down, she had learned the hard lesson that her personal life was way more important than her professional life.

"Hi honey, I'm home!" Liam interrupted her thoughts, as he let himself in the front door and made his way to the kitchen at the back of the house. Their Fred Flintstone greeting had become an everyday occurrence, which she loved. Their little tradition, which they would carry on into the future.

She smiled as she tipped the steaks onto their two plates and stood back to admire her handiwork.

"Ta-dah!" she said.

"Bloody hell," said Liam. "What have I done to deserve this? A cook in the kitchen and a whore in the bedroom eh? This is what a man's dreams are made of."

"Oi cheeky. Anyway, don't call me a cook until you've tasted your steak."

"It looks beautiful, thank you," he said, kissing her softly on the lips. "Just like you. You scrub up well sometimes, don't you?"

Charlotte laughed, pushed him away and flicked his chest with the tea towel. "Sit down, you cheeky bugger!"

Just as she hoped, the steak was perfect and half an hour later, with all the dishes loaded into the dishwasher, she settled herself next to Liam on the sofa in the living room, his arm around her shoulder. There was no place on earth she would rather be. Even the bright lights of London hadn't drawn her as much as the tiny lights from the dozen candles on the fireplace did when Liam was with her.

"So, I've got some news for you," he said suddenly.

"Good news or bad?" asked Charlotte.

"Well, good I think. Yes, pretty good, I think, yeah."

"You don't seem too sure." Charlotte pulled away slightly, so she could turn to face him. He dropped his arm from her shoulder and held onto her hand.

"I've been offered another job, in Manchester," he said, a huge grin spreading across his face.

"Manchester?" Charlotte didn't need to ask whether he had accepted the job or not. It seemed from the expression on his face that he was happy about it, so she presumed that he had said yes. "What kind of job?"

"Hotel manager. It's a brand-new hotel. They're expanding from London and Edinburgh. It's high-end, luxury, penthouses, the lot."

"Oh wow."

"Yes, exciting, isn't it? I mean, I love Warkworth House, but this is a massive opportunity for me."

Charlotte's thoughts whizzed about in her head at a hundred miles an hour. She would never have considered relocating, especially not so soon after her move from London, but as long as they were together, she didn't really mind where they lived. She would have preferred to live in a small village community and she loved being so close to the beach, but Manchester wasn't that far away from the coast, was it? She used to love going to Lytham and St Annes when she was a little girl. She remembered the beach was just as nice as the one at Warkworth and the shops and cafes were worth a visit. They could be there within an hour and a half.

"I didn't realise you were looking around, but I can see you running a posh hotel. You'll have to have a posh suit. So tell me about it." But as he talked, she found it hard to concentrate on what he was saying. She had so much to think about. They needed to start making plans together. She didn't know anything about Manchester suburbs. She would need to research where was the best place to live. Maybe they should rent a flat in the city for a while until they found a place of their own. She looked around her beautiful living room, with its delicate grey furniture, soft cream walls and wooden shutters. She would miss it, but it could easily be rented out as a holiday home. A small income would be nice. She would need to Google a holiday let company and see if they could manage it for her. She didn't know the first thing about the holiday rental business.

"It's going to be great, you know," said Liam. "The hotel's four times the size of Warkworth House, maybe more. They've got a high-end restaurant, a coffee shop and a little bistro. And a bar obviously…"

"And a pool?"

"Not a pool as such, but they've got a small jacuzzi and some steam rooms next to the spa. They do all kinds of beauty treatments. You're going to love it. It's right up your street."

Charlotte took a sip of her wine and leaned back against the sofa. "Oh, it's been ages since I've been for a spa day. I can't wait. Get me booked in, Mr. Corporate Manager. I'm going to need a new swimsuit."

"Of course you are," laughed Liam. He couldn't believe how well Charlotte was taking the news. He had been nervous about telling her since yesterday morning when he had received the phone call offering him the job. He had immediately gone to tell his uncle, who still owned The Warkworth House Hotel. His plans had always been to buy the hotel from him, but given the current economic climate, it now seemed out of the question. The repayments on the loan would take virtually all of the profits. When his uncle had bought the hotel many years ago, it had been nothing more than a large house. His loving care over the years had transformed it into a boutique hotel and whilst it was only small, it was still out of reach for Liam to buy. Liam's uncle took the news well and told him not to worry about anything. He said that he would advertise for a general manager to take over his role temporarily, possibly for twelve months, or two years, so that Liam had the option to change his mind. Liam had told him that it was probably time for him to move on and give himself another challenge. Never say never, his uncle had said.

"So when do you start?" asked Charlotte.

"Nothing has been arranged yet," said Liam. "I need to get a replacement for my job sorted out and I need to find somewhere to live. I've told them that I'll need a couple of months and they said that was fine. As long as I'm in there by the end of the summer."

"Okay, wow. It's a big move," said Charlotte. "And are you sure it's what you want?"

"Yes, I've put a lot of thought into it and I'm pretty certain."

Charlotte nodded. "I'm going to have to get myself sorted, with this place, and give a month's notice on the office."

"What do you mean?"

"Well, I don't want to sell the house, but it could be a lovely holiday let, couldn't it?" Charlotte picked up her phone and opened the browser. "That holiday company I rented Holly Cottage from, what was its name, can you remember? Sunset Cottages, was that it?" She looked up at him. "What's wrong, you're looking confused?"

"What do you mean?"

"That's the second time you've just said that," said Charlotte. Then suddenly, the penny dropped. "Oh, I get it." She closed the browser on her phone and put it back on the table. "I feel like such an idiot. A fucking stupid idiot."

"Charlotte." He reached for her hand, but she pulled it away. He moved to the edge of the sofa, holding his head in his hands, as the realisation hit him. It never occurred to him that Charlotte would assume that she would be moving to Manchester with him. That explained why she had taken his news so well. She thought they were going together.

"Manchester's a shit hole, anyway," she said.

"No, it isn't. It's the second most desirable city in the UK, or third, I can't remember, but it's a beautiful city."

"How do you know? When have you ever been to Manchester?" She could feel the tension rising and knew that they were on the brink of an argument, but she didn't seem to be able to do anything to stop it. She was suddenly angry. His plans were settled and finalized before he had spoken to her. Her thoughts on the matter were immaterial.

"I've been a few times, in my younger days." He smiled at her but she didn't smile back. Now wasn't the time for reliving memories from a misspent youth; bawdy weekends away with the lads. "And of course, I saw a bit of it when I went for the interview."

"When?" Charlotte hadn't intended the word to come out so shrieky, so accusatory.

"Last week."

"When though?"

"Wednesday," said Liam. He had the decency to look a little abashed. "I was there and back in a day. You were busy with the office and you had plans with Linda, remember?"

Charlotte shook her head. "No, I don't remember." She hadn't been doing anything that couldn't have been re-arranged, but for some reason, he obviously hadn't wanted her to be with him, which hurt. She couldn't remember their conversation that day, but by not telling her where he had been, he had lied to her. Deceit was never a word she would have associated with him. "So, you're definitely taking it then?"

"Yes, I've told them I will," said Liam.

"So that's it then," she said. It wasn't a question and she didn't give him time to respond. She stood up and walked into the kitchen, grabbing their two wine glasses from the coffee table and taking them with her.

Liam followed her. "Charlotte, baby, it's not it. It's not the end for me and you." He really wanted to ask her if that was what she was worried about, but he bit his tongue. He didn't want to add fuel to the fire by not understanding her. He was hopeless at reading her cryptic language sometimes.

She emptied the wine from the glasses down the sink, rinsed the glasses quickly and put them upside down on the draining board. She should have known that it would come to an end sooner or later. She came to Warkworth to get away from the stress of her job and happened to bump into a lovely man in a cafe on her first day out. What are the chances? It was too good to be true. Never meant to last.

She should be happy for him, shouldn't she? Someone had seen his worth and offered him a prestigious job. That was cause for celebration, wasn't it?

"Charlotte, did you hear me? We can still make it work."

"Are you kidding me?" she barked at him. "You're moving to the other side of the country and you clearly don't want me to come with you, so what exactly are you suggesting? Because if you're about to say that we can see each other on the weekends, well I'm sorry, that's not good enough. I don't do long distance."

Liam didn't know what to say. He was prepared for her being a little upset, but he was confident that they would make it work. Lots of couples have long-distance relationships. With him working long hours and Charlotte's new law practice, they probably wouldn't see each other as often during the week anyway, so they might as well be in another town. The salary increase for him was huge, so travelling back at the weekend wouldn't be an issue. And he knew that Charlotte would get to love Manchester once she had spent more time there. He had assumed that they would take turns to visit each other and that she would enjoy the change of scene.

Charlotte stared out of the window. It would be dark in an hour or so. The garden fairy lights would be coming on soon. It always looked so pretty in the dark. Her own little oasis. She had only just settled in Warkworth and had become used to the slower pace of life than in a city, so she should be pleased that she didn't need to leave it now, after all, as she wasn't invited to join Liam in his new life. But what was the point of living in Warkworth without him?

As she felt Liam's arms around her waist, she pushed him away. "Get off me, Liam," she said. She wiped her tears with the back of her hand, silently cursing for not putting waterproof mascara on.

Don't fuck it up, Hannah had said. Look after your relationship, he's worth keeping. Well, what was she meant to do now? Was she meant to crack open the Champagne and celebrate his wonderful new job that would take him to the other side of the country and away from her? She wasn't the one fucking it up. He was.

"I want you to leave now," she said.

He sighed but didn't protest.

She waited, listening to him gathering up his phone, his keys and his overnight bag and she didn't turn around until she was sure that he had gone.

Chapter Five

The following week, the cold and damp weather that had threatened to ruin the summer completely lifted and the sun shone down on Warkworth. The warmest day of the year so far. The day of Phil's funeral.

By the time Linda reached the church, which was only a five-minute walk from where she lived, she was hot and sweaty and she wished that she had taken up Charlotte's offer of a lift. As she reached the gate at the bottom of the long path that led through the churchyard and up to the main entrance to the church, she stopped to wipe the sweat from her forehead and catch her breath.

She paused, wondering whether to go in on her own. Charlotte told her that she would wait for her outside if she got there first, but she couldn't see her anywhere. The rising panic made her hotter and she cursed Phil for forcing her to attend a funeral on such a beautiful day. She should be sitting in her garden with her book and a cup of tea. Calm and relaxed. Not here, hot and bothered.

Although she shouldn't really complain, as Phil's sister, Susan, had organised everything, so it wasn't as though the funeral was a huge inconvenience. It was a couple of hours out of her day, that's all. Even so, she would rather be anywhere in the world, other than here right now.

Dorothy had agreed to go through the formality of identifying his body and she had insisted on registering the death, telling Linda that was the least she could do, after all the trouble she had caused, by breaking up their marriage. Linda hadn't told her that their marriage had been dead for a long time and that taking her husband from her was no trouble at all; she was welcome to him. She just said thank you very much and let her get on with it. All Linda had to do was turn up today.

The cars, the flowers, the music and the eulogy had all been taken care of. Susan had asked Linda what 'their song' had been and whether she should have that played at the end, as everyone exited the church.

"That'll be nice, won't it?" she had said, "You and Phil were married for such a long time and you were so close."

Susan had thought it had been an amicable divorce and that Linda and Phil had still been friends. She thought they had just drifted apart; one of those things that happen after a couple has been together for so long. When she rang Linda a few weeks after they had separated, she said that it was a sad situation but she could completely understand it, because they had been together since they were both so young. But as long as they remained friends, that was the main thing. Linda didn't have the energy to contradict her. She was a nice woman and they would exchange Christmas and birthday cards in the future, but they had never been particularly close and she was happy to never see her again. Any reminder of her time with Phil wasn't welcome in her life.

Linda had told her that they didn't really have a song. She didn't tell her that they hadn't listened to music in the house for years and they hadn't made a habit of going anywhere where music was played, so in their life, it just wasn't a thing.

"What about your wedding song?" Susan persisted. "It's on the tip of my tongue, what was it again?"

It isn't on the tip of your tongue, thought Linda. She obviously didn't remember it at all, she was just being polite by pretending to. Linda didn't blame her. Who did remember the first dance at someone else's wedding?

Linda told her that she couldn't remember it either, but of course, that was a lie. It was 'You To Me Are Everything' by the Real Thing. It was already an old song when they were married, but it was a good one, which both of them loved at the time, and both of them knew the words, so they could sing along. Phil had suggested it because he said that it was his mum's favourite tune and she'd be happy that he chose it. Linda had wanted 'Heaven' by Brian Adams, because she had believed that they had been brought together by God and because, when she and Phil were first together before they moved into their marital home, she truly felt as though she was in Heaven every time she was with him. But she was happy to grant Phil, and his mother, their choice of song.

As the evening celebrations began and they swayed together in the middle of the dance floor for the first time as a married couple and Phil held her close and sang in her ear, she told herself that this was love. As she heard the drunken words from her husband, 'You know you've got the power girl, to keep me holding on,' she was the happiest she had ever been. She very quickly learned that if she had ever had any power over Phil, then it was only for those few minutes, on that dance floor in the summer of nineteen eighty-six. As soon as the wedding was over and Phil's hangover was a distant memory, all the power had shifted to him, never to be returned. But uneasy lies the head that wears a crown. What good had it ever done him? He had never been promoted at work, he wasn't happy at home and he didn't have many friends. No friends in fact. The men he met in the pub were merely drinking companions, not friends. They never visited him at home. They never had a meal together. Just alcohol.

Linda had told Phil's sister that she was happy for her to organise the funeral as she wished. She was more than happy to pass over the reins. She really didn't care what kind of coffin he was in, what music was played, or what flowers the family arranged. She just wanted this day to be over and for Phil to be out of her life, once and for all. Susan told her that she would be happy to do that 'for her', thinking that Linda's reluctance to get involved was because her grief was too much for her to bear and she was happy to be doing her a favour.

As she walked into the church and shook hands with the vicar, who had positioned himself at the front door so that he could greet everyone as they arrived, Linda spotted Charlotte waiting for her on the back pew.

"I'm sorry I didn't wait outside," said Charlotte. "It's too bloody hot. I was just texting you, to let you know I'm here."

"Oh, it's fine, don't worry," said Linda, sitting down beside her friend, who wrapped her in a tight hug.

"I wasn't sure where you wanted to sit, so I grabbed this one, but we can move further forward if you want to sit on the family pew," said Charlotte.

"This is perfect," said Linda. "I'll just go and speak to Dorothy, I can see her over there."

Dorothy was sitting on the other side of the aisle, three rows back from the front. She stood as soon as she saw Linda approaching and the two women clung to each other silently, each one lost in their own thoughts for a moment. Dorothy seemed to be genuinely upset and Linda was pleased that she had a friend with her, to comfort her. The poor woman. She hadn't been with Phil long, but it was sad that she had lost her husband and had then lost Phil too. No doubt, after the funeral, she would get over him quickly, when she realised that life without him was so much more peaceful.

"I'm going to sit at the back with my friend, Charlotte," Linda explained to Dorothy.

"Are you sure?" asked Dorothy. "Don't you want to be at the front with his family?"

"Not really. I'd rather keep a low profile if I'm honest. I'll speak to you later."

"Okay love, see you in a bit." Dorothy squeezed her hand affectionately and sat back down next to her friend. "Oh, Linda, don't forget…"

"Yes, I know we need to talk about his will."

Dorothy nodded. "I'd just like to get it sorted, that's all."

"Of course," said Linda, as she began to walk away. She knew that it wasn't fair to Dorothy to keep ignoring the issue and, although today might not be the best time, she needed to make a decision sooner or later. Dorothy had texted her a couple of times already and asked to meet her to discuss it, but Linda had lied and told her that she was busy and would arrange to see her when the funeral was out of the way. The truth was that she needed to speak to Charlotte about it, but she had been so busy, with her new office opening and her new clients to deal with, that Linda had hardly seen her. On the one day that they had managed to get together for a quick coffee, Linda hadn't wanted to bring it up. But she would make a conscious effort to chat to her soon and then let

Dorothy know what she had decided. She knew that whether she decided to take the money for herself, donate it to charity or throw it all away on the two fifteen race at Kempton, it wasn't fair on Dorothy to keep procrastinating.

Linda reached her seat, just as the organ music started. Her heart began to beat so fast that she felt as though she had just run up a flight of stairs. She remembered that day last summer when Phil had gone missing and the nice police lady had taken her to the mortuary at the hospital to identify a dead body. A man had been found dead at the park, with no identification on him and the police thought that it might be Phil because he was of a similar age and build. It wasn't him, but the vision of that poor man was now etched on her brain. The stillness of him. The pale grey colour of his skin. Phil was like that now, lying lifeless and grey in his coffin.

The coffin was carried by Phil's brother-in-law and his two nephews and another man that Linda didn't recognise. He was probably one of the funeral directors, or maybe someone that Phil knew from the pub. How could there be people at her husband's funeral that she didn't know? She should know everyone, shouldn't she? She was his wife, just about.

She nodded hello to Susan, who was walking behind the coffin, dressed from head to foot in black. That should be me, thought Linda. I should be the one at the back of the coffin, accompanying him down the aisle and then onwards to his final resting place. The chief mourner. A sudden wave of sadness overcame her and she began to cry. As she watched the coffin being placed at the altar, she sobbed and sobbed, crying for the marriage that she should have had, for the caring and loving husband that she deserved and for all the lost opportunities that had passed her by while Phil had been her husband.

After the first hymn, Susan's husband stood at the podium and told the congregation how much he would miss his brother-in-law and how sorry he was that his life had been cut short. With a speech full of platitudes, he told the congregation that Phil was such a kind man, he would do anything for anyone, the salt of the earth, would give you his last pound and he would be missed by many. Linda looked over at Charlotte in disbelief.

"Are we at the wrong funeral?" Charlotte whispered.

"We must be. He's not talking about the Phil that I know," whispered Linda, resting her head on Charlotte's shoulder and wiping tears from her cheeks.

Chapter Six

A wake had been arranged in one of the meeting rooms at The Warkworth House Hotel. Linda and Charlotte were sat together on a small sofa in the corner under one of the windows that looked out onto Bridge Street, furthest away from the crowd that had gathered at the bar. Linda hadn't wanted to queue for a drink alongside Phil's old drinking pals, so they had taken a cup of tea from a table at the back of the room instead.

"When is it polite to leave, do you think?" asked Linda.

Charlotte looked at her watch. "We can leave now if you like. You don't owe anybody anything."

"I know, but it's only been half an hour. Maybe we should stay a little longer," said Linda.

"Okay, well let's just pretend we're in the cafe. We don't know these people and we're not at a funeral. We're just having a chat. Maybe we're having a little afternoon tea." Linda smiled at her friend's attempts to cheer her up.

"Are we having a prosecco afternoon tea or just tea?" asked Linda, lifting her cup and peering into it.

"Is it a weekday or weekend?" asked Charlotte.

"It's a weekday, I'm afraid."

"Oh fuck. Just tea then. No, sod it, let's pretend it's

Champagne and we've both sneaked out of work."

Both of them giggled for a moment. They sat back in their chairs, each deep in thought, and watched a group of tourists making their way down the road towards the beach. "Tell me what you've been up to with your retirement," said Charlotte, breaking the silence. "You make me jealous. How is your new neighbour?"

"She's nice, from what I've seen of her so far. She's been in the garden quite a lot, so we've been talking over the fence."

"She doesn't seem like the gardening type," said Charlotte.

"No, not at all. She's been sunbathing, not gardening."

"Ahh, good for her. I knew she wouldn't get those manicured nails dirty."

"She's told me all about her split from her husband and that she'd been to see you about it."

Both women sat sipping their tea for a moment, thinking about Jessica, Linda's new neighbour, who had moved in last week, after splitting up from her husband of six months. She was renting the house next door, which was one of the properties owned by the Warkworth House Hotel. She had been to see Charlotte, in floods of tears, after a mutual friend had told her that he was cheating on her. She had also found out that she was pregnant, but she hadn't yet told him. She told Charlotte that she never wanted him to find out about the baby. He didn't deserve to be a dad, she had said. She had asked whether there was any way that she could register the birth without having to put his name on the birth certificate. Charlotte had advised her to take it one step at a time. She might think differently after the baby was born. Reconciliation should never be dismissed.

When Linda had spoken to her over the fence, Jessica had poured her heart out to her, spilling all her troubles for the world to hear. Linda had told her that she should tell her husband about the baby and, if he was worth having, he would be back like a shot, with his tail well and truly between his legs. Jessica had smiled at that thought and seemed happy to grasp the tiny bit of hope being offered to her and said that she would think about it.

"I can tell you what's going to happen with her," said Charlotte. "They'll get back together. I can tell you now. After her scan, when she sees that tiny heart beating on the screen, she'll come to the conclusion that she doesn't want to be a single mother and she'll take him back. All will be forgiven."

"Yes, I think you're right. From my experience, men tend to go from one mistake to the next, and forgiving them seems to be what women do best," said Linda.

Charlotte frowned at her. She hadn't yet told Linda about Liam's plan to move to Manchester; the plan in which she didn't factor at all. "That's not how it should be though, is it? We shouldn't keep forgiving them. Why can't they just behave in the first place?"

"You don't need to talk to me about husbands misbehaving," said Linda. "But surely having two parents together is better than them living separately, isn't it?"

"Not always," said Charlotte. "The baby wouldn't know any different, and it's always better for a child to live in a peaceful household than in one where the parents are tearing each other to pieces every day."

"I don't know how you cope, dealing with people's messy separations and custody battles on a day-to-day basis. The world would be a much better place if husbands were a little kinder to their wives."

"That's very true. But then, I wouldn't have a job, would I?" Charlotte drained her tea and put the delicate cup and saucer on the low table in front of them. "I'm going for a sandwich," she said. "There's an egg mayonnaise over there with my name on it. Do you want something?"

"Yes please," said Linda. "I've not eaten yet. I'd love an egg mayo and one of those little pork pies."

"Sure, leave it with me."

"And a few crisps," said Linda, as Charlotte started walking away.

She was beginning to get her appetite back now. She had lost count of the number of meals that she had missed because of Phil over the years, when he had either thrown the plate against the wall or he had swiped it off the table with his big fat hand, leaving Linda to clean up while he went to the pub. There was always something that triggered him, no matter how hard Linda had tried. Either the food wasn't up to scratch, or it just wasn't what he fancied, she was never sure. Anger was such a regular visitor at their house at dinner time that Linda had given up trying to guess whether it was her cooking or herself as a wife that didn't reach Phil's exacting standards. The dinner she had made was merely the casualty.

She looked around the room. There didn't seem to be any tears anymore from any of Phil's drinking friends. The few that had been shed in the church had now dried. How sad, she thought, that people recovered from the loss of you so quickly, for you to leave no legacy at all. After all, when half a dozen pints had been downed, they would probably enjoy anybody's company. Phil wasn't anything special to them. There they were now, a group of middle-aged, balding, pot-bellied men, each a mirror image of his neighbour, crowded around the bar at the far end of the room, their loud guttural voices overshadowing all the other conversations in the room. Whatever the topic of their conversation, laughter was the result. Maybe they were discussing the fight a couple of weeks ago. Maybe they thought it was hilarious that drunken punches had been thrown, shirts had been ripped and pint glasses had been smashed onto the pavement. A good time was had by all, eh? She wondered how many of them went home to their wives ready for another fight.

At least their number was now lessened by one. The one who had bent double at the side of the road, the agony of a heart attack causing him to stumble and fall would never again raise another pint of beer to his lips or raise another of his fists to a woman.

Charlotte returned with a plate of food in each hand and they both sat in silence for a moment as they ate. A young waitress took away their empty cups and returned with two new ones, filled with fresh tea, which she left on the table in front of them.

"I don't think I want to be a solicitor anymore." Charlotte dropped the words suddenly, as Linda leaned forwards to pick up her cup. She held up her hand to block any protestations from Linda. "No, no, I know what you're about to say, that I've only just opened the office, but honestly, you're absolutely right."

"What do you mean, I'm right?" Linda was shocked to think that she may have inadvertently put an idea into Charlotte's head.

"I can't stand the drama of other people's messy lives. I think I've made a big mistake returning to the law."

"You can't say that now. You need to do something to pay the bills and I can't see you working in a shop or a café.

You might think you could do it, but the wage wouldn't keep you in handbags."

Charlotte shrugged. "I've got enough handbags."

"Well, you don't have to do divorces, you could concentrate on conveyancing," said Linda, half serious, but trying to lighten Charlotte's mood, which had taken a sudden dip. "You did it for my house."

"I did my own too, but it's boring as hell," said Charlotte. She took a sip of her tea. "But that might not be a bad idea, you know. Honestly, matrimonial work is draining the life out of me. I listen to people weeping and wailing and I tell them what their options are and I start working for them and then half of them get back together and all my work has been for nothing. I feel like saying to them when they come and see me, just leave it for now and come back in six months, because I know you would have sorted it out by then."

"But that's not a bad thing, is it? Like Jessica and her husband, if they get back together for the baby?" asked Linda.

"I suppose not, but I don't want to be involved. I think I'd rather deal with criminals. At least you know what to expect from them. They're always going to let you down and they don't pretend otherwise. Last week, this woman…" she stopped suddenly. "Sorry, I'm ranting, aren't I?"

"No, it's okay, you can rant. I know you've been stressed. You've had a lot going on recently. Opening a business is tough."

"You're not wrong," said Charlotte.

"Actually, I've got no bloody idea, but I've watched Dragons' Den often enough and it doesn't look easy."

Charlotte laughed. "I just need a few days off, that's all.

I need to sort my head out. I might go and see my parents for the weekend next week." She sighed heavily. What she really needed was to get away from Warkworth and have no contact with Liam, until she was sure that he had moved to Manchester. She had managed to avoid him since he dropped his bombshell last week and she would do everything she could to make sure it stayed that way.

"There you go! That's all you need, just a little break. When was the last time you went on holiday?" asked Linda.

"Last summer, when I rented that cottage for a week and first came to Warkworth. I was still living in London, remember? That's when I met Liam," said Charlotte, wondering how different her life would have been if she had chosen the cottage in Cornwall that she had been looking at, rather than Northumberland.

"Yes, I forgot about that, well before then, when was the last time that you had a holiday in the sun, where you relaxed, read books, ate good food, did some sightseeing and slept really well?"

"Honestly, I don't know," said Charlotte. "It was probably before Hannah got pregnant. We went to Ibiza three years ago, but it wasn't very relaxing. We stayed out late, went to dozens of different bars and clubs, slept until lunchtime, and had way too much alcohol. It was good though."

"I can't offer you that kind of experience, but how do you fancy a holiday with me, on the cruise?"

"Yes! I would love that," said Charlotte, without hesitation. "Are you sure?"

"Yes," said Linda. "I had planned to go on my own, but the closer it gets, the more nervous I get. It would be really nice if you came with me."

"I could have a look online, couldn't I? They might have some cabins left. I've never been on a cruise before."

"That would be amazing. What are you waiting for? Get checking the vacancies," said Linda. "The departure date is 10th November and the ship is called Harmony."

For the next few minutes, Linda waited patiently while Charlotte clicked her way around the cruise ship's website on her phone, frowning in concentration. Linda kept herself busy watching people chatting in the room. She could hardly bear the waiting; now that she had made the proposal, she would be disappointed if the ship was completely full, although they could always share her cabin and ask for two single beds, rather than a double.

While she waited, she busied herself watching the various people in the room; the little group of Phil's ex-colleagues, whose conversation had long since moved on to more exciting topics than the man who had just been buried, who none of them had particularly liked but whose funeral gave them an excuse to get out of work for half a day; the family group, his sister Susan, her husband and their two grown-up sons, who seemed reasonably upset, because they only knew Phil when he was on his best behaviour; Dorothy and her friend, who were probably silently toasting her narrow escape from the controlling and nasty man that Phil had recently shown himself to be, and then the raucous party of drinking buddies, their shiny middle-aged heads tipping back regularly as their mouths were filled with an unending supply of beer.

"Right, sorted!" Charlotte suddenly shouted. "They only have inside cabins left, but that's okay. I've booked it and paid."

"Are you serious? I didn't even see you get your card

out of your purse."

"What planet are you on, old lady? I'm a frequent online shopper. I know my card number off by heart."

Then they stood and hugged and Linda cried for the second time that day. But this time, they were happy tears. She vowed never to cry about Phil again. It was time to move on. She had a luxury holiday to look forward to and, even though she had persuaded herself that she was happy to go alone, she was so much happier at the thought of her friend going with her. She refused to cry anymore over the woman that she used to be and the regrets that she may have. Today was all about the future.

Chapter Seven

"Hi, how's it going?" asked Liam, as he approached the sofa where Linda and Charlotte were eating their sandwiches.

"It's been okay," said Linda. "Thanks for organising all of this." She stood up and gave Liam a hug.

"Not a problem," said Liam. "I'm sorry I couldn't make it to the church, but I needed to be here to oversee everything, you know."

"Of course, it's fine," said Linda. "You've done a great job. The food is lovely, as always, and we've been very well looked after."

Charlotte tutted loudly and took another bite of her sandwich, without lifting her head. It was immediately obvious to Linda that she and Liam had had an argument about something.

"Is everything all right with the food?" asked Liam, looking directly at Charlotte, who continued to chew, without speaking.

"Have you two had a barny?" asked Linda, when Charlotte didn't reply. "I know you have. You don't need to tell me; you can cut the atmosphere between you with a knife."

Liam shrugged. "Yes, kind of," he said. "Charlotte? I

think we need to talk, do you?"

Charlotte sighed heavily and put her plate down on the table in front of her. "Not today," she said. "It's not the time or the place, is it?" She gave him a disdainful look, as though he had just suggested performing some completely inappropriate comedic circus act in the middle of the wake.

"Oh, for goodness sake, you two," said Linda. "I'm going to talk to Dorothy and Susan while you sort it out and I want you to be friends by the time I get back, all right?"

"There's no point, Linda," said Charlotte. "There's nothing to say."

"Charlotte!" said Liam.

"You might as well tell her what's going on." She stared at him but didn't give him a chance to speak. "Liam's got a new job with a big fancy hotel chain and he's moving to Manchester."

"Aww, how lovely," said Linda, stroking Liam's arm.

"On his own. Without me."

"Oh." Linda dropped her arm and took an involuntary step back.

"Yes, exactly. So that's it really. There's nothing more to talk about."

"No, that's not it at all," said Liam. "It's not the other side of the world, it's a couple of hours away and as far as I'm concerned, it doesn't change anything. I don't want to fall out about it." He looked at Linda, his eyes imploring her to intervene and make Charlotte see sense.

"Isn't it a bit late to say that you don't want to fall out about it, Liam?" said Charlotte. "You haven't spoken to me for nearly a week!"

"You've ignored all my text messages, that's why," said Liam.

"And have you tried to call me? Have you been to see me? No, you haven't." Charlotte knew that she was being ridiculously unreasonable. She hadn't wanted to speak to Liam, even after he had reached out to her. But that didn't mean that she didn't want him to keep trying. "And you're right," she continued. "It's not the other side of the world, no. But it's the other side of the country. It's miles away, isn't it, Linda?"

Linda, who had never been to Manchester in her life, shrugged her shoulders and nodded at the same time. She knew that Manchester was over the other side of the Pennine Hills, but she had no idea how to get there and whether or not there was a decent train service.

"You're moving and I'm not invited. End of," continued Charlotte. "I told you last week that I'm not going to have a long-distance relationship. I'm too old for that, Liam. I want to settle down, not traipse across the country every weekend, like a fucking…"

"Now now, don't get upset," said Linda. "Here, wipe your eyes. I've got plenty of tissues." Linda patted her pockets.

"Thank you," said Charlotte, taking the proffered tissue and dabbing at her eyes.

"Maybe you should talk to her later," said Linda to Liam. "She's right that maybe here isn't the right time and place."

He nodded, bent down to kiss Charlotte's cheek, and quickly walked away.

"Why didn't you tell me what was going on?" said Linda, sitting back down next to Charlotte and putting her arm around her shoulders. "Have you been arguing with him all week?"

73

"No, not really. I haven't seen him since last Friday. We're done. There's nothing more to argue about."

"Is that why you said you don't want to be a solicitor anymore? You're not seriously going to close the office, are you, because of him?"

Charlotte shrugged. "I don't know what to do, to be honest. I moved all the way from London for that man and now he's moving away. I just feel a bit lost." She wiped away more tears. Of all the places to have a public crying session over a man, then a wake wasn't a bad option, thought Linda. At least people had no cause to be staring over and wondering what she was crying about.

"Is it going to be a permanent move?" she asked. "Or do you think he just wants some experience of a big hotel?"

"Yes, I think so. Permanent, I mean. He's been dazzled by an all-singing, all-dancing, fancy hotel in the city. I can't see him wanting to come back here too soon, can you? What the fuck am I going to do now?" Charlotte held the tissue over her face and sobbed.

Linda didn't have much experience with men, but she thought that Liam was different. It was disappointing. She thought that Charlotte was the front and centre of his world. But apparently, she didn't seem to feature very highly in it at all. "I don't know what to say," she said. "I'm shocked, to be honest. I really thought I'd be buying a new hat for your wedding in the next year or so. I'll go and get us a drink." Linda disappeared to the bar and returned a few minutes later carrying two large glasses of cold white wine. "I got us Pinot Grigio, is that okay?"

"Thank you," said Charlotte. "I'd take a glass of paint stripper if it made me feel better."

Linda handed her the glass as she sat down on the sofa.

"Are you okay?" asked Linda.

"I will be," said Charlotte, taking a large gulp of wine.

"Can't you move to Manchester with him?" asked Linda.

"I would do yes," said Charlotte. She turned to face Linda and placed her wine glass on the table in front of them. "Only, he made it pretty clear that he was going on his own. I don't think it occurred to him that we might go together."

"Okay, well we'll have to change his mind, won't we? Because giving up on what you two have isn't an option," said Linda.

"I'm not begging," said Charlotte. "If he hasn't thought about taking me with him, well he obviously doesn't want to. So I'm done."

"No, you're not," said Linda. "He probably hadn't given it any thought, that's all. It's a temporary blind spot. All we need to do is make him see the light."

"How?"

"Well, I don't know. You're the one with the brain and all the experience."

They both laughed. "I appreciate your optimism, but I can't see it happening," said Charlotte. She wiped her eyes and took a deep breath. "I've been worrying about it all week. I don't want to lose him, honestly, I don't, but I don't want that kind of relationship where we only see each other once a week. I mean, what if I want to go and see my parents one weekend? That means I won't get to see him for a fortnight."

"Well, he can go too, can't he? He can meet you there."

"And then if he has to work at the weekend, am I expected to sit around in Manchester on my own?"

"You're worrying too much about the tiny details. It won't add a single hour to the span of your life," said Linda.

"Here, dry your eyes and drink some more wine. It will all work out in the end." She passed the glass back to Charlotte, who obediently took a sip. "Don't worry about tomorrow, for tomorrow will bring worries of its own. Today's trouble is enough for today."

"You're so wise, Linda. Where do you get all these little nuggets from? I thought you'd led a sheltered life."

"I have," said Linda. "Those are the words of someone much wiser than me. I'm just quoting Him. But it's true. It will all work out in the end, but you do need to talk to him."

Charlotte nodded. The last thing she wanted was for them to break up. They had done that once already and the days that they had been apart had been torturous.

"I knew I should never have dated someone younger than me. He just isn't in the same place as me yet."

"Why don't you send him a message and arrange to talk to him later?" said Linda.

"Maybe. Anyway, let's talk about this cruise. I need some clothes," said Charlotte. "I have a couple of suitable dresses, but I haven't got any swimwear and not nearly enough shoes."

"I need some things too," said Linda. "I need a few dresses for the posh dinners."

"Great. Let's go to Newcastle. One day next week? I need retail therapy. I can close the office for a day," said Charlotte.

"You're not going to close it permanently though, are you?"

"Don't worry, I won't do anything rash for now. I can see how it goes over the summer and I'll do some thinking while we're away on the cruise. Right now, I don't know my arse from my elbow."

Linda nodded. "I can understand that," she said.

When they had finished their sandwiches and their second glass of wine, as Linda was saying her goodbyes to everyone, Charlotte sent a text to Liam, after some persuasion from Linda, asking him to meet her for a talk. She couldn't help smiling when his reply came within seconds, saying that he had missed her and that he would love to see her tonight, or tomorrow, or whenever she was free. She told him that she would call round to his house tomorrow, around eight o'clock. It wasn't that she was playing hard to get, but making him wait wouldn't do him any harm. She wasn't at his beck and call, after all. Under normal circumstances, she would have been excited to add that she had just booked a cruise and she wanted to spend the rest of the day with Linda, so they could chat about it and do some online shopping. But for now, she kept that information to herself.

They were almost at the front door of the hotel, on their way out, when they heard the small voice at reception asking where the funeral of Phil Matthews was being held. Charlotte looked at Linda and raised her eyebrows, as she stood with her hand on the front door. They were both more than a little curious and wanted to see who was asking. As the voice was female and all of Phil's drinking buddies were already upstairs drowning whatever sorrows they may have had in the hotel's finest artisan ales, Linda could only deduce that the young woman was either an ex-colleague from Johnson & Sons (and given that Phil hadn't worked for a number of years, that was unlikely, as she seemed too young) or one of the barmaids from The Hermitage Inn, his favourite drinking spot. Of course, there was a possibility that she was an ex-girlfriend but when Linda quickly decided that was impossible. Phil may have had some charms in his younger days and Linda had certainly been beguiled by them, but he had lost them all in the last few years of his life. No man approaching sixty with yellowing teeth and a beer belly to match the finest of all his drinking pals was ever going to appeal to the likes of the pretty young woman currently standing at the reception desk.

The woman couldn't have been more than twenty or twenty-five years old. Her ankle-length jeans, grey t-shirt with the logo 'McBusted Tour 2014' and white Converse ankle boots made her look like a teenager. It was only her confident demeanour that belied her age.

"If you take the stairs to the first floor, the room is on your left at the top of the stairs. It's called The Orchard Room," said Maggie, the receptionist. "Would you like me to show you the way?"

"No thank you, I'll manage," said the young woman.

Linda and Charlotte watched her disappear through the door leading to the stairwell.

"Who was that?" Charlotte asked Maggie.

"I don't know," said Maggie. "She didn't give me her name. She just said she was looking for Phil Matthews' funeral, although she's not exactly dressed for it, is she?"

"She'll be a reporter, I reckon," said Linda. "Didn't you say there was a piece in the Warkworth Guardian about him last week, Charlotte?"

"Yes, there was," said Charlotte. "That will be it. She's probably doing a story about his funeral, a testimonial, or something. Do you think we should go and talk to her?"

"Not really, do you?" said Linda. Now she was close to the door, she was eager to make her escape into the warm sunshine outside.

"Yes, I think so," said Charlotte. "But only if you want

to."

"His sister's there, and Dorothy. There are enough people for her to talk to." Linda hesitated, her hand on the glass door, anxious to open it and close the chapter on her awful husband's life forever. "Oh, for fuck's sake. Come on then! Let's get this over with."

Charlotte smiled at her and followed her back up the stairs to the first floor.

As they reached the landing and opened the fire door, Linda whispered, "She's standing outside the door. Why hasn't she gone in?"

"Maybe she just needs a minute to think about what she's going to write," said Charlotte. "I don't know." She walked over to the meeting room door. "Hello, can I help you? Did I hear you say you were looking for Mr. Matthews' funeral?" The young woman turned suddenly, her eyes wide with shock. "Sorry, I didn't mean to startle you," said Charlotte.

"Oh, it's okay. Is this the right room?" she asked.

"Yes, that's right. I can take you in, if you like, and introduce you to the people you need to speak to."

Linda was impressed by the way that Charlotte was taking control. The last thing she wanted to do was talk to a reporter, even though she knew that she inevitably must. After all Phil had done, the last thing she wanted was for the newspaper article to comment on his wife's absence from the funeral. The local gossips had had enough to talk about over the years, when they had spotted her fading bruises and black eyes. She needed to hold her head high and answer the lady's questions with as much dignity as possible and then they could leave, finally.

"Are you with the Warkworth Guardian?" asked

Charlotte.

The young woman shook her head.

"Oh, you're a freelancer?"

"I'm sorry, I don't…"

"You're a reporter, right?" asked Charlotte.

"No, no. I'm Phil Matthews' daughter."

Chapter Eight

"I can't tell you how happy I am to see you," said Liam, the following night, as he opened his front door. "Come here." He pulled Charlotte towards him and hugged her tight. She didn't want to melt into his arms. Not yet. They had a lot to talk about before she felt like she could open her heart to him again.

"I've brought us a bottle of wine," said Charlotte, pulling away from him and pushing the wine bottle into his hand.

"Dutch courage, eh?" he said. "Thank you." She followed him into the kitchen. She had chosen to speak to him at his house so that she could leave whenever she wanted to. She felt the need to grasp hold of that tiny bit of control. She watched him open the drawer, take out the bottle opener, and open the bottle of wine quickly and expertly. He poured some into the two glasses which were ready and waiting on the countertop. Her heart ached a little. Sometimes he could be so thoughtful. She knew that he would have at least a couple of bottles of wine in his fridge, already chilled. He always did. But the fact that he opened the wine that she brought touched her, for some reason. Maybe he saw it as a little gift between them that he had accepted. A peace offering. The proverbial olive branch, reaching between them and pulling them together.

"Shall we cheers?" he asked, as he passed her a glass and raised his towards her. "Okay, maybe not yet." He grinned at her and she couldn't help smiling back, even though his constant enthusiasm and optimism drove her crazy.

"Yes, okay, we should cheers," she said.

"To?"

"Peace talks," said Charlotte.

"Yes, to peace talks." They both clinked their glasses together and took a sip of their wine. "How's Linda?" he asked. "Pretty tough day yesterday, I'd imagine. A few mixed emotions?"

"Yes, exactly that," said Charlotte. She pulled out a dining room chair and sat down, resting her elbows on the table. "She was fine. I mean, she cried a bit but overall she did really well, except that when we were leaving, this woman appeared and told us that she was Phil's daughter."

"What? Phil's daughter? I didn't know he had a daughter."

"Well, neither did Linda, until yesterday."

"Fuck!" Liam sat down on the other side of the table and reached across to hold Charlotte's hand. She allowed him to hold onto her hand tightly and wished that the only serious conversation she would have with him that night would be about Phil's mysterious daughter. "So tell me what happened?" he said. "Linda was shocked, I presume?"

"Yes, of course," she said. "She had no idea. Shocked is an understatement. She ran into the toilets crying."

"What a bastard he was," said Liam. "I've never met anyone like him. Who's the mother, do you know?"

"No."

"You hear about these people who have double lives, don't you? They have two entirely different families and neither of them know about the other one."

"I don't know whether that was the case. Phil was home every night, I think. I really don't know any details about the woman or her mother," said Charlotte. "She had gone by the time we came out of the toilet. She might not even be his real daughter. We have no idea who she is."

"I'd never thought of that," said Liam. "Do you think she was a fraudster?"

"I've no idea. Anything's possible, look we…"

"Yes, I know, I'm procrastinating, aren't I? I know I am."

Charlotte nodded. "I'd rather talk about Linda too, but we do have some issues of our own, don't we?"

"Yes," he said, taking a large gulp of wine. "I love you, you know that, don't you?"

"I don't know," said Charlotte, shrugging her shoulders. "Well, yes, of course, you do, I suppose…"

"You suppose? What's that meant to mean?" Liam pulled his hand away and leaned back in his chair. He held onto the wine glass, twisting the stem between his fingers.

Charlotte took a deep breath. "We can't get angry so early on in the conversation," she said. "We've barely said two words yet. We've got to try and take the emotions out and speak honestly about how we see this working." Charlotte couldn't believe what she had just said. She imagined that she would have been the one getting emotional and potentially storming out. Isn't that why she chose to meet at Liam's house, rather than hers, so that she would have the advantage of storming out? Seeing Liam's emotions so close to the surface gave her a little hope that he did care after all, although maybe not as much as she wanted him to. But she regularly advised her clients to try having an honest conversation without emotions clouding the subject. So that was what she aimed to do.

Liam stared at her for what felt like minutes, rather than the few seconds that it was in reality. "You're right. Let's start again," he said.

"Okay," she said. "So, what I meant was that, yes, I know you love me. But if it was me, and I had the choice of moving hundreds of miles away for a job, I think I would have thought a bit more about how it would affect us, as a couple." As soon as the words were out of her mouth, she realised that they came across as accusatory rather than mediatory, but thankfully Liam remained calm.

"I should have spoken to you about it first," he said. " I get that. I'm sorry."

"It's not even that you should have spoken to me first," she said. "We're not married or anything, but we're still a couple and it's going to affect my life as well as yours and you should have put some thought into that at least."

"I know."

"I don't want to be left in Warkworth without you." The tears came suddenly and unexpectedly. Hot and angry. Liam jumped up and was at her side within a second, kneeling in front of her. She rested her head on his shoulder, while he stroked her back and allowed her to cry.

"I'll go and get you a tissue," he said, disappearing into the downstairs toilet. He returned with a full toilet roll.

"How much crying do you think I'm going to do?" asked Charlotte. She took the roll from him and tore of a section of tissue, wiping her eyes as carefully as she could, aware that it was probably too late to save her make-up.

"I didn't think you would do any," he said. "You were the one who said we need to keep emotion out of this."

"Oh fuck off," she said, throwing the roll at him, laughing.

He filled up their wine glasses and sat back down at the table. "You okay?" he asked after a moment. Charlotte nodded. "I'm sorry."

"Don't keep saying sorry," she said. "You're going to make me cry again."

"I don't want to make you cry, honestly. I've never wanted that. I've never wanted to hurt you." Charlotte did her best to hold in the barrage of tears that she knew was waiting to escape. The more kind and caring Liam was towards her, the more it hurt her to think that she would lose him. She thought that he was her future and to consider for one moment that he didn't see them in the same light was tortuous. She knew that he didn't mean to hurt her on purpose, but the fact was, he was younger than her and he clearly wasn't yet ready for them to take the next step. While she had been thinking about where they would live together in Manchester, he had probably been visualising his batchelor pad, which he would allow her to visit each weekend. While she was collecting images for her Pinterest wedding board and following wedding dress designers on Instagram, he was probably considering how big his TV could be and whether he should fit it onto the wall or buy a stand.

"So where do we go from here?" she said.

"All I know is that we've got something special. Haven't we?" he asked. "I don't know why it needs to end."

"I know you don't. We just seem to want different

things…"

"We don't want different things at all, Charlotte," he said. "I'm sorry, I don't want to raise my voice and get annoyed, but..." He paused and his deep sigh told Charlotte that he was trying to understand her, but they were on completely different pages. "We both want each other, so I don't get why you're turning this into a problem. I know we won't see each other every day, but we don't see each other every day here. We're both working people."

"That's not the issue," she said.

"Well, what's the issue? I'm struggling here."

"It is the issue, but not the whole issue." She knew she was talking in riddles and that he wouldn't understand her, but she was reluctant to tell him the truth, in case it frightened him away. But as she was on the verge of losing him anyway, she decided that she might as well speak her mind. "I would have thought that if you wanted to move to Manchester, you would have wanted me to go with you. To live together."

"But you've just opened your own firm."

"I don't give a shit about the firm. I give a shit about us. About our future."

"So do I," said Liam. "But we've not even been together for a year yet."

Charlotte shrugged. "I know, I just thought we were moving in that direction."

"We are, but…"

"Yes, I get it, it's too soon. For you anyway. But I would have thought that moving to Manchester might have made you reconsider, but I can see that for you, we're just dating."

Charlotte could tell by the look on Liam's face that he was shocked. Hannah's words in her head telling her not to fuck it up this time forced her to stay put while her instincts were telling her to walk out. She wanted to shout and scream at Liam and tell him that he was playing with her heart and that he should take more care. She wanted to yell at him and tell him to grow up; that he clearly wasn't mature enough for a relationship with her and he could move to Manchester on his own and shove his hotel up his arse, for all she cared. But instead, she sipped her wine, took deep breaths, and told herself to wait for him to speak. Being rash and dramatic hadn't served her well in the past. There were only so many times that you could do the same thing over and over and expect a different result.

So, when Liam got up from the table for the second time and took her hand and led her into the living room, telling her that they needed to sit somewhere more comfortable, she allowed herself to be led. As they sat side by side, she held tightly onto his hand. When he told her that he did see her in his future and that he wanted to spend the rest of his life with her, she believed him and then rested her head on his shoulder in an act of capitulation.

But whether she wanted to sit around and wait, was a decision that she needed to make for herself.

***

The following day, Charlotte met Linda for lunch in the beer garden at the back of The Masons Arms. Her busy morning had included preparing a divorce petition for a man whose wife had left him suddenly; discussing a financial situation with a female client and what she could expect to receive following her divorce and then preparing an urgent application to the court for a non-molestation order for a young woman who was terrified of her partner. This, together with her conversation with Liam the previous evening left her emotionally drained and in dire need of a glass of restorative wine.

She had considered speaking to Hannah about Liam, but she couldn't deal with the criticism and judgement that she knew would be hurled at her. Hannah might mean well, but she was too opinionated and Charlotte needed to sort her own head out before she could deal with someone else's viewpoint. She knew that Linda would listen and support her, whatever decision she finally made.

After the waiter delivered their salads to their table, together with a bowl of chips for them to share, and they were sure of no further interruptions, they were free to talk.

"You look exhausted," said Linda. "Is everything okay?"

"I'm okay, thanks. I didn't sleep much last night, to be honest. Nothing's changed between me and Liam. We're friends but he's still going to Manchester and I'm still not invited to go with him so it seems like a long-distance relationship is the only option."

"I'm sorry to hear that," said Linda. "I thought he would have come to his senses."

"Yes, me too. He didn't get it. I think he thinks that I'm the one creating the problem."

"He didn't say that, did he?" said Linda.

"Yes, he did. But then he said that he thought we had something special and he wanted to carry it on. He said that he definitely wants me in his future."

"But he's not ready to move in with you?"

"In a nutshell, no. I don't know what to do, Linda."

"Then do nothing."

"What do you mean?"

"Well, what are your options? Dumping him and moving back to London, or dumping him and staying here?" Charlotte shook her head. Neither of those choices was appealing. "I know you don't want to do either of those things, not really. So just do nothing. Keep the status quo. Stay here for now, carry on as normal, and let life happen to you."

"I don't know whether I can do that," said Charlotte.

"Of course, you can. You've made enough big decisions in the past twelve months, it's time to give yourself a break."

Charlotte considered Linda's advice as she picked at her salad. But was Linda really the right person to ask for relationship advice? She didn't have great experience with men and she certainly hadn't made her own decisions in the past. Was waiting around and doing nothing the right thing to do? Maybe she should have spoken to Hannah after all.

"He said he wants me to go and see the hotel with him next weekend and spend the weekend in Manchester," she said.

"Well, that will be nice. I've heard that Manchester's a great city."

"I suppose it is. I've been a few times. In my younger days, I went to a few clubs in the Northern Quarter, before I went off to uni. I enjoyed it, but…"

"But what?" asked Linda.

"I like it here and I thought that this is where we'd settle. Given the choice, I wouldn't choose to go back to city living."

"It will all work out in the end, you know," said Linda. "A year from now, he'll either be back in Warkworth with you, or you'll be in a Manchester suburb with him. You don't have to live in the city. I know that..."

"Oh for fuck's sake!" said Charlotte, interrupting Linda and turning round to stare at the family behind them. A young couple was having lunch with a small toddler, who had decided to throw himself onto the floor and scream that he didn't want red sauce on his chips. He wanted brown. When his mum asked him to sit back at the table, he told her no, at the top of his voice and in no uncertain terms. "Why do they have to allow kids in pubs? It's so annoying."

Linda pushed the bowl of chips towards Charlotte, encouraging her to eat one, to focus on the food rather than the recalcitrant child. The last thing she wanted was a showdown with a couple of strangers, who seemed embarrassed enough at their child's antics. "Kids were never allowed in the pub when I was little," she said. "In the seventies, we had to sit outside and wait while all the adults went inside and had a good time. If we were lucky, they'd send us out a bottle of Coke and a bag of crisps to keep us quiet."

"Go on, say it," said Charlotte. "Those were the days."

They both laughed. "Yes, those were the days. When you had groups of five and six-year-olds unsupervised next to a busy road, for hours at a time. You can't imagine it these days, can you? Children are never out of their parents' sight for a minute."

"No, but to be honest, if I wasn't in such a bad mood, I'd say that I'd rather have kids inside the pub than roaming free outside. It's not exactly safe, is it?"

"Not really. The pub my mum and dad went to was on a

busy road too. Sometimes, we'd sit on the pavement, me and my friends, with our feet dangling into the road. We were inches away from passing cars. But I managed to grow up unscathed." Linda smiled at the image in her head; memories of long sunny days with the freedom to play outside with a gang of local children, whose ages ranged from three to thirteen. Everyone was welcome to play and nobody was left out. As long as someone provided a ball and someone else provided a jumper to act as a goalpost, then they could play football. She had never wanted to go inside the pub. Being shackled to her parents' table, and having to sit quietly while the adults chatted, would have been her worst nightmare.

Things were so much better in those days, she thought.

Charlotte was appalled at the image that popped into her head, of old and rusty cars whizzing down the road with the drivers engulfed in a cloud of smoke (as everyone smoked in the seventies, didn't they?), struggling to see the vulnerable legs of small children inches away from their wheels. At the last minute, they might spot them and swerve. Or worse still, the driver would slam their brakes on and then go flying through the windscreen because they weren't wearing a seat belt. If the children managed to avoid death on the dangerous road, they were then left at risk of being abducted by the local flasher or serial killer.

Things are so much better these days, she thought.

"Anyway, how did you leave it with Liam? I know you're on speaking terms but are you a couple?" asked Linda.

"Yes, we're fine," said Charlotte. "I'm sure we're just having a bump in the road. We'll get over it. Anyway, how are you?"

Linda paused for a moment. She didn't want to lie and say that she was alright. Meeting someone who claimed to be

Phil's daughter had knocked her for six. After the funeral, she had planned a quiet night, just her and Nutmeg. She had been looking forward to putting her feet up and starting her new book, but she couldn't concentrate. She had read three pages before she realised that she had no idea what the story was about. The words were all jumbled in her head and didn't make sense. So she had put the television on and stared at the screen until bedtime.

"I don't know how I am, if I'm honest," she said. "I know you said that that woman might not be Phil's daughter, but she did look like him, don't you think?"

"I don't know really," said Charlotte. "I suppose she does a bit, now that you mention it."

"I'd rather talk about something else if you don't mind. I don't want to think about it anymore," said Linda. "He's in the past now and I don't ever have to see him, or her, ever again."

Chapter Nine

On the first Saturday in July, Liam and Charlotte set off early for their weekend in Manchester. The journey was tense and although Charlotte was doing her best to appear cheerful, she was struggling to maintain the facade. They had stopped at a motorway services after a couple of hours and, over a coffee, Liam had told her that he would do everything he could to keep their relationship going. He said that he desperately wanted to keep her in his life and he would beg if he had to and, in order to reinforce his words, he had jumped up from his seat and kneeled in front of her, his fists clenched together in prayer. Charlotte was mortified and told him to get up immediately before people began thinking he was proposing. He laughed and said he didn't care what other people thought. As he sat back down, to the cheers from a group of young men at the next table, Charlotte wondered whether he had any intention of ever proposing.

Before he had been offered the job in Manchester, she would have said that they'd be married within the next year or so. Secretly, she had begun to search for wedding dresses online and had a Pinterest board of examples of flower arrangements, invitation cards, seating plans and wedding cars. She thought she might like to get married in April because spring flowers were her favourite. She could see them hosting a rustic country wedding with pink tulips and purple irises in the middle of large oak tables in a huge white marquee on the grounds of a grand country hotel. She would use milk bottles, rather than fancy vases. The wedding favours would be tiny jars of homemade jam, which her guests could enjoy on their toast the morning after. Her mum made beautiful jams every year and she was sure she would love to help her. Her bouquet would complement the table flowers and her bridesmaids would have the same ones, only slightly smaller. Betsy and Hannah would look amazing in a dusky pink, or even a warm beige. Low-key elegance would be the theme.

But now she was confused.

She had told Linda about her plans and during the last few months, their favourite topic of conversation had been anything wedding-related. Linda was enjoying the secret planning as much as she was, but now what was the point? She had almost deleted her wedding Pinterest board last week, but something had stopped her. She wasn't quite ready to give up on Liam. But how they were going to make it work, she had no idea.

They arrived in Manchester just after ten a.m., after a three-and-a-half-hour drive. The early start and the long journey did not assist Charlotte's mood one iota, despite Liam's assurance that everything would be fine. She needed the toilet, she needed a coffee and she was desperate to stretch her legs. She climbed out of Liam's car, which he had parked on the small driveway outside the main door of the hotel, ready for the valets to park it for him, and looked up at the hotel.

"What do you think?" asked Liam.

What do I think? That I'd rather be anywhere else, other than here, that the journey here was twice as long as I thought it would be and if you think I'm driving over here every weekend, you've got another thing coming.

"Yes, it's nice," she said, keeping her thoughts to herself. "The valet parking is an added bonus, isn't it?"

"Yes, it really is," said Liam. "It takes all the stress out of the journey, for the guests, doesn't it?"

But what about me? she thought. When you find a flat, will it have valet parking? Or will I need to park in a ridiculously expensive multi-storey car park down the road? She didn't want to ask. At the moment, she wasn't sure how she would get there. Although she didn't relish the long drive, she wasn't a fan of train journeys either, especially as her journey would involve getting a train from Alnmouth to Newcastle and then changing to another train from Newcastle to Manchester. After a long week at work, she knew that she wouldn't have the patience to deal with a noisy train. She could imagine a carriage full of groups of young people, looking forward to partying in Manchester for the weekend. Pink cowboy-hat-wearing young women on hen parties, drinking cocktails out of lukewarm cans and cackling over willy-shaped chocolates, or gangs of football supporters, gathering in the middle of the aisle in intimidating groups, swearing and chanting football songs in loud baritone voices.

Nightmare personified.

She would have to escape to the first-class carriage, which her bank balance wouldn't thank her for.

As Liam filled out the necessary paperwork to book them into the hotel and introduced himself to the two reception staff, Charlotte texted Linda to let her know they had arrived safely.

The hotel is beautiful and couldn't be in a better location. I can see why Liam fell in love with it :(x

Hope everything goes okay for you. Whatever happens, enjoy yourself x Linda replied.

Thanks. We're going to get some breakfast after we have checked in. I'll keep in touch and let you know how it goes x

Good luck x

You too. What time are you meeting her? asked Charlotte.

Meeting at The Masons at two x

I'll be thinking of you x

Linda had arranged to meet Phil's daughter and Charlotte knew that she was incredibly nervous. She had offered to re-arrange her trip to Manchester so that she could be there with her, but Linda had assured her that she would be fine on her own and it was important for Charlotte to be supportive of Liam, even if she didn't much feel like it.

After the shocking appearance of the young woman at Phil's funeral, Linda had burst into tears and had rushed off into the ladies' toilets. Charlotte had quickly told the young woman that Linda was Phil's wife and that she was unaware that Phil had a daughter, so she could understand that this had come as somewhat of a shock. She had expected some kind of explanation, but the young woman had merely shrugged her shoulders as if to say 'What do you want me to do about it?' Charlotte had wanted to slap her face and scream at her, exasperated by her insensitivity. She might be young, but was she really that stupid? Surely she would be aware that

96

blundering into someone's funeral and announcing that you were the dead man's long lost daughter might come as a shock to some people, especially if the man concerned had been married for thirty-five years and the long lost daughter was much younger than that and therefore had been conceived at some point throughout the marriage.

Charlotte had followed Linda into the toilets, to find her sobbing into a bunch of tissues. She hugged her tightly and when Linda's tears had abated, they spent the next half an hour calling Phil all the names under the sun. Just when Linda thought that Phil was history and couldn't hurt her anymore, he did this. Well, technically he had done it twenty-odd years ago, Charlotte had explained, and she might not even be his daughter. She had tried to warn her that she might be a scammer, someone who preyed on vulnerable widows to get inheritance money. Linda had frowned at her and said that she didn't think that was the case. Knowing Phil and how he was often unable to keep it in his trousers, it didn't surprise her at all that he had a child. It was almost inevitable. For all she knew, he could have children scattered all over the country. Charlotte doubted it. Phil hadn't been at all good-looking or charismatic, in her view, so he wasn't the type to have a woman in every port. Of course, she didn't say that to Linda.

By the time Linda had calmed down and dried her tears, the young woman had gone. Hoping that she never had to see her again, Linda said that she would just forget her and pretend that she didn't exist. After all, she was nothing to do with her. If Phil hadn't died, they would have been divorced within a couple of weeks and then, technically, she wouldn't even be his widow. But the woman had telephoned the hotel a few days later and had left her telephone number with

Maggie, the receptionist, with a message asking Linda to call her when she was ready. Maggie had given the message to Liam, who had passed it to Linda. In the end, after almost two weeks, Linda's curiosity got the better of her, and she phoned her and arranged to see her.

"Everything alright?" said Liam, appearing at Charlotte's side, holding a key card.

"Yes, fine. I'm just checking on Linda. She's going to meet Phil's daughter today at The Masons."

"Oh, she rang her back then?" asked Liam.

"Yes, I don't know why. Well, I do know why, she's just a lovely person and I think that she wants to meet the woman, to give her some kind of closure, if Phil really was her dad. She said she felt a bit sorry for her because she missed the funeral."

"Let me know how she is, will you, when you hear from her?"

"Of course," said Charlotte.

"Come and meet Rani and Nadiya, two of the reception team." Liam led a reluctant Charlotte over to the bronze-fronted reception desk, where she gave Rani and Nadiya her biggest and brightest smile. She told them that it was wonderful to meet them, even though it wasn't and she would much rather be standing in The Warkworth House Hotel and chatting to Maggie. They told her how lovely the spa was and that the Signature Facial was the one she should choose, if she ever went there. She asked them where the hotel's coffee shop was and they told her that the blueberry muffins were 'to die for'.

She was doing a great job at pretending to be happy.

She said goodbye to them and Liam carried their bags over to the lift, like the perfect gentleman. As the lift doors closed behind them, he kissed her lightly on the lips and told her that he was so pleased that she had agreed to come over and see the hotel.

"I'm not here for you," she joked. "I'm here to check out the talent and hopefully put my mind at rest. I didn't want you working somewhere that's full of glamorous women, but now I've met those two..."

"There's nobody as glamorous as you," he said. "Well, apart from all the reception staff. They're pretty hot."

She thumped his arm and he laughed and assured her that Nadiya was married and he had already asked Rani on a date, but she had turned him down. Charlotte thumped him again. As they both laughed and giggled their way to the hotel room, she wished that she didn't love him so much, so that when the end inevitably came, it wouldn't hurt.

The view from their hotel room on the twenty-second floor was breathtaking. The Manchester skyline was beginning to fill up with modern towering glass blocks of apartments and offices, which mingled with the old Victorian mills and hundred-year-old rows of shops, built with brown Victorian bricks, which had now been converted into restaurants, boutiques and nail bars. The canal walkways, once abandoned, unused and overgrown with weeds, were now littered with trendy coffee shops and artisan bakeries.

Charlotte looked down on the tiny people going about their business outside. Couples holding hands, a mother and a toddler, four almost identically dressed young men, a fast-walking woman talking into a phone. Everyone on a journey.

It reminded her a little of London. When she had first moved there, over ten years ago, she was in awe of everything she saw. In her first week, she had taken an open-top tour bus and, even though it had been raining, she enjoyed every second of listening to the knowledgeable tour guide describing what had happened on Pudding Lane in 1666 and pointing out the Traitors' Gate leading into the Tower of London, where condemned prisoners were forced to enter the Tower before being executed. She imagined King Henry VIII living in Westminster Palace. Did he sign the death warrant for Anne Boleyn in the same room that is now used by the Prime Minister? He could have done.

That was what she loved most about London. It was so old. The ancient history of the place was fascinating. Before she had started work and had made new friends, she spent hours and hours walking the streets and soaking up the sights and smells, stopping to buy street food from a vendor on the West Bank or browsing around Borough Market, where she would buy crusty bread, cheese, and homemade brownies to take home to her tiny one-bedroomed flat.

Was she beginning to miss being amongst the excited buzz of a city? Maybe she was. She had some good memories of Manchester and it almost felt like home. Lancashire and her childhood home weren't too far away and it would be easy to visit her family from here. Maybe everything would work out after all, she thought. It would take some adjustments, but maybe she could do it. Manchester had a fascinating history, just like London, and maybe she should learn more about it.

"It's a great view, isn't it?" said Liam, coming up behind her and wrapping his arms around her waist. "That's an eighteenth-century cotton mill over there. And the one next to it. Did you know that Manchester was at the heart of the industrial revolution?"

"Have you been reading books behind my back?" laughed Charlotte.

"Absolutely not. I saw a documentary on telly once."

"You'll be telling me about the Spinning Jenny next."

"Oh, I've met her. What a girl."

Charlotte laughed. "You're a nutter," she said.

She turned around and kissed him and for a few moments, all her worries about them being separated were forgotten.

Chapter Ten

Linda had spent the last couple of hours getting ready, trying on one outfit after another, until she was finally satisfied with her choice of a blue and white mid-length dress with capped sleeves, which Charlotte had helped her to choose during one of their shopping trips to Newcastle. At a quarter to two, she left home and walked the few minutes to The Mason's Arms in the centre of the village. She told herself that it didn't matter what she wore, she wasn't going on an interview and she didn't intend to impress anyone. Nevertheless, she was meeting Phil's daughter, which meant that the young woman would more than likely be reporting back to her mother, someone whom Phil had had an affair with. The last thing she wanted was for the mother to think she was slovenly and old-fashioned. At one time she had been. But not now.

She matched the dress with white trainers, also bought with Charlotte's help from Russell and Bromley, the most expensive shoe shop that Linda had ever been into.

"These are perfect for the summer," Charlotte had told her, lifting one of the trainers off the glass shelf and pushing it into Linda's hand. "I've got them in pink. They'll go with anything."

Linda turned the shoe over in her hands. The leather was

a soft off-white with cream stitching and huge white cotton laces. It was beautiful. Sturdy yet delicate. Classic yet contemporary. Linda had never before held a shoe that was so expensive.

"Buy cheap, buy twice," whispered Charlotte, giving a little nod to the shoe that Linda was cradling like a baby. "I know what you're thinking, but my advice is, don't think. Just buy. I'll ask the assistant for the other one. Go on. Try it on."

Before Linda could object, Charlotte had walked off towards the assistant. Ten minutes later, she walked out of the shop with her new shoes, trying not to think about how long she would have had to work at the care home in order to pay for them. A week at least! But she didn't need to think like that anymore. She had plenty of money in the bank and she deserved nice things. The sting to her bank balance was softened by the fact that Charlotte bought a pair of sandals with a matching handbag, thereby spending twice as much as she did.

Now, as she walked into The Masons Arms, she spotted the young woman she was there to meet already waiting for her at the bar. As she pushed open the door, the young woman jumped off the bar stool and waved at her, despite the fact that they were merely a couple of metres away. The action made her appear childlike and self-conscious and it endeared Linda to her immediately.

She was wearing a cream-coloured linen tunic top, white leggings and white trainers. Her blue eyes shone with youth and excitement and something about them reminded Linda of the first time she had seen Phil, on the day that Prince Charles married Lady Diana Spencer on 29th July 1981. She had liked his eyes, initially. Until the shine had dimmed with the disappointment of marriage, work and domestic life.

"Hi, thank you for coming," she said, holding out her right hand for Linda to shake. As Linda moved closer and took her hand, she caught a whiff of perfume, just a whisper of something delicate and young. Linda didn't know which one it was or how expensive it was, but it suited her.

"Well, I wasn't busy," said Linda. Then, not wanting to appear rude or arrogant, she added. "It's nice to meet you properly." She spotted a small table in the back corner. "Would you like to sit down and I'll order us some drinks?" The young woman nodded. "What would you like?"

"I'll have a coffee, please. A cappuccino, if they do them," she said.

Linda had expected her to order something alcoholic. She looked the type who would drink one of those posh artisan gins, rhubarb or strawberry flavour, served in an enormous glass with lots of fruit. Phil would never have gone into a pub and ordered a coffee. She dismissed the thought quickly. She didn't want to compare everything she said and did with Phil when she didn't even know for sure that he was her father.

She waited at the bar while the barman made two cappuccinos and then carried them over to the table.

"So, you're Phil Matthews' daughter," she said, as she put the cups down on the table and sat down in the opposite seat. It was a statement, rather than a question.

"Yes. I'm sorry for turning up at his funeral the other week. I didn't know how else to reach you. I read about his death in the paper. There was a copy lying about at work. I'm sorry for it being such a shock."

"It's fine," said Linda. "You don't need to apologise. It isn't your fault that your father was a married man." She put

104

her hand over your mouth. "I'm not saying it was your mother's fault…"

"No, no, it's okay."

"I mean, it was Phil who was playing around. Although it takes two, as they say. Sorry. This is strange, isn't it?" said Linda. "I don't really know why you wanted to see me, to be honest."

"I just wanted to know a bit about my dad, I suppose. I don't know anything about him, other than his name."

It was obvious that this was the reason for the visit. Why else would she want to meet her dad's wife, other than to hear about the man that she never knew, the father that she could have had but missed out on? How much information Linda was willing to divulge was something she had thought about ever since his funeral. It might be true to tell her that he was a bully, a nasty piece of work, a complete waste of space. But what good would that do either of them? Linda didn't want to have to regurgitate painful memories and this young woman certainly wouldn't want to hear them. She was at a loss as to where to begin. All the nice comforting memories were evading her, so she asked the question that Charlotte insisted she ask first.

"Do you mind me asking, how do you know that he was your dad? Did you ever meet him?"

"Not that I can remember, no. My mum said that I did meet him once or twice when I was tiny, but then he stopped coming over within a couple of months of me being born. I've got this though." She handed Linda a folded piece of paper. "My birth certificate," she said, watching Linda carefully unfold it.

There it was in black and white. The name of the baby's father was Philip Matthews. He must have been present at the registration of the birth, thought Linda. Whatever relationship he had with the baby's mother must have been important enough to him for him to stand up to his responsibilities, if only for a short time. Linda looked at the date of birth, 2nd of September 2000.

"You were born in September," she said.

"Yes, the oldest in my class at school. My mum was always telling me that if I'd arrived a couple of days earlier, I could have gone to school a year earlier." The woman laughed nervously. "She said that would have made her life a whole lot easier. But I was four weeks early as it was." She took a sip of her coffee, waiting for Linda to speak. "I was all right though, just a little small," she added, as though anticipating Linda asking about her health as a premature baby.

"I'm not that good at maths, but I take it you were conceived around Christmas time?" Linda asked. "Sorry, sorry, that's not a question I should be asking. It's not something you want to think about, is it?"

"Not particularly," she said, shrugging her shoulders. She took the birth certificate back off the table, folded it neatly, and bent down to put it away in her bag, under the table. As she bent down, Linda noticed the tattoo on the top of her back. Pink and blue flowers and butterflies danced across her left shoulder and disappeared down into the neck of her tunic top and up into her hairline. Linda had never met a woman with tattoos before. To her, they represented youthful rebellion and were often accompanied by short hair and nose piercings. The woman in front of her had quite long hair, tied into a ponytail, and she didn't have any piercings that she could see, not even in her ears. She wondered what she did for a living, but didn't like to pry. She looked like one

106

of those creative types. An art student or someone who worked at a gallery and knew all there was to know about the Renaissance. If she did have artistic tendencies, she must have inherited them from her mother, certainly not from Phil.

"So, my dad, what was he like?" she asked.

"I don't know where to start really," said Linda. She picked up her coffee cup and took a large sip, wishing that she had ordered a glass of wine instead. If Charlotte were here, they would have ordered a bottle and by now, her nerves would have been on their way to being quashed. "I've got to admit that you look like him. There's no doubt that he's your father."

"Do I?" The young woman smiled, as though handed a compliment.

"Yes. Your eyes are the same colour blue and he had lovely dark hair like yours when he was younger."

The woman touched her ponytail. "My mum told me that. She said that's what attracted her to him. I know he was married, I'm sorry. She shouldn't have done it, but she said she liked him and fell in love with him really quickly. She was pretty hurt when he stopped coming over."

Linda nodded. "I had an inkling that something was going on," said Linda. "He had a couple of affairs that I knew about, but I had no idea that he ever had a child."

"Have you got any other children, you and him?"

"No. I wanted them, but he didn't." Linda paused, unsure whether to tell her the truth. It was none of her business, they had only just met, but there was something about this young woman's aura that put her at ease. "I did get pregnant just before we got married, but he talked me into getting an abortion." Linda blinked rapidly to dispel her sudden tears. "The worst decision I ever made." She wiped them away quickly with her fingertips.

"That's awful."

Linda hadn't intended to confess something so personal and now this woman was judging her for something that happened thirty-five years ago.

"I mean it's awful that he made you do it, if you didn't want to," she said. "I'm sorry for making you upset." She leaned across the table and touched Linda's hand, a warm gesture that would never have occurred to Phil.

"I didn't want to at all. But I loved him, so I did want he told me. I wish I hadn't, believe me."

"Wow. He did the dirty on two of you then, didn't he? You and my mum, I mean. He wasn't nice to her, you know."

"I can believe that," said Linda. "He didn't hit her or anything, did he?"

"Good God no, she would have punched his lights out." They both laughed at the thought. "I just meant that he abandoned her with a young baby and didn't pay a penny my whole life."

"Did she ever ask him for money?" asked Linda.

"I don't know. I presume she did. All she told me was that he didn't want a child and he blamed her for getting pregnant. She stood up to him, obviously, and told him he was talking crap, but you can't get blood out of a stone, can you? She didn't want to take him to court or anything like that."

Linda tried to remember back to the year 2000, the year that Phil became a father, but their lives were so mundane that one year blended into the next, in her memory. She couldn't remember Phil being any more shifty than usual. He had clearly managed to hide this other life from her, the parallel life in which he had become a parent without her.

She could remember New Year's Eve as though it was yesterday. It was like asking someone if they remembered where they were when Elvis died, or when Princess Diana died. It was a special night that the whole country was looking forward to and she remembered it clearly. The end of the old century and the start of the new one. She was only thirty-three and he hadn't yet managed to stamp on all her hopes and dreams, although Phil was slowly but surely doing his best.

She could remember a couple of weeks before Christmas asking him if they should go out somewhere special, not just the pub. They could book a table at a nice restaurant, and treat themselves. She even offered to drive home, to save money on a taxi. She didn't mind staying sober. They could always have a drink when they got home. She would buy some Champagne and have it waiting for them in the fridge, so they could toast the new century together.

But Phil had told her that it was a stupid idea. Restaurants would be already fully booked by now, packed to the rafters and charging twice as much. And all the good chefs would have the night off. You'd get your steak cooked by one of the juniors, who'd burn it or serve it raw. So she suggested that they eat at home and then walk to the pub for last orders. They could enjoy standing outside on Bridge Street and watching the fireworks at midnight. Someone was sure to be letting fireworks off. The pub would have some arranged, wouldn't they? She could see that Phil was at the end of his patience, so she let the matter drop. Most of the arguments they had were caused by her 'going on at him'.

When New Year's Eve had finally arrived, she bought a couple of fillet steaks from the butchers on her way home from work, together with a sachet of red wine sauce, which she would heat up in the microwave. She didn't want to risk ruining a sauce that she made herself. She planned to serve the steak with tiny roast potatoes and Phil's favourite beer. She hadn't bought any Champagne. He had never been a lover of wine and wouldn't thank her for spending money on 'that fizzy crap from France', despite its celebratory connotations.

By the time Phil arrived home, the potatoes were peeled and in a pan of cold water. The steaks were resting on a plate on the countertop.

"What's this?" he asked, walking into the kitchen, throwing his plastic lunch box into the sink for Linda to wash later, and peering at the steaks.

"I've treated us to some steaks. They weren't expensive, but it is a special occasion, isn't it?" To defuse the temper that she knew instinctively was on the rise, she reached out and grabbed his hand, hoping to convey that they should be looking forward to a romantic night of passion.

"I thought you wanted to go out." He tugged his hand away and walked over to the fridge. He pulled open the door, took out one of the bottles of beer, opened it, and drank from the bottle. "Are you going to answer me or not?" He threw the bottle opener back into the utensil drawer, slammed it closed, and took another swig of beer, followed by a large belch.

"I didn't know we were going out," said Linda. She wanted to say that he told her that everywhere was too expensive and that New Year's Eve was a rip-off and that this one especially was just a 'licence to print money' for the pubs and restaurants. But she didn't want to add fuel to the fire. "We can have these tomorrow night. It's not a problem. I'd like to go out. That'll be nice."

As she was putting the steaks back in the fridge, Phil had stamped around the kitchen, shouting about how she never listened to him and about how he worked night and day just so she could have a roof over her head and buy her 'all this shite', waving his arms up and down in front of her, as though he was making reference to an expensive evening gown, rather than the threadbare t-shirt, cardigan and old jeans that she was wearing. He gulped down his beer, threw his empty beer bottle in the bin, and walked upstairs. With each angry step, he reminded her of how hard he worked, how selfish she was, and that he couldn't bear to look at her right now. He said he would have to ring the restaurant and cancel their table because she had ruined everything again and now he wasn't in the mood. Ten minutes later, as the front door slammed behind him, she knew that she would be spending the last few hours of the twentieth century alone.

He hadn't come home until after eleven the following morning. By then her parents had arrived for New Year's Day lunch, so she hadn't questioned him about where he had been and he hadn't offered any kind of explanation. She just wanted to get through the first day of the year without any animosity.

"I haven't asked your name," said Linda. "I was so busy looking at Phil's name on your birth certificate that I didn't notice yours."

"It's Storm," said the young woman.

"Oh."

"Yes, that's the usual reaction I get," said Storm.

"Sorry, I didn't mean to say that. It's a lovely name, honestly," said Linda. "Very unusual, that's all. It's just that I would never have expected Phil to choose a name like that.

It's very, I don't know, modern, for want of a better word."
An image of Jesus calming the storm flashed into Linda's mind. With a small boat full of disciples fearing for their lives, Jesus reached out his hand and calmed the roaring sea. She wondered whether Storm had the same fiery temper as her father and if she did, who was the one to calm her.

"He didn't choose it," she said. "He didn't like it at all, my mum said. But she did, and she was the type of woman to get her own way."

"I like it," said Linda. She smiled to herself as she imagined the argument between Storm's mother and Phil. Phil would probably have accused her of wanting to be above her station, because only celebrities gave their children unusual names, like Apple or Peach for a girl or River or Hunter for a boy.

"And I actually like the sound of your mum. Anyone who could stand up to Phil is a winner in my eyes."

"From what she told me, she definitely did stand up to him," said Storm, pausing to take a drink. "He wasn't a nice man, was he?" asked Storm.

"Not really, no," said Linda. "I think you know that already, don't you?" Storm nodded and her expression told her that she understood exactly what kind of man Phil was. "So, were you born on a stormy night, or did your mum just like the name?"

"Actually yes, it was a bit rainy, but Mum told me that she had already settled on my name before I was born."

"Well, I'm very pleased to meet you, Storm," said Linda. "I'm sorry that you didn't get to meet your dad, but honestly, you wouldn't have liked him."

"That's exactly what my mum said, but I kind of wanted it to be confirmed, I think. Now I know that I didn't miss out on anything by not having him around."

"Oh, believe me, you were better being out of his way," said Linda. "I don't think you've missed out on anything at all."

Chapter Eleven
New Year's Eve 1999

As church bells and clocks all over the country chimed midnight on 31st December 1999, Millennium Eve, and millions of people up and down the country held hands and swayed, singing Auld Lang Syne together and exchanging drunken kisses, Linda opened her front door and, wrapping her old towelling dressing gown tightly around her waist as the bitter wind swirled around her ankles, she took a sip from her glass of brandy and looked up and down the street.

If anyone had been watching her, they would have thought that she was celebrating New Year's Eve like everyone else who had chosen to stay at home. They would assume that she had had a nice meal, possibly a celebratory steak or a fine sea bass with a creamy sauce, then a little drink by the fire, a glass of Pinot Noir or even some Champagne, and then as soon as Big Ben announced that the new Millennium was finally here, here she was, spending a few minutes on the doorstep, peering through the midnight sky, hoping to see some distant fireworks. The perfect ending to a perfect evening, they would say.

Except that Linda and Phil's dinner was still in the fridge, uncooked. She didn't have any expensive sophisticated wine or Champagne for a toast, just a little bit of the supermarket's own-brand sherry left over from Christmas when she made the trifle. The truth was, she wasn't too bothered about seeing any of the fireworks. What was the point in getting excited by them if there was nobody with you to share the joy? She didn't really know why she was standing on the doorstep at all. The merest flicker of hope that she might catch sight of her disappointing husband as he made his way home to her was extinguished swiftly when she told herself that she was being stupid. Hell would freeze over before Phil would choose her company rather than the company of his drunken friends. She imagined him in the busy pub, squashing a willing female against the bar, while he wished her a Happy New Year. As they snogged, neither of them would give her a single thought. They would each blame alcohol for the poor choices that they made as the new century began.

"Happy New Year, Linda," said a voice from next door, just as Linda was about to close her front door. It was Ava, her next-door neighbour.

"Happy New Year, Linda," repeated another voice.

"Happy New Year, Ava, and you too Brian," she said.

"Are you on your own?" Ava stepped off her doorstep and peered towards Linda's front door as if expecting half a dozen party-goers to spill out onto the path. "Phil not with you?"

Linda's hackles rose, but she fixed the smile on her face. Ava was the nosiest person she had ever met and the last thing that Linda wanted to do was give her something to gossip about. "He's gone to spend the night with his mother," she said. "She isn't well and, you know, with it being a special night, he didn't want her to be on her own." It was the first thought that came into her head and she admonished herself for not being pre-armed. She should have known that Ava would ask questions and she should have had her story ready.

"That's nice of him." Ava's forehead creased into a frown and Linda knew that further questions would surely be coming her way. Ava wasn't one to give up until she had all the facts at her disposal. "Didn't you fancy going with him?" she asked. "You should have said you were on your own, you could have spent the evening with us."

Why? So you could fire questions at me all night and poke and pry into my marriage? No thank you, thought Linda. I'd rather stay on my own and stick pins in my eyes.

"She knows she's welcome round here anytime, don't you, Linda?" said Brian. "Just knock on, anytime at all."

"Yes, anytime, of course," said Ava.

They had both so often practised at being good neighbours that they had the appearance down to a fine art. Although Linda wondered why they hadn't asked her to join them earlier. An invitation to join them when the evening celebrations were practically over was of no use nor ornament. As much use as a chocolate fireguard, her mother would have said. They knew she was on her own, didn't they? They must have done. Surely they had heard the raised voices and the slamming of the front door hours ago. They would have seen Phil storming down the path, into the street. He wasn't a quiet man and his presence was felt by everyone, whether they liked it or not. If Brian hadn't heard their argument, Ava most certainly would have and she would have filled him in with all the details, as much as she was able to gather through the wall. Linda could imagine them both, their heads together over the dinner table, discussing their neighbours' shenanigans, smug in their own love for each other. Any concern for Linda would have been quickly dismissed before it spoiled their evening.

Ava was happy to chat with Linda over the fence while her young boys played in the garden and occasionally they had shared a cup of tea when Phil was out, but Linda knew that, despite her words, Ava wasn't someone she could rely on in a crisis. Once, a few months ago, Linda had confided to her that her marriage was going through a rocky period and she and Phil were arguing more than usual and, although Ava had soaked up her every word like a voracious sponge and had offered her more tea and plenty of biscuits until Linda's tears had eventually dried and she had told her that she felt much better, thank you, Ava hadn't checked on her the following day. Or the day after that, or the day after that. If the roles were reversed, Linda was certain that she would have called around to see if she was all right, with a hug and a shoulder to cry on. But she hadn't seen Ava for weeks, by which time the argument was forgotten and neither of them spoke about it.

"Anyway, it's too bloody cold to be stood here in pyjamas, so I'm going in. Ava, you coming?" said Brian.

"Yes, I'm coming," said Ava. "Well, I'll more than likely see you tomorrow, Linda. Happy New Year again."

She followed Brian inside and shut the door, containing their perfect marriage and their perfect family - with their two boys and their small dog - indoors. She hadn't pressed Linda on why she hadn't gone to Phil's mother's with him, which Linda was grateful for. She wasn't that good at thinking on her feet and was even worse at telling lies. The truth was that she had no idea where Phil was and on New Year's Eve, especially a special night such as the Millennium New Year's

Eve, the likelihood of Phil being sat inside with his elderly mother was zero. She knew that he would be in a pub somewhere, either in Warkworth or in Amble. He wouldn't be far away, as he would be walking home. He was too tight to pay for a taxi on a normal evening and he certainly wouldn't dream of paying double fare after midnight. He would rather walk for an hour than pay a couple of quid for a ride home.

Linda took a deep breath and had one last look up and down the street before she retreated back inside. The door had been open long enough. If Phil came home now and felt the cold air blustering around the hallway, he wouldn't be pleased and she would have to endure another lecture about how much electricity cost and how many hours a week he had to work to earn enough money to keep them, just for her to burn it 'willy nilly' by letting all the warm air escape from the house. "I might as well get a ten-pound note and burn it on the fucking fire." She could hear his voice in her head, bellowing for all the world to hear, impervious as to who might be listening.

As she entered the living room, the last of the fireworks in London were bursting all over the television screen and Linda sat and watched them for a few minutes before she turned it off. She debated whether to leave the lamp on or turn it off. Her fingers hovered over the switch, as she tried to decide. Phil wouldn't like to come home to the house in darkness. Leaving the light on would make it warm and welcoming. On the other hand, he would see it as a waste of money and he might be angry that she was being extravagant. Whatever she did, she'd be in trouble for it. Of that, there was no doubt. Deciding to leave it on, more so that the neighbours might think she was still up enjoying herself, rather than a symbolic welcome home for her errant husband, she took herself up to bed.

She climbed into the cold bed and tried to distract her mind away from what Phil was doing by losing herself in a book. She couldn't bear to think about what he might be doing and who he might be doing it with.

Half an hour later, at the exact time that Linda closed her book, turned off her bedside light, plumped her pillows, and pulled the duvet up to her neck, finally giving way to a restless night's sleep, Phil together with his latest interest, Rosie, was making a baby. Not intentionally. Phil had no desire for children and he certainly had no desire to make one with someone who wasn't his wife, but after a long night out involving huge quantities of alcohol, neither of them had remembered the condoms. The conception was quick and perfunctory and was followed by a fitful sleep. Phil's alcoholic stupor woke him often during the night. His conscience reminded him that he was meant to be at home. The tiny voice in the back of his head told him that Linda would be worried about him and might think that he had been in an accident or a fight or something. But he merely stirred, turned over, and went back to sleep.

The unopened condom packet was the first thing that he saw the following morning when Rosie's three-year-old son bounced into the bedroom and flung himself on the bed, far too early for Phil's liking.

"Is that a sweetie? Can I have it?" he said, reaching over for the condom which was on the bedside table.

"Not right now," said Phil, grabbing it quickly and putting it underneath the pillow.

Rosie sniggered and pulled her son into the bed between them. "You're a little monkey, you are," she said, covering his face with kisses and tickling him until he squirmed and kicked.

You're an annoying little shit, thought Phil. When one of his tiny feet kicked him hard in his back, he bit his tongue and squeezed his lips together, forcing himself to smile. Although the child was incredibly irritating and the situation would be much easier if he didn't exist, Rosie suited his purpose, so he tolerated him. For now.

Every other weekend, when the child was with his dad, Rosie was a free agent and, if Phil managed to get away from Linda, usually by manufacturing an argument which enabled him to stomp out of the house, telling her he was off to the pub, they would have a night on the town. She was happy to accompany him on a pub crawl, matching him pint for pint, which was something that Linda was incapable of. They would then queue in the kebab shop and they would take home two lamb kebabs with chips, which they would eat in companionable silence while Phil watched the last few minutes of Match of The Day. Afterwards, she would lead him upstairs to the bedroom and make him believe that he was the best man she had ever had.

"I need to get back," he said, throwing back the covers and sitting on the edge of the bed. He held his head in his hands for a minute, until the spinning room came to a halt. He had no idea how much he had had to drink last night, but the pounding in his head was telling him that it was much more than usual, although the fact that he had still managed to perform between the sheets was something he could be proud of. He patted himself metaphorically on the back.

He hadn't planned to stay the night. Usually, he managed to sneak back into the house and into bed without waking Linda. If she ever asked him what time he had come home, he lied. Always. Today, he would have to tell her that he had decided to stay overnight at his mother's house. Although she might not believe him. She knew that he was much too big for his old childhood single bed, but he was confident that she wouldn't dare interrogate him too much.

Nevertheless, he was annoyed with himself. He would have to try and think of an excuse now and hope that she hadn't already phoned his mother, checking on his whereabouts. He contemplated getting her a bunch of flowers from the supermarket on the way home. Not because he was sorry that he had stayed out all night without telling her, but to wish her a Happy New Year. Then it occurred to him that it was New Year's Day and all the shops would be closed. Never mind. She wasn't used to having flowers, so it was probably best not to fuel her suspicion.

"Can't you stay for breakfast?" asked Rosie. "I've got some sausages in the fridge."

"Sausages, sausages!" shrieked the child. "Can I have some?"

"Of course, you can darling. Shall we share them with Uncle Phil?"

"No thanks," said Phil, picking up his underpants and shirt from the floor, as quickly as his banging head would allow. "I told you, I need to get back."

"Your loss," said Rosie.

He hated the way that she dismissed him so quickly. Who did she think she was? They were too old and too long in the tooth to play hard to get, but sometimes Rosie made him feel that she wasn't bothered whether she saw him or not. He didn't have the strength to challenge her, but if she said anything like that to him again, he would pull her up about it. That's for sure.

She reached for her nightdress which was underneath her pillow, pulled it over her head and got out of bed. She lifted the child onto her hip and strode out of the room and into the bathroom. Phil heard the door lock and had to stop himself from screaming at her to hurry up. He needed a piss and he needed to get home. But, telling himself to be careful and not to rock the boat, he waited patiently on the side of the bed until Rosie and her son went downstairs.

Chapter Twelve

By the time Linda came out of The Masons Arms following her lunch with Storm, the clouds that had spotted the sky earlier that day had completely gone. The late June sun was blazing in the blue sky. She wished she could have stayed longer in the pub, maybe relocating to the beer garden, where she would have been happy to sip cool wine for another hour or so. But Storm said she had to go. She was studying fine art at Edinburgh University and had a job as a waitress during the summer break, so she needed to get ready for work.

On her way home, Linda took a small diversion to the river. She stood in the middle of the bridge that crossed the River Coquet and, leaning on the six hundred-year-old stone, she watched the sunlight sparkling and dancing on the moving water, as it slowly made its way through the village towards the sea. A family of ducks jumped into the water from the shore, each of the chicks following their mother one by one as she floated down the river. She had seen that family before and had watched the chicks grow over the past few weeks. She was pleased to see that there were still six of them, waggling their tiny tail feathers and quacking in ignorant bliss of the dangers that might lie ahead of them in their life's journey.

She took her phone out of her pocket to text Charlotte. She knew that she'd want to know how her meeting with Storm went. But then she put it back. She didn't want to disturb her. She would leave her to concentrate on Liam.

It was such a beautiful day, she contemplated going for a walk on the beach, but somehow she couldn't face being alone amongst the families and happy couples. Loneliness engulfed her, as it so often did on sunny days. The winter had cossetted her, with its blanket of frost and darkness, but now that the summer was here, she was vulnerable and alone. There was a huge gap in her life where her family should be. By now, she should have grown-up children. She should be spending her weekends surrounded by the loud laughter and conversation of them and their partners. She should be looking forward to welcoming grandchildren. Instead, what did she have? A retirement of solitude. Much as she liked her own company, and revelled in it sometimes, she didn't want that to be the norm.

She suddenly felt overwhelmed by a mixture of sadness and anger. Having walked out of Phil's funeral with the decision to move on and never let him control her emotions again, less than a month later, he was still doing it. She had tried to move on and dismiss any thoughts of him that had intermittently entered her head, but she failed each time they appeared. How could she ignore the fact that he had taken her dream of becoming a mother and stamped on it, whilst becoming a father himself? How cruel was fate? Whatever lesson she had to learn from this, she had no idea. Was she fated to live a life dominated by Phil, even after his death? Throughout her marriage, she had been fated to be a domestic hermit, tied to the home because of Phil's demands. Was it now her fate to be tied to her own home because of her poor social life? She couldn't help feeling jealous of Phil. Despite his early demise, he had lived the life of his choosing. He had gone out whenever he wanted, with whomever he wanted. He hadn't let anything or anyone hold him back. Even though his dreams were small and parochial, he had followed them and for that, she couldn't blame him. She should have done the same. She had nobody to blame but herself.

She needed to pull herself together. She didn't want to send herself on a downward spiral of depression, just when she was looking forward to her new life of freedom. Oh, beware my lord of jealousy! It is the green-eyed monster which doth mock the meat it feeds on.

It was time to shake off the monster. After all, she knew that she was luckier than most.

Four months ago, when she had walked into her bungalow to view it with the estate agent, she knew that she wanted to live there and she was over the moon when her offer was accepted by the vendors, an older couple who were moving to Spain to be close to their son, who owned a bar out there. It had felt like home instantly. The living room at the front had an old-fashioned log-burning fire, which the owners had lit prior to the viewing. Scented candles, plenty of brightly coloured cushions and a large potted palm were clearly added as props, and although Linda told herself to ignore the internal decorations, she couldn't help falling in love before she had even seen the rest of the house.

The square kitchen overlooked the long garden at the back and, being south-facing, was filled with light, even on the dull day in March when she had first seen it. The owners' large oak table in the middle of the room was surrounded by six oak chairs with padded cushion seats and Linda could envisage the couple having raucous dinner parties with delicious food, loud laughter and plenty of flowing wine. They seemed the type to have lots of friends. The wine rack was full of bottles and one wall in the hallway was crammed with photographs of a smiling couple, mainly on holiday, but always surrounded by lots of other smiling people. Socialites, her mother would have called them, as though that were an insult.

As she strolled past the table, being led to the garden by the young estate agent, Linda had stroked the back of one of the chairs. Sighing deeply, she had blinked away sudden tears that appeared out of nowhere. She didn't begrudge the couple their lavish lifestyle, with their long list of friends and family to entertain; she simply wished that she was in the same position. It would be nice to have similar memories of parties and holidays to look back on and cherish.

On the evening of her moving-in day, when the removal company had left and she was finally alone, she had closed the curtains, switched on a table lamp, and sank into her soft new sofa and she knew that she was on the right path.

Since she had moved in, through her dedicated ministrations, she had watched her garden change from a desolate and unloved eyesore to a beautiful and calming space, filled with colour and fragrance. She had covered every shelf in the tiny greenhouse in the back garden with trays of seeds, sprinkled them with water every day, and waited patiently for them to grow strong enough to be planted outside. Her efforts had left her with a colourful garden bursting with red poppies, purple sweet peas, blue delphiniums, multi-coloured pansies and pink cosmos. Charlotte had said that it was like a country cottage garden oasis. Linda had topped up her wine glass and told her that that was exactly what she was aiming for. They had both sipped their wine, listening to the river making its way to the sea, its gentle splashing soothing their souls.

As a housewarming gift, Charlotte and Liam had bought her a set of four extremely comfortable chairs, a table and a parasol for the garden, which Liam had installed for her, on the patio close to the house. It was the perfect viewing point to sit and read amongst the flowers and was close enough to the house to pop back inside whenever she needed to top up her drink. It had quickly become one of her favourite places to read, although she was often taken away from her books by a weed that needed pulling or a dead flower that needed to be snipped away.

Meeting Charlotte had unquestionably changed her life, but she couldn't rely on her for all her social activities. Charlotte had Liam and now that Liam was planning to move to Manchester, Charlotte would be less available. Maybe it was time to renew her own love life. Slowly but surely over the past few months, she had begun to rebuild her self-esteem; to a level that she had had when she was a young woman, when she was confident in her own skin and assured of her youthful beauty. Charlotte had partly assisted by helping her to renew her wardrobe, which was now filled with fashionable new dresses, jeans, jackets and lots of new shoes following their shopping trip to Newcastle. Recently she had begun to feel happier when she looked in the mirror at a face that was wearing foundation, a dash of bronzer and mascara. She looked ten years younger than she had this time last year.

This afternoon in the pub, she couldn't help but notice the handsome man at the next table who had looked across at her a few times. She had sensed someone watching her and when she looked over and met his eyes, he had smiled and cheekily raised his eyebrows and his drink, in mock cheers. She had smiled politely but then looked away quickly. Was he flirting with her? She wasn't sure. She was so un-used to getting someone's attention. But there was no doubt about it, the man had a choice of keeping his eyes fixed on his two friends and their dogs, or looking at someone else and he had chosen to look at her. It had felt good.

Charlotte had told her that it was time for her to get 'back in the saddle' and, whilst she didn't agree with the terminology, maybe Charlotte was right. Maybe it was time. But what if she ended up with someone who was just like Phil? A new man might appear to be pleasant initially, but gradually his true colours would show through and she would be back in the same position, except with someone of a different name. No, she would rather be on her own, thank you very much.

It seemed that Phil continued to be her kryptonite.

As she began the walk back towards her house, she spotted Jessica, her next-door neighbour, in her front garden, gently pulling weeds from between the bedding plants. She stood when she saw Linda and brushed the soil from her hands.

"You're doing a good job there," said Linda.

"I'm not a lover of gardening, to be honest," said Jessica. "It's ruining my nails. But I'm also a bit of a neat freak and the weeds were getting on my nerves."

"I've got some gardening gloves you can borrow," said Linda. "I'll go and get them from my shed, if you give me a minute."

"That'd be great for next time, thanks, but I've had enough for today, to be honest. It's too hot now."

"Do you fancy a cup of tea, or a cold drink?" asked

Linda. "If you're not busy?" Linda knew that Jessica loved to talk, more about herself than anything else, but she didn't want to be alone, and getting to know her a little better would be nice.

"Sure. Let me go and wash my hands and I'll be right over."

A few minutes later, as they settled themselves on the patio chairs, sheltered from the harsh sun by the parasol, with two cups of tea and a plate of biscuits in front of them on the table, Linda began to tell Jessica about her meeting with Storm, the unexpected daughter of her dead husband. After agreeing with Linda about how much of a pig Phil must have been, first of all to have the affair and then to have a secret child, Jessica told her that she was very brave to have gone to meet her, with the possibility of opening up old and extremely painful wounds. She didn't think she could do it. She cradled the tiny bump of her unborn baby, telling Linda that, whatever kind of arsehole her own cheating husband was, at least she had come away from that marriage with a baby to look forward to. She would have been devastated if he had been the one to have a child with someone else. Although that was undoubtedly true, Linda smarted a little at her insensitivity, before telling herself that she was being silly and Jessica hadn't meant anything by it.

Jessica told her that she hadn't heard from her husband for over two weeks now, after he initially bombarded her with messages asking her to go back to him. She admitted that she couldn't help but look at his photos on Instagram on an almost hourly basis and found out that he had been out with a group of mates in Newcastle last weekend, spending hundreds of pounds no doubt, but then he didn't reply to her when she asked him for some money to contribute towards the baby's pram. She said she had seen a pram online which was in a promotional sale and all she asked him for was eight hundred quid. He would earn that in a couple of days. The pram should be over a grand, she had said, so it was an absolute bargain. But the bastard had ghosted her.

Linda was about to ask when she had told him about the baby, because the last time they spoke, Jessica had said that she didn't want him to know that she was pregnant, as apparently he didn't deserve to know, but she could hear her phone ringing from the depths of her handbag, which she had left on the hall table.

"Do you mind if I get that? It'll be my friend, Charlotte," she said. "I'll just tell her I'll ring her back later." She got up and then added, "Flick the kettle on if you like, Jess. I'll make us another brew."

Jessica followed her inside and filled the kettle with water, while Linda rushed to her phone, which she managed to reach before it went to voicemail.

"Hi Charlotte," she said.

"Hi, how did it go?" asked Charlotte. "I've been thinking about you."

"Really well actually," said Linda. "She seems lovely. She's an art student. I guessed she was. She looks the type, doesn't she?"

"Yes, she does."

"Phil didn't have a single creative bone in his body. She obviously takes after her mum."

"Is she definitely Phil's daughter?"

"Well I didn't ask her for a DNA test," said Linda, smiling, knowing that Charlotte would want ultimate proof of Phil's paternity, "But she showed me the birth certificate with his name on. And before you ask, she didn't ask me for any money or anything."

Charlotte laughed. "There's time yet."

"You old cynic!" She was well aware that Charlotte and Liam were both concerned that she would be scammed by this woman who was purporting to be Phil's daughter, who somehow had found out that someone had died and was preying on his vulnerable relatives, in the hope that she could steal money from them. No doubt that happened to some people. Linda had watched her fair share of Crimewatch programmes and she had read the newspaper often enough, but she had been willing to take Storm at face value. There was nothing about her that made her suspicious of her actions in any way. She trusted her instincts and from what she could tell, Storm was simply an abandoned daughter who wanted more information about a father that she never knew. "Look, I'll have to go, Jessica's here for a brew. Is everything okay with you and Liam? Have you seen much of the hotel?"

"Yes and yes. He seems really adamant about his decision, so I can't stand in his way, can I?"

"Probably not, no."

"He seems certain that we can make it work and when he's ready for the next step, I suppose I'll be moving to Manchester eventually. I haven't told him that though."

"I knew you'd work it out. Sending love to you both. I'm sure you'll be fine. Just before you go, guess what Phil's daughter is called."

"Philippa?"

"No."

"Perpetua?"

"No, but it's equally unusual. She's called Storm."

"What the fuck! Storm? I didn't expect that. Wow!"

"I know. I like it actually. She said Phil didn't like it and didn't want to agree to it, but her mum went ahead with the name she wanted."

"Brilliant," said Charlotte laughing. "That's really cheered me up. I love the name but I love it more because Phil didn't."

Linda laughed too and asked Charlotte to text her later, to let her know she was okay. By the time she said goodbye and returned to the kitchen, the kettle had boiled and Jessica was standing at the back door, looking into the garden, with her back to Linda.

"Do you want another tea?" asked Linda, "Or a coffee? I've got decaf."

"I'm going to have to go actually," said Jessica, turning around. "I've remembered something I've got to do. This baby brain of mine is useless." She tapped the side of her head with her finger, as though to prove a point, and rushed out of the kitchen towards the front door, saying a quick goodbye and that she would see Linda again soon.

Maybe she had a text from her husband, thought Linda as she closed the front door behind her. She seemed upset and in a rush to get away. The poor girl was at the start of her long and winding emotional journey to divorce. She thanked the Lord that her own journey had ended and she could now get on with the rest of her life.

Nutmeg suddenly appeared at the entrance to the kitchen. She had been sleeping in her usual place on the back of the sofa. She miaowed as she sauntered over to Linda, who bent down and picked her up. She kissed the top of her head, as the cat purred with delight.

Linda's phone pinged with an incoming text. She put it down on the countertop, so she could open it with one hand. It was from Storm.

It was lovely meeting you today x

Thank you. It was lovely to meet you too x Linda replied

I'm sorry my dad treated you so badly. My mum told me he wasn't worth knowing and now you have confirmed it x

He did have some good points. When I remember them, I'll let you know x

She sent a smiley face emoji to let Storm know that she was only joking and was relieved when Storm sent one back. She couldn't believe that the lovely person she met this afternoon had Phil's genes, but it just proved that nurture is more powerful than nature.

With thoughts of young Storm in her mind, she went back into the garden for an afternoon of gentle pottering interspersed with the counting of her blessings.

Chapter Thirteen

The next day, Linda finally agreed to go and see Dorothy to collect Phil's will. Since the funeral, Dorothy had called her and had left umpteen messages, asking Linda to meet her, but Linda had replied that she was busy, she had this prior arrangement or that prior arrangement. In truth, she hadn't had anything planned except for her meeting with Storm in The Masons Arms, but one Phil-related meeting at a time was more than she could cope with.

As she sat in her garden, her chair gently warming in a patch of the early morning sun, cradling a large mug of tea and listening to the birds singing, she would have done anything to postpone the meeting with Dorothy, but she told herself that she was being unkind and she shouldn't keep putting it off. Dorothy had done her a huge favour by agreeing to be the person to identify Phil's body and then she had registered his death at the Registry Office. The least Linda could do was to go and see the poor woman when she had been invited, especially when the trip involved her being given some inheritance money.

She closed her eyes and lifted her face to the sun. Just five more minutes, she thought. She had agreed to be at Dorothy's by ten o'clock, so there was still time to enjoy the peace and tranquility of the garden for a little while longer.

Her thoughts drifted to Phil and she wondered why he had written a will at all, and what had prompted him to leave all his money to her. Why hadn't he left it to Dorothy, or even to Storm? He knew that he had a daughter and even though he didn't have any contact with her, it made more sense to leave it to her, rather than to his ex-wife.

She wondered whether he had ever felt the slightest bit guilty for not having financially supported Storm and for not spending any time with her when she was growing up. Despite the fact that he had always been adamant that he didn't want any children, when accidents happen, surely that's the time to step up to your responsibilities?

But twenty-two years ago, if Phil had told her that he had fathered a child with someone he had been having a secret affair with and that he intended to pay a monthly allowance to the child's mother for the next sixteen or eighteen years, would she have been happy about that? She wasn't sure. Probably not. Although, Storm seemed like a nice person and she could imagine that she had been a sweet child, who she could have grown to like, or even love, given half the chance.

After the initial shock, she probably would have been quite pleased to see her, if Phil had brought her home for a visit. They could have gone to the park together, as a family, or she could have baked cakes with her in the kitchen while Phil watched a football match on the television. After that, they could have settled down together for a home-cooked meal, before Phil took her back home to her mother. She could even have stayed over at their house when she was older, six or seven maybe. Linda would have read her a night-time story while she drifted off to sleep in the double bed in their spare room, snuggled deep down in the huge duvet.

Linda would have liked that.

But not only had Phil denied her a child of her own, he had also denied her a stepdaughter.

Her thoughts were interrupted by the loud buzz of a bumble bee. She opened her eyes and watched it land on a lavender stem, busily drinking nectar with its tiny proboscis. Nutmeg was watching it too. She began to crouch low to the ground. She crept across the grass, over to the lavender bush on her tiptoes, leaping on it, seconds after the bee flew away.

"It will serve you right if you get stung, you stupid cat," Linda said. She got up from her chair and picked Nutmeg up, holding her tight to her chest. The cat nuzzled her head on Linda's chin, purring softly.

"Hi, Linda." It was Jessica from next door. "You okay?"

Linda walked over the low fence that separated the two gardens. "Yes, thank you, are you? You're up early."

"Bit of morning sickness, but it's nothing too bad. It usually clears after a cup of tea and some toast. Have you got time for a brew? I've just put the kettle on."

"I've got to go and see someone actually, but I'll only be an hour or so. I'll come round when I get back if you like."

"Yes. Well actually, do you mind if I come over to yours?" asked Jessica. "Your garden furniture is much more comfortable than mine. It'll be nice to sit out in the sun for a bit, won't it?"

"Yes, that will be nice. I'll let you know when I'm back."

Linda was making her way inside when Jessica asked her who she was going to meet and whether she was going to see her husband's daughter again. Linda told her that they hadn't made any plans to see each other again, and in fact, she was off to see her husband's girlfriend. Jessica laughed and said that it was about time that that two-timing rat was out of her life, but he seemed to be hanging around like a bad smell. Linda laughed and told her that she wasn't wrong and that she really didn't want to go, but Phil had left her some money in his will, so she was going to pick up a copy of his will and his bank details etc.

They said their goodbyes and, after a quick shower, Linda got dressed and drove to Dorothy's house.

When she arrived, Dorothy was prepared for the visit. The kettle had just boiled, there was a plate of shortbread biscuits in the middle of the kitchen table, and next to it was a large brown envelope, which Linda presumed contained the will, the death certificate and Phil's bank card.

"I'm sorry I've not been round before now," said Linda, as she took a seat at the table.

"Don't worry," said Dorothy. "I understand that it's all been a bit over-facing."

Linda nodded. "I thought I was rid of him, that's all. I was quite happy, starting my retirement in my little bungalow and I feel as though he's dropped a bomb on it all."

Dorothy smiled empathetically. "Yes, I can see that. But this is the last bit that needs sorting and then you can move on."

"We both can," said Linda.

Dorothy's eyes filled with tears. She picked up a tea towel that was neatly folded on top of the oven and wiped them away. Linda reached over and stroked her arm. "I'm fine, honestly," said Dorothy. "I've been a bit tearful the last few days. I don't know what's wrong with me."

"Well…" Linda was about to say that it was obvious why she was crying. She had just said goodbye to the man

137

she had been living with for the past six months, the man that she had presumably planned a future with.

"I'm not crying over Phil, if that's what you're thinking," said Dorothy, as though reading Linda's mind. She gave a sardonic laugh. "I'm glad he's gone, if I'm honest with myself."

"Yes, me too," said Linda.

"It's just that my David would have been so disappointed in me. In my choice of men, I mean." She poured hot water into a large teapot - a blue one, dotted with white circles that Linda had seen in John Lewis - and placed it in the middle of the table, along with two small china cups on saucers. "We had the chance to talk about how I'd cope after he'd gone, and he told me that he wanted me to meet someone, even though I told him that I didn't. He didn't want me to be on my own for the whole of my retirement, he said."

"That was nice of him," said Linda. "He sounds like a lovely man."

"Yes," said Dorothy. She sat down opposite Linda, poured the tea into the cups, and placed them both on ceramic coasters. Linda poured in the milk for both of them. "Sugar?" asked Dorothy.

"No thanks," said Linda.

They were silent for a moment while they drank their tea. Linda could see that Dorothy was on the brink of a deluge of tears and she wasn't sure whether talking about her husband would make her feel worse, or better. So, she waited while Dorothy dabbed at her eyes and tried, and failed, to compose herself.

"I've let him down so much," she said eventually. "If he knew what Phil had been like with me, I swear he would have killed him."

"I can't sit and tell you that you did the right thing by choosing Phil, but you need to cut yourself a bit of slack. You didn't know what he was like when you first met him. He was a charmer. He could have charmed the hind legs off a donkey. What he did wasn't your fault."

"But I should…"

"No buts," interrupted Linda. "It's over now. If your husband is looking down on you right now, what do you think he would say to you?"

"That I'm an idiot," said Dorothy.

Linda smiled softly. "But he wouldn't want to see you cry, would he?"

"No," said Dorothy.

"And would he say that he loves you?"

"Yes, of course. He loved me with all his heart."

"You're so lucky to have had that. So hold onto that and, after today, don't give Phil Matthews another thought. I'm going to do the same thing. Well, after I've sorted his bank account out, that is."

"Well, it's all here for you," said Dorothy. "Apparently, all you need to do is take the will and the death certificate to the bank and they'll transfer the money to your account. I've also put his wallet in there. There's a couple of hundred quid in it. Two hundred and thirty to be exact."

"Thank you," said Linda. "He always preferred paying for things in cash, I don't know why. Probably because he didn't want me to know where he'd been and what he'd spent his money on, as though I was bothered." She picked up the envelope and put it into her handbag. She still had no idea what she wanted to do with the money. She didn't need it. She had plenty of money of her own from the sale of her father's house, but she supposed that extra money would make her life more enjoyable.

She was looking forward to the cruise with Charlotte later in the year and if they enjoyed it, she could perhaps suggest that they go on another one next year and she would pay for it. She knew that Charlotte would protest at that, and she'd insist on paying for herself, but what else was she going to do with her money? She might buy some more plants for the garden, and some books, of course, but that wouldn't cost more than a hundred pounds.

Having money in the bank gave her choices, Charlotte had told her. She had said that she could buy herself a sports car; she could fly to Milan for a day's shopping trip if she felt like it; she could buy herself a designer handbag or spend the day at a Champneys Health Spa, having massages and facial treatments. Linda had laughed at the thought of all those things and said that she didn't need anything like that to make her happy. Charlotte had scoffed at her initially and then she had agreed, telling her that, on second thoughts, she was right, none of those things would make her happy.

Charlotte's old life in London had been peppered with expensive shopping trips and days at the spa. Her wardrobe had been filled with Louis Vuitton handbags, Christian Louboutin shoes and clothes by Chloe and Prada. But she hadn't been happy. She had told Linda that there was no doubt about it, she felt beautiful when she wore designer clothes, but these days, when she walked by the river with Liam in an old pair of jeans and a t-shirt, she was a million times happier than when she used to go out to an expensive restaurant in a dress that had cost her a couple of thousand pounds.

When Linda first told her that she and Dorothy had laughed about giving all the money to a cat rescue centre, Charlotte had said that she wouldn't blame her if she did. But she had to buy herself a new car first. It wasn't that there was anything wrong with her old Ford Fiesta, but she would look great in an Audi TT, like the one she had, and she assured her that it was guaranteed to bring her pleasure every time she drove it. Linda had laughed but now, with access to another hundred thousand pounds, which was Phil's share from the sale of their house, she could buy herself whatever car she wanted.

"My friend has told me to buy myself a sports car," she said.

Dorothy laughed. "Why not?" she said. "That would be amazing. I can see you whizzing up and down the coast road in a convertible. Look, I know we laughed about giving it all away to charity, but don't do something you'll regret. You might need that money at a later date."

"I know," said Linda. "I'm just going to sit on it for a while, while I do some thinking. I'm going on a cruise with my friend in November, so I can spend some of it on some day trips."

"Yes good idea," said Dorothy.

When it was time to leave, Linda gave Dorothy a hug and told her that they should go out for lunch soon. Dorothy told her that would be lovely. She said that she was part of a book group that met every fortnight, taking it in turns to meet at different houses, and that Linda would be welcome to join them, if she liked reading, although most of the time they didn't talk about the book much at all. They chatted about all sorts, got through too many bottles of wine and put the world to rights. Linda told her she would love that and Dorothy said she would send her a text with all the details and the address of their next meeting, which was next Wednesday afternoon.

"Thank you for being so understanding with me," said Dorothy, as she opened the front door.

"What do you mean?" said Linda, thinking that Dorothy was referring to her earlier crying episode.

"You've been so lovely. I did go off with your husband, after all, so you have every reason to hate me."

"Oh don't be daft," said Linda, laughing. "You were very much welcome to him. We had broken up anyway. I should have told you sooner." Linda felt a flash of guilt that she had allowed Dorothy to identify Phil's body, as though as an act of penance for being a scarlet woman who had stolen another woman's husband, when she was nothing of the sort and she had nothing to be sorry about. "Please, don't be sorry about anything," she added.

***

Just as Linda arrived home, her phone pinged with an incoming text, which she presumed was from Dorothy, giving her the details of the book group. She scrambled in her handbag for her phone and was surprised to see Storm's name on the screen.

Hi Linda, it's my day off today, are you free for a drink at some time? x

What does she want? thought Linda, not relishing an afternoon of more chat about Phil. But, despite Charlotte warning her of the chance of being scammed out of any money that she had inherited from Phil, she had actually enjoyed her time with Storm in the pub. She seemed like a nice person. She had a good vibe, as Charlotte would say.

Yes, I'm free, she replied. *I've just arrived home and I'm still in the car, so shall I come over to you? X*

She didn't actually know where Storm lived, but it couldn't be far, as she had travelled to The Masons Arms yesterday on the bus.

I'm at my brother's in Alnmouth, but the house is a bit hectic. I'd rather come over to Warkworth if you don't mind x

Linda told her that she didn't mind at all and she was welcome at her house. She said that she would make them some lunch, if she wanted some. Storm replied that it would be good and she would be there around one o'clock. Linda sent her the address and then walked round the corner to the deli on Bridge Street, where she stocked up on different cheeses, black and green olives, black pepper wholewheat crackers and a handmade extortionately priced feta and tomato quiche. She wasn't sure whether Storm ate meat, so she played it safe by keeping the meal vegetarian.

As she was unpacking her shopping, she heard a knock on the front door and it was only when she opened it and saw Jessica standing there, that she remembered that she had invited her over for a drink.

"Oh hi," she said. "Come in. Come through to the kitchen, I'm just unpacking my shopping. I've been to the deli and spent an arm and a leg."

"It's gorgeous in there, isn't it?" said Jessica.

"It is," said Linda. "It's very expensive but worth every penny. Storm texted me just now and is coming over for some lunch. You're welcome to stay, if you like. I've got enough food for five thousand."

"You're seeing her again?"

"Yes, I know. I hadn't planned to, but I don't mind. I quite like her actually and if talking to me helps her to deal with whatever issues she has relating to her dad, then I'm happy to do it."

"Is that what she wants, to talk about her dad?" asked Jessica.

"I don't know. I presume so. Why? You're frowning. What are you thinking?"

"Nothing," said Jessica. "It's just that she might think that she's in line for some inheritance. Didn't you say that your husband had left you some money?" Jessica eyed the brown envelope that Linda had left on the table.

"Yes he did, but she doesn't know that."

"I bet she'll ask you about it."

Linda didn't reply. She wasn't comfortable with the way that Storm's reputation was being tarnished by people who had never met her. Charlotte, Liam and now Jessica all assumed that the only thing she was interested in was money. "What would you like to drink?" asked Linda, anxious to shut the conversation down. "I can make some tea, coffee or I've got elderflower juice."

"Tea would be great, thanks," said Jessica.

Linda filled the kettle and then put the rest of her shopping away while she listened to Jessica's latest emotionally charged dealings with her husband. She did her best to listen, but the details of their tit-for-tat conversations went in one ear and straight out of the other. Her mind was whirring with thoughts of Storm. For a second, she contemplated texting her back and saying that she didn't want her to come over. But what reason would she give? That her cynical friends were afraid that she would be taken advantage of and were basically calling her a thief, even though they didn't know anything about her? It was absurd. She was old enough to be her own judge of character. But apart from that, when she had been wandering around the deli, choosing nice food for their lunch, she found herself looking forward to seeing her again.

She made the tea and as they carried it outside onto the patio, she remembered that Jessica hadn't actually said whether she wanted to stay for lunch or not. At the moment, she was still ranting about her husband, so when she took a breath, she would ask her. Linda hoped that she wouldn't stay. Her comments about Storm had irritated her and she wanted her to go home. But instead, she sipped her tea and listened politely, nodding here and there when appropriate.

When they had finished their tea, Linda collected the empty cups. "I'll just take these into the kitchen and then pop to the bathroom. I won't be long." A few minutes later, when she returned, she asked Jessica again if she wanted to stay for lunch and was relieved when she said thanks, but she would leave them to it.

"Just be careful though," said Jessica, as she made her way to the front door. "Don't turn your back on her and don't leave your purse lying around."

Linda did everything in her power not to slam the door behind her.

Chapter Fourteen
February 2000

After twelve years of marriage, Linda had become accustomed to the disappointment of Valentine's Day. While thousands, if not millions, of bunches of red roses were purchased by men anxious to demonstrate their love to an equal number of lucky women, not one of those bunches had ever reached Linda's house. Her cut-glass vase had remained empty on 14th February every year.

For the first few years, having been told on numerous occasions by Phil that Valentine's Day was a money-making scheme invented purely by the card shops and the florists, (although she wasn't sure whether he was suggesting that the bosses of those two particular industries got together in huddled meetings to discuss how to dupe the public into spending money that they didn't have, so soon after Christmas) she remained sanguine. However, even she wasn't so dim as to expect a floral gift after five or six years of there being none.

In their first year of marriage, she had bought him a card, which she had handed to him in bed, together with an expensive bottle of whisky. He had thanked her for the whisky, telling her that 'it would go down nicely', but he hadn't read the card. She could tell that the words that she had carefully chosen in the card shop were not resonating with him in the same way that they had with her. He had ripped open the envelope and discarded the card on the bed with the excuse that he needed to get ready for work, as though reading some printed words of love for twenty seconds would make him late.

Linda hadn't asked him where her card was. She had simply gone to work, filled with young love and optimism, and hoped that he would come home struggling under the weight of the biggest bunch of red roses that she had ever seen. She had washed her two vases and put them ready on the windowsill above the kitchen sink. She had worried that they might not be enough and so had carefully washed the milk bottles, which she left on the kitchen window sill. Just in case.

When she heard Phil whistling his return at six o'clock, she rushed into the hallway to take his coat, ready to thank him for the flowers. Even his empty hands didn't diminish her spark initially. She thought that he might be playing a trick on her by leaving the flowers on the doorstep. But he hadn't.

She didn't ask him why he hadn't bought her anything. That would be churlish, she told herself. She knew that Phil loved her. He didn't need to show his love just once a year. He loved her every day, didn't he? He could buy her flowers on any day of the year. He had married her and he was here with her, eating his tea across their small dining table every night. With her. He had chosen her.

As her inner voice spoke, she knew that it was talking rubbish.

It was true that Phil might love her, in his own way. But it wasn't true that he could buy her flowers at any time. He never had and she was to learn that, throughout their marriage, he never would.

Valentine's Day of 2000 was no different from all the others. They always had sausage and mash on a Monday and Linda wasn't about to break the habit. She had contemplated going to the big supermarket and getting one of their special Valentine's meal deals, with the little chocolate puddings in heart-shaped pots and a cheap bottle of wine, but she knew that Phil wouldn't appreciate it. Unless the meal deal was a heart-shaped sausage and mash, there was no point.

By six o'clock, the sausages were perfectly done and were keeping warm in the oven, the gravy was already in the jug and Linda was mashing the potatoes when Phil arrived home. She no longer rushed to greet him in the hallway but concentrated on getting his tea on the table promptly. That was Phil's love language, which she was beginning to understand.

"I've got to go out tonight," he said, as he took his jacket off and hung it on the back of the chair. She would pick it up later and remove it to the cupboard underneath the stairs. He had passed the cupboard on his way to the kitchen, but in twelve years of marriage, it never occurred to him to hang his own coat up on the way past. That was Linda's job.

"Okay," she said, placing his plate in front of him as he sat down. She had long since given up arguing with him about why he was going out on a particular night and with whom. Whatever she said had never made a blind bit of difference. At least if he was out, she could binge-watch Coronation Street and Emmerdale. Then she would treat herself to a long bubble bath with a book and an early night. She was looking forward to him being out of the way.

As they began to eat, she expected him to spin her a yarn about some bloke down the pub who was fundraising for some charity and who needed people to pledge their money to him tonight, or one of his drinking buddies was having a birthday drink or he had to attend some special snooker tournament that he had forgotten all about. She wouldn't believe any of the explanations. But he didn't offer one, and she never asked.

When he came downstairs an hour later, fresh from the shower, wearing a clean shirt and smelling of cheap aftershave, she told herself that it didn't mean anything. Just because a man was clean, did not mean that he was cheating. And just because a man wore aftershave on Valentine's Day to go out with his friends did not mean that he was cheating.

Except that in Phil's case, of course, it did.

Half an hour later, Rosie was pouring Phil a beer in the kitchen of her small house, five miles down the road. She carried it through to the living room and handed it to him as he sat down on the sofa. She squeezed herself next to him and crossed one leg over the other, so that she could stroke his leg with her foot.

"So," she whispered in his ear. "I thought I'd mark this very special and romantic night by giving you some special news." She couldn't wait any longer. She'd been excited to see him all day.

"What's that then," he said. "Have you had a winning on a lottery card?" He laughed at his own joke.

"Better than that," she said. "I'm pregnant." She pulled away so that Phil could see the huge grin on her face. She had been counting down the minutes all week so that she could tell him the best news in the world. The news that she hoped would mean that he would finally leave that boring wife of his and move in with her.

"You're what?" said Phil, jumping up as though scalded.

"I'm preg-nant." She emphasised the two syllables separately, saying them loudly and clearly. She stood up from the sofa and leaning into his face, this time with no smile in her voice, and said. "I know it wasn't planned, but don't look at me like that."

"Like what?"

"Like I did it on my own," she shouted. "I thought you'd be pleased."

"Why would I be fucking pleased? Did I tell you that I wanted a kid? Did I?"

"Don't fucking shout at me like that! Who do you think you're talking to? My name is Rosie, not Linda." She pointed at herself in the chest with her thumb. "And I don't tolerate being shouted at in my own house."

Phil had never met anyone like Rosie. Her temper was as quick to flare as his and he wasn't sure how to deal with it. Shouting at her didn't work. She never backed down as Linda did. She shouted back and she never seemed to be scared of him. It was disconcerting, although sometimes it was exhilarating. But not right now. He couldn't deal with her anger, together with this news. What the fuck was he going to do? Linda would be devastated. He had never meant for it to go this far.

"Yeah well, you can get rid of it," he said. His voice was quieter but nonetheless threatening and aggressive.

"What? No chance!"

"How many weeks are you?" he asked.

"Oh fuck off! As though you care!" Rosie flounced into the hall. A few seconds later, she returned carrying Phil's coat, which she threw at him. It landed at his feet. "Get out and close the door behind you!" she said. She folded her arms defiantly and stood in the middle of the room, waiting for him to obey her orders.

Phil considered his options but then bent down, picked up his coat, and walked out.

As he got into the car and started the engine, he shook his head, unable to believe what had just happened. In all his years, he would never understand women. She caught him off balance like that and when he asked a reasonable question, such as how far gone was she, she suddenly went demented and threw him out. Unbelievable!

Bitch.

Knowing her, it probably wasn't even his child.

Within a couple of minutes, he was back home. Linda was watching one of her soaps on the television. The look on her face told him that she wasn't too pleased about his early arrival home. She smiled, but it was too late. He had seen the flash of irritation on her face.

That was all the excuse he needed to go back out and spend the evening in the pub, slamming the front door on his way out.

Linda was in bed by the time he got home.

Chapter Fifteen

Storm arrived at Linda's house with a huge smile and a bunch of beautiful long-stemmed pale pink roses. Her warmth and geniality were very welcome after tolerating half an hour of Jessica's bitching and moaning.

"These are for you," said Storm, holding the huge bunch at arm's length.

"They're beautiful, thank you," said Linda. "What have I done to deserve these?"

It was a rhetorical question, one which many women ask when they are handed flowers, when they usually already know the answer. "Well, you put up with my dad for, like, forever." Storm laughed. "From what my mum said, you deserve a medal."

As Linda led Storm into the kitchen at the back of the house, she felt a tiny stab in her heart. Not one that was big enough to stop her in her tracks, but a tiny pinch. She told herself not to take any notice of it, but she couldn't help feeling a little aggrieved. She didn't like the thought of Storm and her mother, whatever her name was, discussing her, and giggling about her and questioning why she was still married to Phil. She wondered whether they gave her pet names, such as 'doormat', 'drudge' or 'dogsbody'. Well, she had called herself a dogsbody, so she supposed she couldn't blame them. But to think that their conversations would have such negative connotations was more than a little hurtful.

When she was a teenager, she used to love Debbie Harry from Blondie. She wanted to grow up like her. Debbie would never have been called someone's dogsbody. She would never have allowed it. Glamorous, exciting, alluring, those were the words that popped into your head when someone said Debbie Harry. All the things that Linda had never been and, more than likely, never would be.

If Storm had picked up on Linda's sudden, but very temporary, dip in mood, she didn't let it show. "I wanted to get you something to say thank you for chatting to me and answering my questions," she said.

"You really didn't need to," said Linda.

"Yes, I did," said Storm. "So, I went into the florist and asked her what colour rose you give someone when you want to say thank you. She showed me these. Pink is for appreciation, apparently."

"I never knew that," said Linda. "You learn something every day." Linda put the flowers down on the countertop while she filled her vase with water. The roses were already tied beautifully with a pink ribbon, which Linda carefully snipped, trying her best to keep the arrangement that the florist had done. "I'm not much good at flower arranging," she said. She bit her tongue so that she didn't add that she hadn't had much practice over the years. She didn't want to give Storm and her mother something else to talk about. "But they look beautiful, don't they?" She placed them in the vase carefully.

"Here, let me take them for you. Where would you like them to go?" said Storm.

"In the living room, I think. It's north-facing, so these will be just the thing to brighten it up. This way."

Storm followed her down the hallway to the front of the house, carrying the vase carefully in front of her. "This is a lovely room," she said. "And that bookcase. Wow!" She put the vase down on the window sill and wandered over to the bookcase. "Have you read all of these books?"

"No, I've read the ones on the top shelf. I'm keeping those because I love them. The other shelves are mainly books waiting to be read."

"I've got a TBR pile as long as your arm," said Storm. She took Linda's hand and raised her arm into the air, as though she was a contestant in a boxing ring. "Actually, it's about ten times longer than your arm." Her infectious childlike giggle made Linda laugh too.

"Whatever does TBR mean?" asked Linda.

"To Be Read," said Storm. "I think it's a social media term. I've also got a DNF pile, which means didn't finish; a JFH pile, which is just for holidays and a HFYM pile." She giggled again. "My friend made that one up. It means hide it from your mum because it's got dirty bits in."

"Oh, I don't think you'll find any HFYM books on there," said Linda, laughing.

"My mum wouldn't have bothered anyway," said Storm. She ran her hands along the spines of the books on the top shelf and paused when she reached a small hardback copy of Little Women. "She was pretty easygoing."

"Did you say she was?" asked Linda, noting the use of the past tense.

"Yes, she died. Just over a year ago now," said Storm. She smiled tightly and gave an almost imperceptible shrug.

"This was one of her favourite books, Little Women. She used to read it to me at bedtime."

"That's nice," said Linda, thinking that she would have read it to her too, if she had known her as a child. She wondered whether her mother had read other childhood classics to her, such as Bedknobs and Broomsticks and Alice in Wonderland.

"I couldn't really follow the story, if I'm honest. But I just have this memory of me and my mum squished side by side in my single bed. She read to me every night until I fell asleep. To this day, I don't know what the story's about, other than three sisters."

Linda wanted to tell her that it was four sisters actually, but instead, she said, "I'm so sorry to hear about your mum. It must be hard losing her when you're still so young."

"Yeah. But at least she got to see me go off to university. She was proud of me for that."

As they wandered back into the kitchen, Storm sat at the table while Linda prepared their lunch. She told her that her mum had been artistic too. "She used to run a small business making pottery, vases, bowls, cups, that kind of thing, until she got too poorly and had to give it up. Sometimes people asked her for specific things, such as a particular fruit bowl or vase, and sometimes she made as many things as she could and sold them at artisan craft markets." She didn't make a fortune, but she told her kids that being her own boss was worth more than all the money in the world. Linda asked her when her love of pottery had begun. Storm explained that when her brother was born, her mum had a job as a sales assistant in a boutique wedding dress shop. She told Storm that she used to look at the wedding dresses and examine the seams and the cut of the cloth and she had a dream that one day she would design some herself and own her own place. She was pretty fixed on that but then, as a Christmas present one year, a friend of hers bought her an afternoon making pottery, just as a bit of fun. They both went together, for a day out. And that was it. That was the beginning of her love of pottery. At the time, her mum and dad told her she was crackers. Nobody ever made money out of making things from bits of clay, they told her. But her mum was stubborn and headstrong, Storm said, and if someone told her she couldn't do anything, she would go out of her way to prove them wrong.

"And she did prove them wrong, didn't she?" said Linda. "Because she made it her living and she enjoyed it."

"Yes, we were skint though, growing up," said Storm. "I mean, she paid the rent and everything and we always had food on the table, but we didn't have many holidays. I've only been abroad a couple of times. I think that's why I've got such a passion for travel now. As soon as I finish my degree, I'm taking myself off around Europe."

Linda sliced the warm quiche and put it on a plate in the middle of the table, next to another plate of cheese and crackers, a bowl full of green salad with avocado and cherry tomatoes, and a small bowl of olives.

"This looks amazing, thank you," said Storm.

"Help yourself, please. I've got some crusty bread too, I'll just cut it and bring it over."

"Oh not for me, thanks," said Storm. "I try not to eat too much bread."

"And that's why you've got a figure to die for and I've got middle-aged spread." She patted her stomach, laughing.

"Rubbish, you're lovely. Just as you are, as Mr Darcy said to Bridget."

"What an amazing film," said Linda.

"And an amazing book," said Storm. "You have so much in common with my mum, you know," she said, as she filled her plate with salad and reached for a slice of quiche. "You would have got on really well. She loved reading too."

"Would we?" asked Linda. She doubted that. In reality, Storm's mum wouldn't have given her the time of day. She sounded too cool and sophisticated. She would have been one of those women whom Linda aspired to be like, whilst at the same time knowing that she didn't have a hope in hell's chance.

"Absolutely. You've got a kind soul, I can tell. My mum said you should always judge a person by the way they treat others and you've treated me with nothing but kindness, even though it must have been a shock meeting me."

"It was a bit of a shock, I'll admit that," said Linda. "So, you've got a brother?" Linda was anxious to change the subject. Talking about her own strengths of character was not something she was totally comfortable with and this was the second time today that she had had a compliment about how nice she was.

"Yes, Reuben. He's almost four years older than me. He looks after me, we're very close."

"Does he still live at home, at your mum's house, I mean?"

"No, she was only renting that house, so when she died, I had to move out. I couldn't afford the rent on my own." She gave that tiny shrug again, as though losing your mum and then losing your home were everyday occurrences that could be shrugged off, when the reality is that her heart must have been breaking. "My brother's been living with his girlfriend in Alnmouth for a couple of years, so I moved in with them."

"I'm sorry to hear that," said Linda. "I mean, I'm sure he's lovely, but to have to give up your home…"

"I know, but it's okay," said Storm. "I'm only there at holiday time anyway. During term time, I'm away in Edinburgh at university, so he gets his spare room back. That's another reason why I want to go travelling. Don't tell him, he's been the perfect host and everything, but I need my own space. Even if that space happens to be a small tent that I have to carry around on my back for months. Tortoises manage to put their house on their back, don't they?"

"True," said Linda. "And snails."

"Exactly, so if they can do it, I can do it."

"You said you fancied travelling around Europe?" asked Linda.

"Yes, I'd love to see Switzerland and France, maybe Italy if I can afford it. Any country that has snow on the mountains and art galleries in the cities is a must for me." She sat back in her chair and looked up, as though her hopes and dreams were floating about around her; she just had to reach out and she could grab them, as easy as that. "Can you imagine the art galleries and museums in Paris? I've been researching where to go. They're just something else. And Rome. Oh, and Berlin, they have some wonderful galleries, apparently. I want to go all over."

"It sounds wonderful," said Linda.

"Yes, I can't wait. But I need to save up first. That's why I'm working all the shifts I can at the restaurant. I'm hoping to be able to go when I've finished my degree."

"People didn't really do that kind of thing when I was young." Well some did, but she didn't. "You'll have a great time. Oh hang on, what's that bloody stupid cat doing? She's chasing bees again." Linda jumped up and ran into the garden. "Nutmeg! Nutmeg, what are doing? You're going to get stung, I told you this morning." Nutmeg, on realising that there was a high likelihood of her games being brought to a premature end, skipped out of Linda's reach and ran to the back of the garden. Linda followed her, reaching out her hands, whilst at the same time trying to convince the cat that she wasn't about to grab her. But cats have their fair share of intuition and it was well over five minutes before Linda managed to get hold of her and take her back inside.

"You did a great job there," said Storm. "It only took you half an hour to catch her."

Linda laughed. She closed the door and put the cat on the floor. Nutmeg immediately trotted over to Storm and wrapped herself around her legs.

"I know, I'm not the nimblest person you'll ever meet," said Linda. "She's going to get stung though. I wish I could tell her to stay away from the flowers, but she wouldn't listen even if I did."

The next couple of hours passed much too quickly and as four o'clock approached, Storm said that she had to go, as she had another shift at the restaurant. As they got to the front door, Linda told her that she had really enjoyed her company and invited her to come back whenever she liked. She didn't tell her that she hoped it wouldn't be too long before she saw her again and that she had been a breath of fresh air, as it felt inappropriate, but she couldn't help the thoughts from forming.

"Just one thing before you go," said Linda. "Wait there a second." She dashed into the living room and came out with the copy of Little Women in her hand. "I'd like you to take this. It'll remind you of your mum."

"Thank you," said Storm. Her tiny voice was full of emotion. She hugged Linda tightly and said that she had had a lovely time. "Next time, you should come over to Alnmouth. There's the best seafood restaurant ever on the high street. You'll love it."

"I'd love that," said Linda. "Thank you."

It was only when Storm had gone and Linda was clearing the plates from the table and stacking the dishwasher that it occurred to her that they hadn't spoken about Phil once.

Chapter Sixteen

"Any drinks or snacks?" the smiling air steward asked, as she held onto the trolley in the middle of the aisle of the British Airways plane. Charlotte and Liam were on an early flight to Verona. Liam had arranged it, assuring her that they needed a dirty weekend away, to relax and reconnect before his move to Manchester the following week. It was the last weekend in August and throughout the summer, he had been telling her that all would be well and she had nothing to worry about. But crisis talks were needed, in Charlotte's opinion, and Verona was as good a place as any for those talks to take place.

"Oh yes please," said the woman seated in the aisle seat, next to Liam, with the effervescent over-enthusiasm of someone who had just been offered a free holiday of a lifetime to the Maldives, together with fifty thousand pounds spending money, like one of those day time TV competitions that Charlotte sometimes entered. 'Text WIN from your mobile and you could be our next winner.' Although she never was.

"What can I get you?" asked the steward. Charlotte marvelled at the infinite patience required to ask the same question over and over again, until they reached the back of the plane.

"Ooh, I'd love a coffee please," simpered the woman. "Black and as strong as possible."

Charlotte squirmed, waiting for her to add a comment about liking her men the same way, but thankfully she didn't. "And two of those dinky bottles of Sauvignon Blanc please."

Charlotte wouldn't have minded a glass of wine herself, despite the fact that it was only half past nine in the morning, but now that the woman had ordered some, Charlotte felt like supercilious abstinence would taste much better.

The woman touched the payment machine with her card, collected her wine and coffee, and flashed the steward an expensively veneered smile, one of those that cost thousands of pounds, but are much cheaper to buy in Turkey. Charlotte couldn't understand why the woman was irritating her so much. Her sister, Betsy, had had work done on her teeth and they were beautiful, so she couldn't criticise her for that.

"Cheers," the woman said, holding her miniature bottle of wine towards Liam's bottle of water. "I don't want to be too naughty and open it now. I'd better have my coffee first."

That's why.

The absolute height of bad manners was flirting with someone else's boyfriend, especially when his girlfriend is sitting right there. Hello! I'm here, Charlotte wanted to say. You little bitch, keep your fluttery false eyelashes to yourself. We've got enough troubles at the moment. We don't need you stirring the pot, thank you very much.

Liam held his bottle of water aloft with one hand while squeezing Charlotte's thigh with the other. "Cheers," he said, politely. He looked over at Charlotte and winked and she couldn't help smiling at him. She felt the irritation slowly leave her. She had nothing to be worried about. This was Liam. Not Miles. He may have his faults, (lots of them in fact, the biggest one being that he had arranged to live on the other side of the country without her) but flirting with other women wasn't one of them.

"Have we reached France yet, do you think?"

Seriously, does this woman ever shut the fuck up? thought Charlotte.

"As soon as you see the coast, if you look down, you'll see my parents' farm." She pointed a red-manicured fingernail in the direction of the small window, next to Charlotte. "They know I'll be flying over this morning; they might have put the flags out, literally." She giggled and leaned towards the window, her breasts hovering too close for comfort to Liam's left arm. What would she say if I pulled the blind down, rested my head on it, and pretended to sleep? Charlotte wondered.

"Mmm, that coffee's just perfect. It was an early start, wasn't it?" she said.

"Well, not too bad for us really," said Liam. "We stayed overnight at one of the airport hotels, so we didn't have to get up ridiculously early."

"In fact, we had a luxurious lie-in, didn't we, darling?" said Charlotte. "Breakfast in bed and everything."

"Oh how wonderful," said the woman, finally pulling her eyes away from Liam's face and sipping her coffee. If she had noticed that Charlotte was there previously, she hadn't shown it and Charlotte felt she had no option but to make her presence felt. She refused to sit for the next hour and a half and listen to a strange woman chat up her boyfriend. The reality was that they hadn't had a luxurious breakfast in bed at all; they had rushed to the airport and grabbed an almond croissant from Pret a Manger, but she didn't need to know that. Liam, she could tell, was finding the whole episode highly amusing. Charlotte, however, was finding that even her deep breathing techniques were failing to keep a lid on her rising temper.

"Hello Anna-Belle." One of the pilots appeared from the cockpit to talk to her and was now leaning against the seat of the person in front. "How are you? Christian told me you were on the flight."

"David, hi. I'm absolutely fabulous, thank you."

Did she just say that, really? Why couldn't she just be fine or okay like everyone else? Why did over-enthusiasm have to be the order of the day?

"You don't look a day older than the last time I saw you," said the pilot. "It must be nearly ten years now." Charlotte wondered if they had had a thing.

"Oh don't be silly. I've been up since the crack of dawn. I must look dreadful," said Anna-Belle, twisting a lock of her hair with her fingertips.

Yes, they'd definitely had a thing. The pilot seemed to be struggling to maintain eye contact with her. He smiled at her breasts lasciviously. An awkward silence followed, which was surprising, given the fact that the woman had plenty to say only moments earlier.

"Well, I'd better get back," said the pilot eventually. "It was good to see you. We should…"

"Yes, good to see you too," Anna-Belle interrupted. "Can I give you this?" She handed him her empty coffee cup. "Pop it in the bin will you, darling? Thank you ever so much."

Pilot David took the cup reluctantly and returned to the cockpit.

"Is he an ex?" asked Charlotte, as soon as he was out of earshot. The woman nodded. "I thought so. Nice move with the coffee cup." Both women burst out laughing and when Anna-Belle held up her hand for a high five, Charlotte was more than happy to reciprocate. A little show of girl power.

"Women!" said Liam, laughing. "Always ready to dish out cold revenge."

"Absolutely," they both said in unison.

The rest of the flight passed quickly. Anna-Belle told them that she was on her way to meet her husband in Verona, who had been working for an international bank for the last six months. She said that she hadn't seen him for over four weeks. He had booked them a suite at the Vista Palazzo as a treat for her birthday, rather than staying in his apartment. Charlotte knew from her internet searches that that hotel was beautiful and she told Anna-Belle that she was in for a real treat.

By the time the plane had landed and the passengers were on their way to Border Control, Charlotte had swapped numbers with Anna-Belle, who had promised to send her some photographs of her hotel suite. She wasn't so bad, after all, and Charlotte remonstrated with herself for being so uptight. She really must relax. She was worrying about problems with Liam before any had actually arisen.

"Benvenuti a Verona," said Charlotte, as they exited the airport and stood in the Italian sunshine.

"Good accent," said Liam. "Are you going to practice that this weekend?"

"No, I think my Italian/Lancashire accent works very well actually. No improvement necessary."

"I agree," said Liam, pulling her into a tight hug and kissing her.

As they settled into the taxi for the short journey from the airport into Verona, Liam held tightly to Charlotte's hand and thanked her for the second time that day for being so understanding about his move to Manchester.

When he had suggested that they have a weekend away, just the two of them, without the distraction of other people and work, Charlotte had readily agreed. They could talk about the logistics of his move and how everything was going to work. But now she was here, she would rather bury her head for the next couple of days and simply enjoy his company. She didn't want to agree to him living in Manchester. She wanted him to live in Warkworth, just a few minutes away from her. She wanted to call him on a random Wednesday lunchtime and go for a quick coffee, before they both rushed back to work. But, now she would have to settle for a phone call. She wanted to shout at him and tell him he was the most selfish man she had ever met and he was ruining what they had. But what was the point of travelling thousands of miles just to argue?

"Okay, il tuo hotel," said the taxi driver, a short time later, stopping outside the most beautiful old hotel that Charlotte had ever seen. So far, Liam had done a good job. Their hotel was in the centre of Verona, overlooking the arena and within a minute's walk of bars, restaurants and lovely shops.

"Grazie," said Liam. The taxi driver got their suitcases out of the boot and Liam passed him a bunch of Euros in return. "Arrivederci."

"Ciao," said the taxi driver.

"This is beautiful," said Charlotte. "You couldn't have picked a more perfect location."

"I know," said Liam. "I want this weekend to be perfect because I love you." Charlotte could feel tears pricking at her eyes and tried to blink them away before he noticed. They were travelling back to England on the same plane, after their trip. But what about the next trip? Would he be flying back to Manchester, while she travelled alone back to Newcastle? "Don't cry, please," he said. He had already noticed, even though she hoped he hadn't. Sometimes, Charlotte loved the fact that she could be herself around him and didn't have to hide anything, but at other times, it was infuriating that he knew her so well.

"I'm sorry, I don't want to, but we're in one of the most romantic cities in the world and I just wish it was under different circumstances."

"But you're here with me, what do you mean?"

"I know, I want to be here with you, but I don't want to spend the whole weekend talking about us, our relationship and how it's going to work. I don't want it to end in an argument. I wish we didn't need to."

Liam nodded solemnly. "I know, but don't worry, things will be fine. Let's book in, drop the luggage, and then go for a coffee and then we can talk. After that, we can enjoy the rest of the weekend." He walked towards the hotel's revolving glass door, dragging the suitcases behind him. If only it was that simple, thought Charlotte.

***

"Did you know that Romeo and Juliet was set in Verona?" asked Liam, a few minutes later, as they left the hotel and turned left towards the centre of the city, passed the Roman ampitheatre. He took hold of Charlotte's hand and squeezed it.

"Yes, I did actually," she said. "I'm meant to be the educated one. What do you know about Shakespeare?"

"About as much as I know about the industrial revolution. I've seen the film." He laughed and winked at her and, although she laughed back at him, her heart wasn't in it. She wanted to have a good time and she wanted to enjoy the sights and sounds of this wonderful city, but all she could think about was that this time next week, he would be leaving her and packing to start a new life in Manchester.

"Shall we go and see the famous balcony?" he asked. "I know it's cheesy, but we have to see it, don't we?"

"Of course we do," she said, trying her best to summon up enthusiasm.

"It's just around the corner. You turn right when you get to the market square and it's just on the left-hand side somewhere. I asked the receptionist at the hotel."

"You've certainly done your homework."

"I'm trying, Charlotte." Liam stopped walking suddenly, causing two tourists who were walking too close behind them to curse in French, as they negotiated the crowd and walked around them. "I know you're not happy about my new job, but we will work it out somehow." He pulled her towards him and kissed the top of her head. She rested her head on his shoulder and breathed in the scent of his aftershave, before pulling away.

"I know," said Charlotte. "Sorry, I didn't mean that to come out as sarcastic as it sounded. I do appreciate the effort you're making."

"But?"

"There's no but. Come on, let's see this balcony. If we don't move, we're going to get arrested for blocking the highway."

They walked on through the slow-moving crowd, each of them concentrating on their own thoughts, until they reached the famous balcony. The entrance to the tiny cul-de-sac was packed with tourists and the air was full of different languages. Couples, groups of students and families all seemed to be chattering excitedly at the same time.

"Isn't it amazing that tourists from all over Europe, Japan, America, and goodness knows where else have all come to see this? Shakespeare would be pretty chuffed about that, don't you think?" said Liam.

"I suppose so," said Charlotte. "To be honest, I can't believe that all these people are here in a tiny Italian street, staring at an old stone balcony that a fictitious character from hundreds of years ago was meant to have stood on."

"She's not fictitious. What do you mean, fictitious?" Liam looked shocked. Whether it was genuine or he was kidding, Charlotte couldn't be sure. They often played the same game, where Liam pretended to be stupid and uneducated, when in fact he was nothing of the sort.

"She wasn't real, Liam," she said.

"Of course she was. Both families were real and then Shakespeare wrote about them."

"Like the Kardashians, you mean?"

"Exactly," he laughed. "If Romeo and Juliet were alive today, they would one hundred percent be in their own Netflix series."

Charlotte still didn't know whether he was serious or not, but she couldn't help laughing at his sincerity.

"Anyway, if they weren't real, why does everyone do this pilgrimage to an old balcony?" he asked.

"I've absolutely no idea," said Charlotte. "It's not even that impressive, is it?"

"Well, I suppose it's okay for an old one. It's not my cup of tea," said Liam. "Come on, let's go and get some lunch."

Charlotte led the way back through the crowd to the main street. The comforting feel of Liam's hand on the small of her back let her know that he was right behind her. The phrase 'he's got my back' jumped into her head and she wished that it were true.

"Fancy a pizza?" he asked.

"Absolutely. I proper Italian one, with tonnes of cheese and garlic," she said.

Five minutes later, they were seated at a small round table at a pavement cafe, waiting for their pizza and salad. Liam poured them a glass of Chianti each and replaced the bottle in the metal wine cooler. Neither of them spoke for a couple of minutes. Charlotte pretended to be busy people watching, a fixed smile on her face, so that anyone passing would think that they were just another couple in love, having a romantic weekend away, rather than a couple on the brink of a relationship crisis that could ultimately break them up.

"So," said Liam, interrupting her thoughts.

"So, what?"

"I know what you're thinking," he said.

"You do?"

"Yes. You're thinking that we need to talk and get this over with, but you don't want to be the one to start the conversation."

Damn it. He had hit the nail on the head. Why did he always do that? He had a knack of reading her thoughts. He was right that she didn't want to be the one to start the conversation. She didn't want to have the conversation at all. Full stop. But right here, in this beautiful cafe surrounded by dozens of people, with dozens more walking within inches of their table. was not the place. She didn't want the conversation to be in hushed tones, conscious of anyone overhearing them and she certainly didn't want to cry in public. She knew that whatever happened, it would end in tears. He might start off by holding her hand and telling her that he would come home at the weekends and that they would speak on the phone every day, but it wouldn't be the same. Before they knew it, they would drift apart, he would be busy at the weekends, or would have some social event that he wanted to go to and eventually, he would meet someone else. Maybe he doesn't intend to. But it will happen.

Charlotte took a deep breath. She picked up her glass of wine and took a large drink to prevent her unspoken fears from escaping. She waited for Liam to begin.

Chapter Seventeen

"Isn't that the lady from the plane?" said Liam, pointing at someone walking towards them on the crowded pavement.

That wasn't what Charlotte had been expecting him to say. She turned around and spotted Anna-Belle in the crowd, conspicuous in a knee-length red sun dress with thin shoestring straps and a large sun-coloured straw hat. Round Gucci sunglasses shaded her eyes. If she was trying to achieve the Audrey Hepburn look, she was doing it very well. She waved to her as she approached their table. "Anna-Belle! Hi."

"Hello, how nice to see you," said Anna-Belle, standing by the side of their table. "Are you enjoying Verona, so far?" She took off her sunglasses and placed them on top of her hat.

"Yes, thank you," said Charlotte. "Are you? Is your husband with you?" She looked over Anna-Belle's shoulder, expecting to see a tall handsome man, well-dressed in a designer casual kind of way. The type that wears good shoes and expensive aftershave. Anna-Belle didn't seem the type that would settle for anything less.

"Not at the moment," said Anna-Belle. "He's working."

"Do you want to join us for a drink?" asked Charlotte. "We've got a bottle, so you're very welcome." She avoided Liam's eye, not wanting to see any reproach that might be there. She knew that the last thing he would want would be the company of a stranger when they were meant to be having a deep discussion. But she didn't care.

"Are you sure?" asked Anna-Belle.

"Yes, of course, come and sit down," said Liam, standing up. "Here, take my seat. I'll grab a waiter and ask for another one." Charlotte smiled at his chivalry.

"Thank you," said Anna-Belle, sitting down. She hooked the straps of her expensive handbag on the back of the chair and leaned back, securing it between herself and the chair. "You need to keep an eye on your bag," she said to Charlotte. "Just because the sun is shining doesn't mean that there are no baddies around."

A waiter appeared at their table with another glass and Charlotte poured the wine and handed it to her. "Baddies," she laughed. "I've not heard that word for years."

"Oh, I use that word all the time. It encompasses so many people, not just thieves and vagabonds, but all the people you don't like, exes, mother-in-laws…"

"Cin cin to that," said Charlotte, raising her glass.

"What's that about mother-in-laws?" asked Liam, returning to the table, followed by a waiter carrying a spare chair.

"Nothing," said Charlotte.

"Just some girl talk," said Anna-Belle. Charlotte was beginning to like her more and more every minute and she was ashamed of herself for having judged her so harshly on the plane.

"Have you eaten? Do you want to order something?" asked Liam.

"No, no, don't worry about me. I don't want to interrupt your lunch," said Anna-Belle.

"Not at all," said Liam. "We can't have you walking about on your own, if your husband's busy. You're welcome to eat with us until he finishes work. We're just having pizza."

He squeezed Charlotte's knee under the table and she could feel her heart beating with pure emotion. She loved him so much. He was a nice genuine man. A gentleman. A rare find. Whatever happened, she needed to make sure that she didn't lose him.

Anna-Belle said that it would be lovely and ordered a Margherita pizza. As expected, the lunch was delicious, the waiting staff were attentive and the conversation was interesting and amusing. Charlotte felt herself relax and begin to enjoy herself. The temperature in the city rose to almost thirty degrees, but they were kept cool by the large canvas canopy that stretched across the pavement tables, protecting them from the harsh sun.

With the first bottle of wine empty, Charlotte suggested that they order another bottle and Anna-Belle readily agreed. As the waiter uncorked the bottle and poured a little into Charlotte's glass for her to try, Anna-Belle surreptitiously glanced at her watch.

"Do you need to get back?" asked Charlotte. "I wasn't thinking about the time."

"No, not really," said Anna-Belle. Her mood seemed to have taken a sudden dip, as a veil of sadness descended over her. She blinked rapidly, as though fighting back tears. Charlotte, having seen that expression so many times on women sitting across the table from her at work, wondered whether she had argued with her husband that morning and that was the real reason that she was out walking on her own. He wasn't working at all. Why would he be working when he had made a special effort to invite her over for the weekend? It didn't make sense.

Charlotte told the waiter that the wine was lovely and waited for him to pour it into their glasses.

"Is everything okay?" she asked. She didn't care that she might be asking this relative stranger a personal question. She could tell when a woman was putting on a front. Anna-Belle gave her a sad, tight-lipped smile and took another mouthful of wine. With a quick nod of the head, Charlotte somehow managed to convey to Liam that it was a good time for him to leave them alone for a few minutes, which he was quite happy to do. Emotional women were not his favourite company.

"I'm just going to pay the bill and then I think I'll have a wander round the market, if that's okay with you ladies?" said Liam. "I spotted a stall with some souvenirs for the staff at work." He got up, kissed Charlotte on the cheek, and left the women to talk.

"He's not leaving because of me, is he?" asked Anna-Belle. She dabbed at a tear with her napkin. "I'm sorry, I think I'm hormonal or something."

"Don't worry about him. He loves rummaging around a market. Hormones or not, do you want to talk about it? I'm a good listener," said Charlotte. "Or if you just want to sit and cry into your wine for a few minutes, that's fine too."

"I absolutely do not want to cry," said Anna-Belle. "This eye make-up took far too long to put on. I'm not going to have it ruined because of a man."

"I thought a man might be the root cause," said Charlotte. "They usually are."

Anna-Belle looked shocked. "You two are happy though, aren't you? He's besotted with you, you can see it in his eyes, the way he looks at you. Pure love."

Charlotte laughed sardonically. "Maybe he is, but not enough for him to turn down a job on the other side of the country. We live in Northumberland, but he's moving to Manchester in a couple of weeks. We've come away this weekend so we can talk about how it will work. He's told me 'not to stress'." She indicated air speech marks with her fingers and rolled her eyes. "But I am stressing about it, though. He's accepted the job without thinking about me and now he just wants to put my mind at ease, I think, so he can go off without worrying about me."

"It sounds like you'll have to put some effort in to keep the relationship going. But if it's meant to be, you can work it out," said Anna-Belle.

Charlotte shrugged her shoulders. "If you don't mind me asking, how do you and your husband manage? Didn't you say on the plane that you hadn't seen him for weeks?"

"Yes, I did say that."

"That's what I'm worried about. I miss Liam if I don't see him for a couple of days. I can't bear the thought of not seeing him for weeks."

"I was lying." Anna-Belle put down her wine, sat back in her chair, and seemed ready to give her confession.

"What?" Charlotte leaned in and rested her elbows on the table. She knew there was more to this woman than first met the eye. She just needed to give her a chance to talk.

For the next half hour, while Anna-Belle cried, despite her best intentions, and both of them finished the second bottle of wine, she told Charlotte that it was true that her husband was a banker, but he didn't work in Verona for an international bank. He worked in London, which was where he was now. She was in Verona on her own, to get some desperately needed thinking time. She had booked the trip herself, as a last-minute get-away.

She said that they lived in Beckenham with their two boys, aged five and seven, who were staying with her best friend for the weekend. Last Sunday night, just as the children had been put to bed and she was settling down next to him on the sofa, wondering what drama they could watch on the television, out of the blue he told her that he wanted a divorce. While she sat next to him, open-mouthed and in shock, he told her that he wanted to put the house on the market. He told her that he could take on a small mortgage and she would be able to buy somewhere smaller for her and the boys. House prices had risen considerably in that area, he justified, so she shouldn't have any problem. He would continue to pay the school fees, of course, but she might need to increase her hours at work. He swore to her that there was nobody else involved but he just didn't love her anymore. He apologised and said that there was nothing he could do about it and he hoped that she 'wouldn't be difficult about it.'

After nine years of marriage, that was it. He was ending it. Their own personal drama had begun.

Charlotte reached across the table and held her hand. "Do you have a lawyer yet?"

"No, he said I don't need one. It should be straightforward, as long as we both get to see the children. He said he'll pay a generous allowance every month, as well as their school fees, so I'll be okay."

"You should get legal advice though. And what about the house? Do you want to sell it, because you know you don't necessarily have to."

"Yes, I did know that."

"Plus, whatever he is telling you now about paying for the children etc might not be what he agrees to in the end. People do change their minds, especially where money's concerned."

"I know, you do hear horror stories, but honestly, we're trying to keep it amicable. Look, I'm sorry for dumping all of this on you. I didn't mean to…"

"But it feels better to talk, doesn't it?" asked Charlotte.

"Yes, it does."

"And to have someone who will listen to you?"

"Yes, that too."

"And what if I told you that I was completely on your side and that I would always be here for you if you needed to ask any questions?" Anna-Belle looked confused. "I'm a solicitor," said Charlotte. "And I specialise in divorce."

"Honestly?"

"Yes, honestly. I used to work at Wise & Bancroft in London, have you heard of them?" Anna-Belle shook her head. "Well, I don't work there now, I've got my own practice in Northumberland and I'd love to help you, if you'd like me to. I don't charge the earth, but I can give you the best advice there is."

"But don't I need someone local?"

"That's up to you," said Charlotte. "If you're happy to chat via Zoom and on the telephone, I can work for you. I'm due a visit to my friend in London soon, so I can come and see you at home and I'm happy to come down to London whenever there is anything to sign."

"Thank you," said Anna-Belle. "You're right, I think I do need someone in my corner."

And I need you, thought Charlotte, to give me something to focus on when Liam starts his new job.

By the time Liam arrived back at their table, Charlotte had arranged to speak to Anna-Belle on Zoom next week.

"Okay, I'm going to leave you two love birds on your own," she said. "Thank you so much for lunch, Liam."

"It's a pleasure," he said. "We'll probably bump into you again over the weekend."

"Yes, you might. Charlotte, I'll speak to you next week," she said, kissing Charlotte on both cheeks and hugging her tightly. "Thank you. I can't tell you how much better I feel now. You've literally taken a huge weight off my shoulders."

"You're welcome," said Charlotte. "The next few months will be hard, I'm not going to lie. But I'm here for you and we'll get through it together."

Chapter Eighteen

Liam came out of the bathroom with one of the hotel's soft white towels wrapped tightly around his waist. His hair was wet and dishevelled. Tiny tufts stuck up at the back of his head and Charlotte wanted to stand close to him and tidy his hair while looking deep into his eyes. She wanted to wrap her arms around his neck and kiss him passionately. She wanted the towel to fall accidentally on purpose to the floor. But instead, she turned away, pretending to be taking in the view of Verona from the window, taking deep breaths to stop herself from crying. She didn't want to find him irresistible. She didn't want her body to react to his in the primal way that it usually did. She didn't want to love him.

She had decided that she needed to take a step back. For her own protection.

He had already decided that his work was more important than their relationship, and it was time that she accepted that. She couldn't really blame him. He had only just turned thirty-one and any man was at the peak of his ambition at that age. She should have known that he wouldn't be happy to stay in Warkworth for the rest of his life, especially not after having been brought up in London. The bright lights of the city were sure to lure him back sooner or later. She should have seen it coming.

She had no idea how their relationship would work once he made the move. All she knew was that she wanted it to work, which was why she had agreed to come along on the weekend away. When Liam suggested it, it proved to her that he wanted it to work too. But the nagging voice at the back of her head was telling her that he was too young to settle down. He hadn't yet finished his dating life and there were beautiful women waiting to meet him in Manchester. It was only a matter of time before he strayed. They all did.

She knew that she would lose him in the end. He had always been too good to be true.

She remembered her mum's face when she had taken Liam home to meet her family for the first time at Christmas. As they had walked into her parents' hallway and dropped their bags onto the floor, her mum couldn't wait to reach out and greet him. She had rushed forwards before he had even taken his coat off and pulled him into a warm hug. Luckily, Liam was a demonstrative person and he had wrapped his arms around her mum and hugged her back, telling her how much he had been looking forward to meeting her. It was true, too. All the way there in the car, Liam had chatted animatedly, occasionally singing along to the songs on the radio, and not once had he shown any signs that he was nervous about meeting his girlfriend's parents. He was used to mixing with people at work but, not only that, he actually liked them. He spent time talking to the guests in the hotel, not out of duty, but because he was genuinely interested in their lives and what had brought them to Northumberland. There were dozens of leaflets in the hotel about the local area, but rather than just handing them out, he spent time telling the guests where was best to eat and how to get to the places that had the best views across the beach. She had always loved that about him.

"I'm so excited to meet you," Charlotte's mum had said. And the huge grin on her face had told Charlotte that was true.

She had ushered them into the kitchen, where Charlotte's dad had his head in the fridge. He emerged with two bottles of beer, one of which he offered to Liam, along with a firm handshake. Liam had taken it gratefully, telling her dad that he much preferred beer to wine. Her dad had commented that wine was okay at weddings and possibly on Christmas Day to toast the turkey, and he wouldn't say no to a Sangria on holiday, but apart from that, it was beer all the way. They had bonded immediately.

Later that day, when they had had lunch and Liam and her dad were watching a football match in the living room, Charlotte's mum had told her that she thought Liam was lovely. He was much nicer than that slimy Miles from London, she had said. He seemed like a very ordinary, down-to-earth and pleasant young man.

Charlotte had frowned. "You don't think he's too young then?"

"No, not at all," said her mum.

"You know he's five years younger than me?"

"He doesn't look it, but that doesn't matter, does it? Not in these days, equality and all that."

"It isn't that," said Charlotte. "I'm just worried that he isn't ready to settle down and I am. We're at different stages in our lives. You know men take a long time to catch up."

"Some do, yes," said her mum. "But he's in his thirties."

"Only just."

"Yes, but he's out of his twenties, that's the main thing. Your dad and I had been married for five years by the time he was thirty and had a child and another one on the way."

But times were different then, Charlotte had thought. And you lived in a village. Lives were smaller. There wasn't so much choice. Nowadays, your partner can literally be made to order. Dating apps ask you how tall you want them to be, what colour hair you want them to have and some even ask what salary you want them to earn. Rather than asking about moral values and goals, it was all so superficial. Consequently, heads could turn so easily, and they frequently did. There was always something better just around the corner, or at the swipe of a screen.

Charlotte hadn't voiced any of her worries to her mum, who seemed to know what she was thinking. Her mum had gently pushed her hair behind her ear, kissed her cheek and told her not to worry. Live in the moment, she had said. Liam wasn't Miles. He was a good one. She could feel it in her bones, her mum had said.

"Are you ready, beautiful?" Liam was close behind her. He rested his hands on her shoulders and gently kissed the back of her neck. She leaned back against him for a moment, before stepping away.

"Yes, but you're not," she said. "Unless you want to go out like that. Give the Veronians a little thrill."

"Veronians? Who are they?"

"The people of Verona, stupid," said Charlotte, in an attempt to lighten the heavy mood that was weighing her down.

"Is that the name for the natives, or all the people in the city?" he laughed.

"Everyone," said Charlotte. "I'm a Veronian for the weekend."

"Well come here then, if you want a thrill." He opened his towel and flashed at her and she turned away, squealing with laughter, and hid her eyes with her hands. She loved it when they laughed together.

"You should get dressed," she said, suddenly serious. "We need to talk."

"I know," he said, reaching for his clothes, which he had laid out on the bed.

She walked back to the window and turned her back on him while he dressed.

"I'm ready," he said, a couple of minutes later. He was wearing cream-coloured linen shorts and a black linen shirt with short sleeves. As he pushed his feet into his trainers, Charlotte's heart ached. He looked so handsome in black, which showed off his tan and his brown eyes. But she forced herself not to reach for him. "There's a cocktail bar in the hotel; shall we have a drink before dinner?" he said. Charlotte nodded. "Come on." He grabbed her hand tightly and kissed her cheek.

As they entered the bar, tucked away at the back of the hotel and dimly lit by candles on each of the tables and small lamps dotted along the bar, Charlotte spotted a table for two in the corner. She went to sit down, while Liam ordered their drinks at the bar. She asked him to bring her something fancy and brightly coloured with plenty of alcohol and smiled when he walked over with two pink Cosmopolitans in small triangular-shaped glasses, decorated with twirled orange peel and a tiny red paper umbrella.

"You know me, never afraid to show my feminine side," he said, as he gently put the cocktails down on the table and sat down. "Cheers." He lifted his glass and waited for Charlotte to lift hers, so they could clink them together. She watched as he took a sip of the sweet cocktail and pulled his face. "Lovely," he said, licking his lips. She knew he would much rather have a beer, but he was joining her in a cocktail in an unnecessary show of solidarity. Drinking the same drink did not make them a happy couple.

Now that they were here in the bar, settled in a quiet corner with their drinks, there was no escaping what they had travelled thousands of miles for. She wanted, more than anything in the world, to chat about cocktails and what they would have for dinner, but she waited quietly for Liam to start the difficult conversation.

"So, let's get this over with, shall we?" he said, taking his cue.

Over with? What the fuck was that supposed to mean. Was talking about their relationship something that he just had to rush through? Something to endure? He wouldn't have to do it if he had given them a single thought, before he agreed to take the job in Manchester. Charlotte took a large gulp of her cocktail, to avoid saying something she would regret.

"Look," he continued. "I've been thinking all day about what to say and I've prepared a little speech in my head, so if you don't mind, I'll go first." Charlotte nodded. "Is that okay?" he said.

"Yes," she said.

"I just want to tell you how much I love you," he said.

"I love you too," she said, sighing heavily. She wished he would just get on with it. This was torture. She felt as though she was in a session of couples' counselling, where they had to declare their love for each other before they tore each other apart, emotionally.

Liam drained his cocktail as though it was lager. He put the glass down and pushed it to one side, reaching across the table to grab Charlotte's hand. "I've got to say that I don't think you're going to like what I'm about to say, but truth is the basis of all relationships, don't you think?"

"No," she said. "Communication and trust should be the basis, shouldn't they?"

"And truth," he said, shrugging his shoulders.

He was really beginning to irritate her now. Was he grinning? He looked like he wanted to, but was trying to hide it. Maybe it was nerves, but this was certainly not a laughing matter. What was he talking about, fucking truth? Like when she asked him if she looked good in her new jeans, was it okay to tell her that her arse looked big? That's truth, isn't it? Or that she looked tired without her make-up. Or that he would rather watch the football with his mates than with her, if she didn't mind. Or that he would rather live on the other side of the country and actually, he wanted to do that on his own. And the truth was that he wasn't ready to move in with her yet, despite the fact that he was a grown-arsed man and he should be settled down by now. No, thank you. She didn't want that kind of truth in her relationship.

"Carry on," she said tersely waiting to hear what kind of bollocks was waiting to come out of his mouth. She pulled her hand away from him and sat back in her chair.

"Well, like I said, I don't think you're going to like what I'm about to say to you, but I just want you to know that I'm doing it with the best intentions."

"Oh get on with it, Liam," she said, feeling her anger rising.

"Okay, I don't want to keep you in suspense any longer." He too sat back in his chair, mirroring her, although he appeared to be completely relaxed, while Charlotte's stomach churned and her heart beat as fast as it did during a workout.

The door to the bar opened and she watched a middle-aged couple walk up to the bar, hand in hand. As they waited for the bartender's attention, the man dropped his partner's hand and put his hand on the small of her back. Such a loving gesture. She wondered whether they were married and how long they had been together. They looked so comfortable with each other. She guessed they had been married for a long time. The bartender approached them and the man ordered the drinks without asking his partner what she wanted. He clearly knew what she liked and didn't need to ask. Charlotte was envious of the love that had clearly spanned the decades. Was she ever going to find that kind of love?

"So, like I said, I know that you're not going to like it, but," he paused, taking a deep breath. She forced herself not to scream at him to spit it out. He wasn't a judge on the X-Factor, there was no need for the dramatic pause.

"Liam, for fuck's sake!"

"Okay, okay. I'm not going to Manchester," he said. "I've turned the job down. So you're going to have to put up with me hanging around Warkworth."

"You've turned it down? What do you mean?" Charlotte's attention was now fully on Liam.

"I'm not going."

"But…"

"I'm staying in Warkworth." He grinned at her, as though he had just handed her the best gift in the world and he was waiting for her appreciative thanks.

"You're staying in Warkworth? And you've got your job back at the hotel?" she said.

"Yes. Well, technically I never lost it. My uncle still hasn't advertised my job yet, so…"

"You can't do that!" Charlotte was aware that she shrieked when she was angry or exasperated, or both, so she tried to whisper. The last thing she wanted was for the happy couple at the bar to look over at them with pity. She didn't want their commiserating glances. She knew that they should have had this conversation in the privacy of their hotel room, but Liam insisted that they came out and talked over a drink. At the time she thought that it might be a good idea, but hindsight told her otherwise.

"Of course, I can," said Liam. "I've already done it. I thought you'd be happy about it."

"Well yes, I am," said Charlotte.

"Do you want to tell your face that?" Liam grinned and reached for her hand again. This time she let him take it. "Talk to me," he said. "Because this conversation isn't going the way it did in my head. By now we should be whooping and hollering around the table and hugging each other. You say you're happy, but you don't look it at all."

Charlotte shook her head. "You don't get it, do you?"

"No, to be honest, I don't." That's because you're from Mars and I'm from Venus, she thought.

"So what happens in a few months' time, when the holiday season's over and the hotel goes quiet and you get bored again?"

"I'm never bored…"

"You are, Liam. Stop lying to yourself. That's what this whole thing's been about, isn't it? You got bored and you wanted a new challenge."

"Well, yes," he said. Confusion knitted his brows together. "But I always find something to keep me busy at the hotel…"

"Then you'll blame me when you get bored."

"No, I won't."

"Yes! When the Christmas party season starts, you'll start to wonder what you're missing in Manchester and what's going on at the fancy new shiny hotel and you'll blame me for holding you back." Liam shook his head. "I don't want to hold you back. You need to take the job, Liam."

"As long as I live, I'll never understand women," he said. "Do you want another drink?" He stood up, collecting the empty glasses from the table. "Same again?"

"Whatever," said Charlotte. She couldn't be bothered to make a decision about something as trivial as a cocktail.

The bar was busy and as Liam queued, she phoned Hannah. She needed to vent to her best friend. Someone who knew her dating history and who would give her straight and honest advice. Hannah answered almost immediately. She knew that Charlotte was away for the weekend with Liam and she was on standby to offer a shoulder to cry on.

"Are you okay?" she asked, as a perfunctory greeting.

"He's not going to Manchester," said Charlotte.

"He's not going? Why?"

"He said he's just changed his mind. I mean, what the fuck was all this about if he never wanted to go in the first place?"

"Well, he clearly did want to go in the first place," said Hannah. "But maybe he's had time to think and he's now choosing you."

"Yes, but he can't do that," said Charlotte.

"Why not? Of course, he can. He's doing precisely what you wanted him to do, albeit a month or so late."

"Because now he'll always think of me as the woman who held him back. I don't want to stand between him and his dreams."

"Have you ever thought that you might be his dream?"

"I've got to go. He's on his way back. I'll text you later." She hastily ended the call and put her phone back in her handbag, hoping that Liam hadn't spotted it, but obviously he had.

"Who was that?" he asked, handing her a Mojito. The glass was packed with ice and mint and it smelt divine.

"No one," said Charlotte.

"Okay," said Liam, sitting down. He had bought himself a beer and took a long drink, before placing it on the table. "Look, I know you're angry with me, but I don't really know why." He looked defeated and more than a little sad and Charlotte felt her heart expand with love for him. He didn't get it. How could she explain to him that yes, of course, she wanted him to stay in Warkworth, so that he could see her three or four times a week and speak to her every day? The truth was that she wanted to live with him. She was ready to move their relationship to the next level. She wanted to share their everyday lives; their home; their bills; their supermarket shop. She wanted him to be her husband. But he wasn't ready yet and she was slowly coming to terms with that. In the meantime, she would have to wait.

"I don't want to stand between you and your dreams," she said, repeating what she had said to Hannah moments ago. Even though she could hear Hannah's words in her head that she might be his dream. "You'll hold it against me at a later date."

190

"If I said you had a beautiful body, would you hold it against me?" Liam sang the old Dr. Hook song. "If I said you were an angel, would you treat me like a devil tonight?" His infectious laugh made her laugh too.

"You're crazy," she said. "And you know you can't sing for toffee?"

"You can't beat a bit of country music," he said. "If I said you had a beautiful…"

"Shut up!" laughed Charlotte, as she threw the cardboard coaster across the table at him.

Chapter Nineteen

The day after Charlotte and Liam returned from Verona, Charlotte couldn't wait to meet up with Linda for a de-brief. She needed to tell her about her trip and Liam's u-turn decision about his new job. She had a telephone appointment with a client at eleven, so Linda suggested an early morning walk on the beach before she started work. They collected their takeaway coffees from Bridge End Cafe as soon as it opened at nine o'clock and made their way over the bridge, towards the steep hill that led to the beach.

As they clamoured over the sand dunes and took their first sight of the expanse of soft light brown sand and the gentle blue waves, they both stood for a moment, taking in the sight while they sipped their coffees. The only sound was the splashing of the waves onto the beach interrupted intermittently by a small dog barking as it excitedly ran in and out of the sea.

Charlotte took a deep breath, trying to calm her racing mind, which had refused to settle since Liam had told her that he no longer planned to move to Manchester. The morning after his news, after a night of too many cocktails and emotionally charged conversations, she had lain awake next to him in their hotel room for hours. The city roused early and she surrendered the pleasure of peaceful sleep, which had alluded her for weeks. Lately, she had become used to lying awake in bed, staring at the darkness. Restlessness, brain whirring early mornings, a myriad of thoughts, feelings and emotions all wrestled for space in her head. Her worries about their long-distance relationship had been replaced by worries about his rashly made decision, which he would undoubtedly hold against her in future arguments.

In Verona's dawn, she had burrowed under the hotel's thin cotton sheet, tugging it up her chin, hoping that it would induce sleep, but within a minute, she was too hot and kicked it off again. Liam must have turned off the air-conditioning at some point during the night and she longed for the icy blast to cool and calm her. After a few moments, she had crept out of bed and tiptoed onto the balcony, where she quietly read a magazine and waited for Liam to wake up. Throughout their breakfast, their last walk around the city and their flight home, she had tried her best to be cheerful.

"We came here on our first date, you know?" said Charlotte. "It's beautiful, isn't it?"

"Yes, it is," said Linda. "Liam is such a romantic, isn't he? He was born in the wrong era. He should have been born two hundred years ago, when he could have thrown his cape down into a puddle for you to step over."

Charlotte laughed. "I don't know whether he would have done that. He's quite particular about his clothes. He might have carried me over the puddle though."

"I'm so glad he came to the right decision about Manchester. I knew you'd sort it out in the end."

"I just hope he doesn't regret it," said Charlotte. Her eyebrows knitted together in a frown.

"Stop saying that. He's a grown man and if he wanted to go to Manchester, he'd go. It's still not too late for him to change his mind."

"I know, that's what Hannah said. Come on, let's walk. I ate way too much pasta at the weekend and I need to burn it off."

They made their way down the sand dune and onto the beach, which was empty except for the dog walker a hundred yards away. The little dog yapped as it chased a tennis ball into the shallow waves, retrieved it, then dropped it at the feet of its owner, who picked it up and threw it into the sea again.

"Obviously your weekend away worked wonders. I knew that eventually he would realise that he'd miss you too much if he moved away, and getting to see you just once a week wouldn't be enough," said Linda.

"It was Anna-Belle that made him change his mind, actually," said Charlotte.

"Who's Anna-Belle?"

"A woman who sat next to him on the plane. We got chatting on the flight and then we bumped into her in Verona and she joined us for lunch and..."

"And what, she spoke to him about him moving?"

"No, no. She told us this elaborate story on the plane about her husband working for a foreign bank and that she was going to meet him for the weekend in Verona. She said that he had booked them into a posh hotel for a dirty weekend. But when we saw her the next day, she was on her own, so we invited her to have a drink with us, and some lunch, and after a couple of glasses of wine, she admitted that she was in Verona on her own. She had made it all up."

"So there was no husband?"

"Yes, there's a husband. He's a rich investment banker - and also another word that rhymes with banker," said Charlotte, putting her hand to her mouth and whispering the second half of the sentence, as though Anna-Belle were somewhere close by and might overhear her. "But he wasn't with her in Verona. I can't go into details because she's going to be a client, but I spoke to her and offered to help her with her divorce proceedings, the kids and the house and stuff. Then Liam told me later that it was that conversation that made him change his mind." Charlotte drained the last of her coffee. "He said it was because he had realised how good I was at my job," she added modestly.

"Well, of course, you're good at your job," said Linda. "You wouldn't have been able to hold down a job in a big firm in London if you weren't any good. That's always been a given."

"I know and, not meaning to blow my own trumpet, that's exactly what I said when he told me. But he said that he had never seen me deal with an upset client before and he saw how relieved she was when she walked away, knowing that I was working for her. The long and short of it is that that made him think that he couldn't expect me to leave my own practice and go and work in a big office in Manchester, which I would have to do if I eventually moved there. He said that wouldn't be fair, because he knows how much I'd hate that corporate environment. Out of the frying pan and into the fire and all that."

"So does that mean that he had planned to stay in Manchester and he was expecting you to move there?"

"Yes, apparently so," said Charlotte.

"So he wasn't just going to try it out for twelve months and then come back?"

"No, he said that when he accepted the job, he envisaged himself staying there permanently."

"That's a pretty big assumption to make, that you would give up your life here and follow him, given that you have your own firm here," said Linda.

"Well, I did kind of lead him to believe that I would," admitted Charlotte. "When he first told me about the job, I started talking about renting out my house as a holiday let and finding somewhere to live in Manchester. I just assumed that I'd go with him until he made it clear that he was going on his own. Anyway, all's well that ends well." Charlotte smiled and although she was doing her best to show that she was perfectly fine with the situation, Linda knew her better than that. Charlotte wasn't fully opening up.

"Are you back on track, do you think?" Linda asked hopefully. Having been through a previous break-up with Charlotte and Liam, she didn't want that to happen again. She knew that they were made for each other. The sooner they both came to the same conclusion, the better for everyone.

"Yes."

The way Charlotte answered the question, curtly and emotionless, confirmed to Linda that there was definitely more that she wasn't saying. She couldn't see her face as they were walking side by side, so she couldn't tell what she was thinking. "Are you sure?" she asked. She stopped, held onto Charlotte's arm, and turned to face her.

"Yes, yes, of course. I'm just a bit shaken by it all. I thought we'd have a smooth ride and it's been far from it."

"Ahh well, you know what they say…"

"Yeah, yeah, the course of true love never ran smooth bollocks. Don't start quoting Shakespeare at me. I've had enough of him this weekend."

"What do you mean?" said Linda with feigned exasperation. "Romeo and Juliet is one of his best works."

"Yeah, I'm not a fan, I'm afraid to say. She was way too young, she went against her family's wishes and took the whole thing way too seriously. If she'd hung on, and said no to Romeo, she would have been snogging another boy within the week. You don't fall in love at that age, you just think you do. It's all hormones and teenage angst."

"You're a literary heathen," said Linda, laughing. "But you've got a point."

"Seriously though, the 'me and Liam' thing, I'm still processing it all. I feel massively let down because of his decision to go to Manchester on his own. I thought we'd be making plans to get our own place soon."

"Yes, I know," said Linda. "Sounds like he's not quite ready to give up living on his own. He is worth waiting for though, don't you think?"

"Maybe," said Charlotte, sounding completely unconvinced. "So, what have you been up to? Have you heard anything more from Storm since your lunch?" said Charlotte.

"She has texted me a couple of times and suggested that we get together again soon, but I haven't really had time to arrange anything yet."

"Why? What have you been doing?"

"This and that. I'm retired now, my time's my own and I didn't feel like committing to anything." Linda laughed and tried to sound light-hearted.

"Look, if you don't feel comfortable seeing her, you know, if she reminds you too much of Twat Face, then just tell her. She'll understand. She's an intelligent woman," said Charlotte.

"It's not that," said Linda. "It was lovely to see her. She was telling me all about her university course and her plans to travel to Europe. She's really friendly. We were chatting away as though we'd known each other for years."

"And that's fair enough, but if it's not right for you, then she'll just have to go and get therapy like the rest of us."

"That's a bit harsh," said Linda. She laughed, knowing that deep down Charlotte didn't mean anything by it. She was one of the most caring people she had ever met.

"You know I've got doubts about her, I can't lie," said Charlotte. "I want you to be careful, that's all, if you do meet up again. You do hear of people, criminals, targeting the newly bereaved and trying to get some money from the estate. Just have your wits about you, that's all I'm saying."

"I know, I know," said Linda. "And thanks for the concern, but I believe she's an honest person. She has good energy and if you met her and talked to her properly, you'd know what I meant."

Charlotte could have given Linda a lecture about the ways and means of fraudsters and how they operated, but she didn't want to come across as patronising. How could she tell a woman who was twenty years older than herself that she didn't have enough experience of the world to be able to judge people? Linda was so far removed from being streetwise that she was almost childlike. She took people at face value, which wasn't always the wisest thing to do when they were adept at wearing different masks for different occasions.

Charlotte wanted to grill Linda about whether she had told Storm about her windfall inheritance from Phil, but for now, it was better to keep quiet. She wanted Linda to open up and talk to her, without being judged. She would always be there to help her, if necessary. Maybe it was a moot point anyway. Storm might be under the assumption that Linda was living in the same house that she had shared with Phil. In which case, there wouldn't be an inheritance, other than a few pounds that he may have had left in his bank account.

As it stood, she knew that Linda hadn't yet decided what she was going to do with the money that Phil had left her. Charlotte advised her to leave it where it was, safe in a bank account for now. She didn't need to make any rash decisions. If she wanted to give it away to a cat's home, or take it all out of the bank in twenty-pound notes, tie it in a hessian sack, and throw it in the river, that was okay, she could do whatever she wished. It was her money. But Charlotte needed to make sure that Linda wasn't coerced into doing something that she didn't want to do by someone she had only just met.

In the meantime, she would tread carefully.

"Had she tried to trace her dad earlier?" she asked.

"I don't know," said Linda. "I didn't ask her that."

"So, had she always known who he was?"

"Yes, I suppose so," said Linda. "I mean, his name is clearly on the birth certificate."

"Yes, I know, but did she always know that he was your Phil? You know what I mean, the Phil Matthews who lived in Warkworth?"

"As opposed to?"

"Well, another Phil Matthews. It's a pretty common name, I'd imagine, and he could have lived anywhere."

"Oh I see what you mean," said Linda. "I don't know." She felt stupid for not asking more questions. Now that Charlotte raised these questions, it seemed obvious that she should have asked for more information. Maybe Storm wasn't Phil's daughter after all. Just because her dad is *a* Phil Matthews, didn't necessarily mean that he was *her* Phil Matthews. Is that possible? The thought cheered her a little. She knew that Phil had been a liar and a cheat, but for him to have also been a father was a bitter pill for her to swallow. But when she pictured Storm's face, she could see the remnants of Phil. Her hair was the same glossy black and her eyes were the same deep blue. But it was more than that. The dimple in her right cheek was the same as his and the way she raised her right eyebrow when she talked, was exactly what he used to do.

In her mind, there was no doubt. Her personality may have been from her mother, but Storm was Phil's daughter, whether Linda liked it or not.

She knew that Charlotte was concerned about a stranger showing up at his funeral and claiming to be family. She was scared that Linda would be taken for a ride and she would lose all her money in an elaborate scam. But Charlotte had worked with criminals, represented them in court, and interviewed them in tiny windowless cells in police stations, so she was bound to see the worst in people. She had a warped view of the world.

Linda would keep her guard up, but until Storm gave her cause for concern, she wouldn't worry.

"She is the image of him," said Linda. "I know she's a girl and everything, but she looks just like him. He was quite handsome when he was younger."

Charlotte nodded, although she couldn't imagine a handsome Phil at any age, not even when he was a bouncing baby boy. His wickedness and cruelty erased any attractive features he may have had, in her eyes. All she saw was an ugly bully. "Well, it will all come out in the wash, as my mum says."

Linda knew that, by that, Charlotte meant that Storm would turn out to be a thief sooner or later, but she didn't respond. There was no point in arguing over something that in all likelihood would never happen. "We'd better do an about-turn," she said. "I don't want to make you late for your client."

They turned around and started their walk back to the village. As they navigated their way back over the sand dunes and onto the path that led to the village, Linda tried to quieten the little voice in her head that was concerned about the money that had gone missing from Phil's wallet. She told the little voice that Storm had nothing to do with it, but it didn't seem to be listening and she couldn't get the thought out of her head.

When Dorothy had given her the brown envelope containing Phil's will, his death certificate, his bank card and his wallet, she had told her that there were two hundred and thirty pounds in his wallet. She remembered having the conversation with her about Phil always preferring to use cash, rather than his card. They had laughed because Phil had tried to make sure that Linda wasn't able to keep a check on where he had been spending his money. She had been so busy preparing a nice lunch for Storm, a fatted calf in the guise of a feta and tomato quiche, that she had let her guard down and had left the brown envelope containing Phil's wallet on the kitchen table. Storm had had plenty of opportunity to take a look inside and to procure some of the cash from the wallet while Linda had been engaged chasing the cat around the garden and trying to protect her from a bee sting.

What an idiot she had been. Firstly, trying to stop a cat from chasing bees was just like trying to hold back the rising tide on Warkworth Beach. It was never going to happen. Secondly, trusting someone you have only spoken to once and allowing them into your home was pure stupidity.

She had first discovered that some money had potentially gone missing a few days after her lunch with Storm, when she needed to get some shopping from the supermarket. She decided that she might as well take some of Phil's cash with her, rather than using her bank card. She reached for the envelope, which she had put at the back of the kitchen cupboard over the kettle, and took the wallet out. The wad of cash didn't feel like two hundred and thirty pounds, not that she had ever held that much cash in her hand, and when she counted it, her fears were confirmed. There was only one hundred and sixty pounds.

Even so, she didn't want to jump to any conclusions. Just because Storm was Phil's daughter, didn't make her a bad person. And just because she was a student, didn't mean that she was so desperate for money that she would resort to stealing. After all, she had a job in a restaurant and was working all the hours she could.

Dorothy could have been mistaken, after all, and maybe she had miscounted the money. She had contemplated telephoning her to ask if she was sure about the amount, but had decided not to.

She didn't want to disturb her.

Or was it because she didn't want to face the truth?

Chapter Twenty

In true English style, the summer was short and sweet and by the first week in September, it was over. Linda's lightweight summer quilt had barely been on the bed for a couple of months before it was bundled back into its bag and stashed underneath the bed. The thick winter quilt had made an early start.

Before she opened her eyes, Linda heard the rain driving against her bedroom window. Although the garden would be thankful for it, today she certainly wasn't. She was having her hair coloured in Alnwick and had planned to go to the bank, which was at the opposite end of the town, and she didn't relish getting soaked wet through. But never mind, she thought. The inclement weather was giving her an excuse to pop into that lovely, but expensive, gift shop and treat herself to a colourful new umbrella.

She kicked off the duvet and pushed her feet into her slippers. As she passed the living room door, she spotted Nutmeg, curled up in her favourite place on the back of the sofa. The cat opened one eye and gave a little sigh as Linda entered the room and opened the curtains. Linda bent down to stroke her, causing her to open the other eye, reluctantly, and stretch.

"Look what you've done to my sofa, Nutmeg. It's covered in hair," said Linda, as she picked her up and tucked her under her arm. "While you're moulting, I think you're going to have to be confined to the kitchen, young lady. Sorry about that."

She carried her into the kitchen, closing the living room door behind her. Once in the kitchen, she put the cat down on the floor and poured her some milk. She flicked the kettle on, opened the blinds, and stood watching the rain, while she waited for the water to boil. As soon as the kettle switched itself off, the house was quiet and still again. The only sound was the rain against the window, which thankfully had settled into a gentle pitter-patter, rather than the forceful hammering that it had been doing a few minutes ago and the gentle tapping of a branch of the cherry tree against the kitchen window. The kitchen clock ticked its rhythmic passing of time.

"Oh Nutmeg," she said. "It's just you and me. That's Heaven, isn't it? Rain, midnight rain, nothing but the wild rain on this bleak hut, and solitude, and me."

She wondered sometimes whether solitude was the gift she had expected it to be, or whether she missed living with someone. Phil hadn't been that bad, had he? Well, not all the time. Especially in the early years of their marriage, he had been quite good company. When they were younger, she used to like having their morning breakfasts together at the weekend. He used to have a boiled egg on toast, or sometimes a bacon sandwich, which she would make for him while he read the paper or watched the television. But as the years passed, more often than not, when she shouted to tell him that his breakfast was ready, he would tell her that he wanted to eat in the living room, so she would take it to him and he would eat with a tray balanced on his knee and his mug of tea next to him on the coffee table. Sometimes she joined him, telling herself that it was better for them to be together, despite the fact that his full attention was on Match of the Day, rather than to be on her own in the kitchen. But gradually, she began to deliver his food to him and go straight back to the kitchen, where her book and her cup of tea would be waiting for her. Artificial friends, but nevertheless, ones that were better company.

All things considered, she would much rather live on her own, she decided.

As she was stirring the teabag around in the hot water, thanking the universe that she only had to make one drink for herself, and she no longer had to make tea or cook breakfast for the unappreciative slob that was her ex-husband, her thoughts were interrupted by a text message on her phone.

Would you do me a favour this morning please and wait in for a parcel to be delivered for me? It was Jessica from next door.

I've got a hair appointment this morning, sorry, I won't be able to do it, Linda replied.

What time is your appointment?

Ten forty-five, said Linda.

Could you nip over here around half-nine? The parcel delivery window is nine thirty to ten thirty and I've got an appointment with Charlotte.

Linda was about to text back and say that usually the courier would try to leave the parcel with a neighbour anyway, when another text arrived.

I wouldn't ask but it's something that needs to be signed for. Sorry!

So Linda agreed that she would be there at nine-thirty, adding that if the parcel hadn't arrived by ten, then she would need to leave so that she could get to Alnwick in time for her hair appointment. That's annoying, she thought to herself. Now I won't have time for a coffee before I get my hair done. But she told herself not to be selfish. It was good to be neighbourly, as you never knew when the favour would need to be reciprocated.

At nine-thirty, Jessica opened her front door to Linda and invited her inside.

"Thank you so much, Linda," said Jessica. "I'm sorry for the inconvenience. The parcel could literally arrive any minute, so as soon as it arrives, obviously you can go."

"If it hasn't arrived, could you ask them to leave it at the back door or anything?"

"No," said Jessica. "It does need to be signed for, but don't worry about it. I'll just have to pop over to the Post Office for it tomorrow. Help yourself to tea or coffee and feel free to raid the biscuit jar."

"Thanks," said Linda. "You get going for your appointment and don't worry about your parcel."

"Do you think you could text me when it arrives?" asked Jessica.

Linda said that she would. She felt sorry for the young woman, being just at the start of her battle with her husband and she was happy to help her, however she could.

Luckily, the parcel arrived within twenty minutes. Linda signed for it and left it on the kitchen table. She sent a text to Jessica, telling her that it had arrived safely, so she didn't need to dash home. She thought that, after what may be an emotional meeting with Charlotte discussing the demise of her marriage, she might be in desperate need of a coffee.

***

After a long appointment in the hair salon, where Linda had every little bit of grey hair covered up by a soft light brown, she entered the bank with a spring in her step. The rain had stopped, but even so, she had called into the gift shop and bought herself a new umbrella. She did live in the UK after all and the rain was a frequent visitor. She had also bought a huge scented candle and some completely unnecessary ornamental wooden hares, one wearing a blue rain hat and one wearing a yellow raincoat. They were adorable and she was looking forward to dotting them around the bungalow to see where they looked best.

She had bought herself a candle once, last year when she had first met Charlotte and they had gone into the gift shop in Warkworth. She burned it secretly in the spare bedroom, which she indulgently called her reading room. When Phil had returned from work, he had stormed up the stairs and blew it out, extinguishing any pleasure that she had gained that afternoon. But never again.

She pushed open the heavy door to the bank and was surprised to find that there were no longer any glass screens between the staff and the public. It looked more like a travel agency. Were there no bank robberies anymore? If someone ran in right now with a sawn-off shotgun and a balaclava, how could the staff protect themselves? she thought. They seemed too vulnerable; like sitting ducks on sandbags full of cash, waiting for it to be taken from them. Some staff members didn't even have the safety of a desk to hide behind; they were walking about amongst the public, helping them to navigate the complicated ATMs or sending them into various tiny glass cubicles along the back wall of the bank, where a small desk was placed between two chairs, presumably for more private transactions. Maybe crime had moved on, she thought. Charlotte was always telling her about cybercrime. Maybe criminals got rich without leaving the house these days.

Her thoughts flitted to Storm and Charlotte's warnings about her, but she batted them down and concentrated on finding someone to point her in the right direction.

"Good afternoon, can I help you with anything? Are you withdrawing or depositing?"

"Neither," said Linda, after taking a pause to work out what the woman meant. "I need to close my husband's bank account. He's dead." She didn't intend for it to sound so cold-hearted, but how else can you say it?

"I'm so sorry," said the bank clerk. "Please come with me and we'll get you sorted out." Linda followed her, past the queue of people waiting to speak to the vulnerable bank clerks, and was led into one of the see-through cubicles. The assistant opened the door and pointed to one of the chairs. "Please take a seat, Mrs..?"

"Matthews," said Linda. That was the first time she had said that since she had left Phil back in January. For nine months, she had remained Linda Matthews without thinking about what that really meant. It hadn't occurred to her until now that she was using her married name. Should she think about changing her name? Maybe she would have done after the divorce, but her maiden name was so long ago abandoned that she wasn't sure that she could rescue it. She was a different person now. She was a widow and it seemed churlish, no, some might say reprehensible, to abandon her married name after her husband's death. It was too late. She would forever be Mrs. Matthews.

"Mrs. Matthews, firstly I'd like to say, on behalf of the Northumberland Bank that I'm sorry for your loss."

"Thank you," said Linda. She briefly wondered whether she should try to be a weeping widow, but decided that she wouldn't be able to summon the tears, which was positive, as the bank clerk would probably feel most uncomfortable if she broke down in front of her.

"So you're here to close down your husband's account?"

"Yes, please," said Linda. She passed her the brown envelope containing Phil's death certificate, the will and his bank card. She had also brought her own brand-new shiny passport, which Charlotte told her she would need, as identification. "I've got all the documents in here."

The clerk took the envelope and, after checking all the documents, she tapped at the computer keyboard for a few moments. "Okay, so I've located Mr. Matthews' account. It's quite a considerable sum. Have you given any thought to where you'd like the money to go? I can see that you have a current account with us, but I'd recommend that you speak to an independent financial advisor, who could advise you how best to deal with the money. There are some good savings accounts, or you might want to invest…"

"Can you please tell me how much is in his account?" interrupted Linda. "Just so I can give it some thought," she added. The clerk's face was expressionless and unreadable and Linda wondered if she thought it odd that, firstly, her husband would have his own bank account and, secondly, that his wife didn't know how much was in it. Sod it, thought Linda. I don't know this woman and I won't have to see her again, so who cares what she thinks of me? Charlotte's influence was slowly but surely rubbing off on her.

"Two hundred and fifty thousand, four hundred and twenty pounds," said the clerk, swiftly, as though she was used to such extortionate amounts falling off her tongue.

"How much?" Linda couldn't help herself. Any pretence that she had known about her husband's financial affairs was now well and truly over.

The clerk seemed a little surprised. "Is that less than you expected?" she asked.

"No, no, it's a lot more than I expected," said Linda. "We kept our finances separate, so I wasn't entirely sure how much he had, that's all."

"Well," said the clerk, resuming her professional persona, "Would you like me to make an appointment with our financial advisor for you? He isn't independent, and I would advise that you get independent financial advice, but he can talk through the products that we have here at the bank, to safeguard the money for you."

"Yes, please," said Linda. "I'm not sure what to do with that amount of money."

"It does need some careful consideration," said the clerk, nodding. Linda wondered how much money she had in her own bank account and how much careful consideration she had to give it. "I'll transfer it to your current account for now and then close Mr. Matthews' account, as you requested." She tapped away at the keyboard again. After a few minutes of silence, she said, "Okay, that's all done for you. It will show in your account immediately."

"Thank you very much," said Linda. Her mind was whirring and all she wanted to do was to get out of this glass enclosure, which had suddenly become extremely hot, and ring Charlotte. She needed financial advice, she was aware of that, but she also needed her friend. She had heard people say that having money was a huge responsibility and she always thought that rich people said that to assuage their guilt about being so blessed. But now, the burden was already becoming heavy and she hadn't been carrying it for more than two minutes. "Could I ring the financial advisor myself, for the appointment?" she said, as the bank clerk picked up the phone. She was desperate to get outside into the fresh air.

"Yes, of course. I'll give you his card. There you are." Linda took the card from her and put it into her pocket. "Thank you for choosing Northumberland Bank and I hope to see you very soon."

She opened the door of the cubicle and Linda was, at long last, released. As soon as she was outside, she rang Charlotte's phone.

"Hi Linda, are you alright?" said Charlotte.

"I'm fuming," said Linda. "I've just been to the bank and closed Phil's account."

"Okay," said Charlotte, thinking that Linda was about to tell her that there was no money in it and, after their conversations about leaving it to a cat rescue society, that Phil had beaten her to it and done that himself.

"He had over two hundred and fifty thousand pounds," said Linda. "The absolute bastard! The bastard!"

"Crikey, that's a lot," said Charlotte.

"Yes, about a hundred thousand too much," said Linda.

"Sorry, I don't follow what you mean."

"When we sold our house, we split the profits, didn't we?" said Linda.

"Yes, I remember," said Charlotte.

"And we had one hundred and seventy-five grand each."

"Oh, I see," said Charlotte. "Sorry, it took a moment for me to follow. So you're saying that he's had seventy-five grand in his bank all this time and you knew nothing about it?"

"Exactly."

"What a bastard!"

"Exactly."

Chapter Twenty-One

The following evening, Linda had booked a dinner reservation for her, Charlotte and Liam at the Seafood Bar and Grille in Alnmouth for seven-thirty. It was her treat. She had already told Charlotte that she didn't want any arguments at the end of the meal, she was picking up the bill and they could order whatever they wanted. In fact, Phil would be paying, she had told her, as she was using some of his money. Charlotte told her that it was about time that he treated her to a meal in a decent restaurant and that this was better still because she didn't have to go with him.

Storm had recommended the restaurant to Linda when they had had lunch together at her house, but that wasn't the reason that Linda had chosen it. She had looked at the websites for half a dozen restaurants in the local area and had chosen this one because it was the most expensive. If Phil was looking down on her, she wanted him to thoroughly disapprove of her frivolousness.

It was also the type of restaurant where the customers made an effort to dress up. The type of place that Phil would have hated and would have felt extremely uncomfortable in. The unspoken dress code meant that the men's shirts were ironed and shoes were cleaned and the women all looked beautiful in elegant dresses or silk shirts and trousers. Linda wore a simple navy blue cotton dress with a long pale grey cashmere cardigan, that Charlotte had talked her into buying as 'an investment piece'. With her new hair colour and her expensive clothes, she felt amazing.

As she studied the menu, she pretended that she was au fait with the various dishes. In truth, she had only heard of half of them. But she was willing to be adventurous. She didn't want to be the only one on the dinner table on the cruise who didn't know how to eat mussels, so she chose them as her starter. She knew that Charlotte and Liam wouldn't judge her if she wasn't sure what to do or which fork to use. For her main course, she chose sea bass in a salt crust, with a herb butter sauce. Charlotte and Liam both ordered mussels, followed by the lobster thermidor. Linda asked the sommelier to recommend a wine and told him that she was happy to be guided by him. She didn't care how much it cost. For once in her life, she was going to enjoy the experience of eating out, without giving the price a second thought. When the bill came, she vowed that she wouldn't look at it. She would just enter her pin number into the card machine nonchalantly, as though she paid hundreds of pounds for a meal every week.

"Do you want to toast to Phil?" asked Liam, when the waiter had poured their wine. "To thank him for paying for the meal?"

"Absolutely not," said Linda. "Let's toast to good friends."

"And to Warkworth being the best place to live," said Charlotte, giving a sly wink to Linda.

"You're not going to let me forget about Manchester very easily, are you?" said Liam.

"I don't see why I should," said Charlotte, laughing.

"To friends and to Warkworth," said Linda, clicking Charlotte's and Liam's glasses in turn.

"So where do you think Phil's money came from?" asked Liam. "Charlotte said he didn't have a particularly well-paid job. You don't think he won it on the horses, do you?"

"Maybe some of it," said Linda. "He did like a little flutter at the bookies at the weekend. But I think I've worked it out. About eighteen months ago, his dad died and I think he left him some money and he never told me."

"That's awful," said Charlotte. "Was it from the sale of his house, do you think?"

"Yes, he lived in a flat, but I don't know how much it sold for. Phil let his sister deal with the sale and he told me that there was no money left, after all his dad's bills and debts were paid and they'd paid for the funeral. He paid about eight hundred pounds into our joint account, that's all."

"And you didn't think any more about it?"

"No, to be honest, I trusted him and because the flat was only small, I believed what he said. But now I think about it, his dad wasn't the type to have any debt and the flat was in a great location, overlooking the sea, so it was probably worth quite a bit of money. Obviously, it was."

"What I don't get," said Liam, "Is why he would put the rest of the money into a separate account when you were both still together. It's not like he could buy himself a new car and hope that you wouldn't notice."

"Who knows," said Linda. "Control, I suppose. Or possibly he knew that we'd split up eventually and he wanted his own stash of cash. But I've got to say that it has made me feel much better about having the inheritance now, because some of it should have gone into our joint account much sooner."

"Well, at least he did the right thing in the end, by leaving it to you" said Liam.

"Yes, I don't know why though," said Linda. "I would never have found out about it. I can only assume that he felt guilty and that's why he decided to make me his beneficiary."

The waiter arrived at the table carrying a large bowl of mussels in each hand and balancing a third on his left arm. As he placed them expertly on the table, the sommelier topped up their wine glasses and Linda asked him to bring another bottle.

As they ate their food and chatted about this and that and found the conversation increasingly more amusing the more wine they consumed, Linda wondered whether to tell Charlotte and Liam that she had bumped into Storm yesterday afternoon. Just as Linda had ended her conversation with Charlotte on the phone after coming out of the bank, Storm had walked up behind her and, after checking it was her, gave her a huge friendly hug and told her how lovely it was that they had bumped into each other.

Within seconds, the heavens opened yet again, and knowing that they had the choice of either saying a rushed goodbye or sheltering from the rain in a coffee shop somewhere, Linda chose the latter. Storm told her that she never said no to a coffee and suggested that they go to the bookshop cafe, which was a little further to walk than the Starbucks across the road, but it was worth it. Linda knew exactly the place that she meant and said that she was happy to walk there.

They had both sheltered under Linda's new umbrella, with Storm linking her arm to Linda's as they walked.

As the rain had been almost constant all day, forcing the less hardy shoppers to remain indoors at home, the bookshop cafe was quiet. They walked through the book part of the store, into the cafe at the back and found a nice table surrounded by four comfortable leather armchairs. Storm said that it was her turn to pay and insisted that Linda sat down while she ordered their coffee. She waved her card in the air, as proof that she had means, but Linda told her that her turn would come when she found herself in full-time employment and, until then, on a student grant and a part-time wage from the restaurant, she needed to keep her money to herself, thank you very much.

A few minutes later, Linda returned to the table with two cappuccinos and two blueberry muffins. "I didn't ask if you wanted one," she had said. "But they looked too good to resist, so I just bought them." Storm had politely told her that blueberry muffins were her favourite and she picked hers up and immediately took a large bite.

As they sat opposite one another, drinking their coffee, eating their cake, and making conversation, Linda was distracted by the inheritance weighing heavily in her bank account and wanted, on more than one occasion, to tell Storm about it. After all, the money was her father's and she had a right to at least some of it. She wanted to ask Storm how much her rent was for her student accommodation. She could easily pay for it, right now, with Phil's money. She had a banking app on her phone. Maybe Storm's rent was paid for by her student grant, but she could still use the money for something else. Did they still have grants these days? Linda had no idea, but she presumed that students from low-income families had some kind of government assistance. So, if she didn't need her rent paying, maybe she would need some new clothes, or just some paintbrushes or some oil paints. They were expensive, weren't they? Should she offer to buy them, or would that be weird? She had no idea what the protocol was. She didn't think there was a guidebook on how to deal with an adult stepdaughter that you have only just met.

But then the annoying little voice in her head shouted up again, telling her she was being stupid and that she needed to keep her mouth shut and keep the money where it was, safe and sound in the bank. At least until she knew Storm a little better.

Right now, if Charlotte had an inkling of what she had been thinking, she would tell her that she was being gullible and she was 'being taken for a ride' by someone that she knew nothing about. Liam would agree with her, no doubt.

But Storm had never asked her for any money. In fact, she had never asked her for anything, not even any of Phil's belongings. She could have asked for his watch, something to remember him by, but she hadn't.

As Linda had sipped her cappuccino and nibbled her blueberry muffin, she had watched Storm and tried to study her body language. She wasn't an expert, of course, she wasn't, but she wasn't stupid either. She knew when a person couldn't be trusted. She knew when someone was telling lies and was being deceitful. She had had enough experience of that throughout her marriage to Phil. She also knew when someone was good and kind and honest and the young woman sitting in front of her in the cafe was all of those things, as far as she could tell.

Linda had asked her about her university course and what she would be studying when she went back for her third year. Storm told her about the option to take a year out and study at a European university, but she said she couldn't afford to do that, as another year of student debts would be crippling. So, she would carry on with her course in Edinburgh and would save as much as she could, so she could go travelling when she graduated.

Linda watched her face light up when she spoke of the galleries and the art museums that she planned to visit in Reykjavik, Berlin, Madrid and, of course, Paris. She said she had been trying to top up her school-girl Spanish, which was rusty at best. She had been doing an online course, so that she could get a job in a café or restaurant in Spain, which meant that she could stay there longer. Linda had told her that she seemed like an intelligent girl and she was sure that she would be able to do it and that she had the world at her feet, so she should grab every opportunity she had.

Storm had yawned then and apologised profusely, saying that she had had a late night, working at the restaurant. Linda asked her how her saving up was going and she said that she couldn't put any money aside this month, as she needed to buy some new brushes, ready for the start of the new term. "I'll get there, eventually," she said. She sighed with the resignation of someone who had almost given up on her dream. It was heartbreaking for Linda to think for one moment that she wouldn't be able to fulfil a simple goal, such as travelling to Europe. She, herself, hadn't been yet, but now that she had nobody holding her back, she intended to travel somewhere interesting every year and Storm should be able to do that too.

"So tell me about Storm?" asked Liam, as though reading her mind. "Do you think she's genuine?"

"In what way?" asked Linda.

"Do you think she's really Phil's daughter?"

"Yes, absolutely," said Linda. "She's shown me her birth certificate and she looks just like him." A look passed between Charlotte and Liam that she couldn't read. "What's that for?" she asked.

"What?" said Liam.

"That look between the two of you. You don't trust her, do you?"

"We're just looking out for you, you know that," said Charlotte.

"Yes, I know," said Linda. "And I love you for it, but I do think that she's genuine."

Linda took another drink of her wine and decided that now wasn't the time to tell Charlotte and Liam about the money that may or may not have gone missing from Phil's wallet. She didn't want to admit that she had turned her back on it and left it on the kitchen table while Storm was there. She also didn't want to tell them that she had looked for her gold necklace and the matching bracelet that Charlotte and Liam had bought her for her last birthday and that she couldn't find them anywhere. She thought the box had been in the top drawer of the chest in her bedroom, but even though she had taken out every item of underwear from that drawer, it wasn't there.

But just because she had misplaced it, which she must have done, as it wouldn't have simply vanished into thin air, didn't mean that Storm should be under any kind of suspicion. Right now, if she told Charlotte and Liam about her missing jewellery, they would have Storm convicted without a trial.

Storm had only been to her house once and although Linda had to concede that she may have had the opportunity to take some money out of the envelope that was on the table right in front of her, an opportunist crime some would call it, she wouldn't have had the chance to go rifling through her drawers in her bedroom. Linda had only been in the garden for a matter of minutes and, for a start, she wouldn't have known where to look.

She wouldn't have done something so brazen. There had to be a simple explanation for both missing items. Dorothy had miscounted the money from Phil's wallet and Linda's jewellery wasn't missing; it was misplaced.

Storm wouldn't have done something so brazen. Would she?

Chapter Twenty-Two

On Sunday morning, Charlotte woke up alone in Liam's bed.
The smell of bacon cooking downstairs and the sound of him
singing to himself told her that his hangover obviously
wasn't as intense as hers. She turned over slowly, reached for
her phone, and sent him a text.

My head's exploding!!!

"You're awake then!" he shouted up the stairs, which
opened out into the kitchen. "Do you want a coffee?"

"Yes, please," she said. She lay back down and
covered her eyes with her forearm. She listened to the kettle
boiling and the sound of Liam pottering around in the
kitchen, preparing the coffee. Just as she was considering
whether she was able to get up unaided, or whether she
needed someone to hold her head still for her as she walked
to the bathroom, she heard him coming up the stairs.

"There you go, my delicate princess," he said, putting
a mug of coffee on the bedside table at her side of the bed.
"Do you think you're capable of sitting up without puking?"

"Fuck off," she said, smiling.

"You can't be that bad if you still have the capacity for foul language." Liam walked round to the other side of the bed, put his coffee down on the bedside table, and climbed into bed next to her. "There are some painkillers in the bathroom. Do you want me to get you some?"

"In a bit."

"I was going to ask you if you wanted the curtains opening, but I thought that might be a step too far."

"Yes, just a little," she said, rolling over onto her side and snuggling into him. She rested her head on his chest and wrapped her arms around him.

"Another ten minutes for the bacon," he said. "Are you up to eating any breakfast?"

"Possibly," she said. "What are you laughing at?" She pushed herself up on her elbows and sank back against the headboard to drink her much-needed coffee.

"You, of course. I don't think I've seen you this hungover before. I usually can't shut you up in the mornings, but you're apparently struggling to put a sentence together today."

"Why did you let me do it?" she said. She reached over for her coffee. "I need lots of coffee today and lots of greasy food."

"And maybe an afternoon nap?"

"Oh, yes definitely one of those," she said. "Preferably in front of some trashy Netflix film with a box of chocolates on my knee."

"I'll see what I can do," he said. "I'd better go and rescue the bacon. Do you want breakfast in bed, or are you coming down?"

"What do you think?" She smiled at him and he gave her a quick kiss on his way out of the room.

"Okay, I'll be back in a few minutes. Ketchup?"

"Yes, please," she said.

While Liam was downstairs, Charlotte dragged herself to the bathroom, where she took two painkillers, along with a pint of water. After she had brushed her teeth, feeling half-human again, she got back into bed and switched on the television. She was flicking through the channels when Liam appeared with their bacon sandwiches.

"It's Gardener's World or Peppa Pig," she said.

"Tough choice," said Liam.

She flicked back to Gardener's World.

"I feel better already," she said, with a mouthful of bacon. "It's amazing what some food and two Paracetamol can do. Thank you for looking after me."

"I love you, of course, I'm going to look after you," he said.

"I think I might be ready to face some daylight now," she said a few minutes later, having taken the last bite of her sandwich.

"Madam, your wish is my command." Liam jumped out of bed and opened the curtains. "Well, that's moderately disappointing. It's not what you'd call sunny. Fancy a walk on the beach later?"

"Are you kidding? What happened to the Netflix plan?"

"We can do that too, but after a little stroll. Come on, it'll do you good. Let's re-live our first date." Charlotte frowned at him. "I admit it may not be as warm as it was on that day, but I just fancy a little walk. Just you and me and the fresh air."

Charlotte had no choice but to accept his offer. She knew that he was making an effort for her and for the sake of their relationship and, hangover or not, this was his way of making it up to her. There was no harm in rekindling some romance, after the rocky road they had just travelled. So she agreed that she would make an effort and would get dressed. Liam told her that there was no rush. He collected the plates and mugs, kissed her again gently on the top of her head, and told her to take her time.

"Why don't you have a bath?" he said. "You can relax in some bubbles before we go out."

"Are you sure?" she said. "It's not going to rain and ruin your plans, is it? Should we go now while it's dry?"

"No, I don't think it'll rain and if it does, it will be more romantic. I'll start running the bath for you. Shall we set off in about an hour?"

She checked the time on Liam's bedside clock and assured him that she would be ready in an hour and, true to her word, fifty minutes later, she arrived downstairs dressed in jeans and her favourite pale blue t-shirt from Pink in Victoria's Secret. Her hair was bundled up into a messy bun. Thanks to a good foundation, two coats of mascara and lots of bronzer, she looked beautiful.

"Liam, I'm ready," she said. Then, "Oh sorry, I didn't realise you were on the phone."

Liam walked into the kitchen from the living room, his mobile phone held to his ear. "Okay, that's fine, well if you wouldn't mind sorting that out then, I'll leave you to it," he said into the phone, before ending the call.

"Who was that?" asked Charlotte.

"Just work," he said. "Just something that needs sorting out for later today, but nothing you need to worry about."

"Do you need to go in?" she said. Since Liam had turned down the job in Manchester, she was worried that his uncle would see him as unreliable and flaky and would want to replace him as soon as he could. However much she wanted to spend the day with him today, she wanted to make sure that he held tightly onto the job that would keep him in Warkworth. So, if he had to go to work, then so be it.

"Not at all," he said. "Come on, you can't get out of the walk that easily. But I'll tell you what, I won't subject you to the walk up the hill, we'll go in the car, is that all right?"

"Thank God for that," she said.

As they travelled the short distance to the beach, Charlotte wondered whether today would be a good time to talk to him about them moving in together. They needed to be in a place where there were no distractions, so they could talk privately and the beach seemed as good a place as any.

Linda had brought up the subject of their living arrangements last night and, although Liam had seemed happy enough to talk about it, the constant interruptions at the table by the waiting staff, checking if their food was satisfactory and re-filling their wine glasses, didn't help him to reach a conclusion that she was happy with. She knew that they would live together eventually, but she still didn't know when and Liam hadn't been clear.

"So when you two lovebirds decide to move in together, will you move into your place or Oriel House?" Linda had asked him.

Charlotte had almost choked on her wine when she heard the question and she stared at Linda, who was studiously avoiding eye contact. She would have kicked her under the table if she could have reached. She was about to tell Liam that he didn't need to answer the question and that there was no pressure to decide anything, but Liam, seemingly unfazed, began weighing up the pros and cons of each of the properties. He told Linda that he loved the fact that Oriel House had two large bedrooms and two amazing bathrooms, but his house had three bedrooms and the small one at the front would make a perfect study, for the occasions when Charlotte wanted to work from home. Linda mentioned his garden, which was gorgeous and was large enough to have all the family round for a barbeque in the summer, and it caught the afternoon sun. Liam had agreed but said that Oriel House had the wonderful view of the castle, and no other house in Warkworth had such an amazing view. Yes, Linda had said, the view was amazing but it was that little bit further away from the beach than his house. Liam nodded and said that, if you counted up how many times they had actually been to the beach in the last six months, he didn't mind.

Charlotte had listened to the conversation with incredulity, her head moving from one to the other and back again, as though she was watching the Wimbledon Final. The result of this game was absolutely critical.

She blamed her hangover on this conversation. One hundred percent. Whilst she had listened to her friend and her boyfriend discussing where he might live, at some indefinable point in the future, she downed a large glass of wine much too quickly. She couldn't decide whether she was happy to hear Liam talking about their future together, weighing up which house would be better for them, or whether she was annoyed that all he seemed to be focusing on were the practicalities. She would be happy to live in a tent in the middle of the sand dunes, if it meant that they were together, and what's more, she'd do it tomorrow. But Liam's analytical brain wasn't giving consideration to the fact that, for her, the move into whichever house they eventually chose would purely be based on an emotional decision.

By the time Linda and Liam had exhausted the conversation, Charlotte was too drunk to take an active part and the conversation quickly moved on to another subject.

But, now as they got out of the car in the car park at the top of the hill and began the walk to the beach, something was telling Charlotte that today wasn't the right time to talk about it. She had a lovely meal last night with him and Linda, and this morning had been good, despite her hangover, so she didn't want to hear Liam tell her that he wasn't ready to give her a full commitment. She was likely to get upset and it would ruin the rest of the day.

They walked hand in hand to the beach and headed directly to the shore, where they stood for a moment watching the waves crashing onto the sand. It was a gloriously vacant beach. Just the two of them.

"I love watching water, don't you?" said Charlotte. "I used to go for a walk on The Embankment at the weekends, when I lived in London. I'd get a coffee and walk for miles, listening to a book or just thinking. Just being next to water is so relaxing, isn't it?"

"Yes, and the Thames is amazing. Do you miss it?" asked Liam.

"London? Never. Not when I've got something as lovely as this on my doorstep. Yes, the Thames is beautiful, don't get me wrong, and I'll always have a soft spot for London, but I don't miss living there, no." It was on the tip of her tongue to ask him whether he had any regrets about not moving to Manchester, but she swallowed the words back down. Again, she didn't want him to say something that would upset her.

When they first met, Liam had told her that he didn't miss London at all, despite having grown up there. He said that he would much rather have a quiet life in the country. But she didn't believe him now. Even though he had changed his mind about moving to Manchester and he had tried to assure her that he was happy to stay in Warkworth, the city boy that lived deep down in his soul would resurface again, sooner or later. She was sure of that.

"Which way do you want to walk?" asked Liam. "Left or right?"

"Let's go left," said Charlotte. "We always seem to go towards Amble and I like the view towards Alnmouth." She turned away from him and began walking.

Her headache had almost gone, she had had a relaxing morning, being looked after by a man she loved and life couldn't get much better. She promised herself that from now on, she would live in the moment and stop worrying about the future of her relationship. They were solid. He loved her and she loved him and they would be fine. Just because he was younger than her and therefore not running towards a commitment as fast as she was, didn't mean that they wouldn't get there in the end. Did it?

"Where are you?" she said, a moment later when she realised that Liam was lagging behind. She turned around to see where he was.

Liam was ten steps behind her, down on one knee, holding out a small square ring box in his right hand. A huge grin was spreading across his face.

"Will you marry me?" he said.

Chapter Twenty-Three

Charlotte screamed and ran towards Liam, falling on her knees in front of him in the sand. She threw her arms around his neck, without looking at the ring box, and shouted in his ear, "Yes! Yes! Of course, I'll marry you!"

After a moment, they both stood up and he held the ring box out towards her again. "This is for you. I hope it fits," he said. He opened the black velvet box, where the most beautiful diamond solitaire ring set in white gold was waiting for her, cushioned in white satin.

"I can't believe you got me a ring. It's the most beautiful thing..." Suddenly overcome by emotion, she couldn't finish the sentence.

"I hope you're not going to cry, you big softie." Liam laughed. "Here, put it on before I change my mind."

"You can change your mind if you want," she laughed, quickly wiping the tears with her fingertips and holding out her left hand. "But you're never having this ring back." He took it out of the box and placed it on the ring finger of her left hand. It was a perfect fit.

"When did you get this?" she said.

"A couple of days ago," he said. "I took myself off to the shops. All by myself."

"You did a great job," she said. She threw her arms around his neck and kissed him again, not caring that the young couple who had just walked on the beach was watching. "So you do want to live with me, after all?"

"Yes, but not yet. In a year or so maybe," he said. "I'm kidding, I'm kidding," he shouted when she raised her hand to hit him over the head. "Of course, I want to live with you. I thought we'd have a conversation about where to live last night, but you got too pissed." He laughed.

"Yes, whatever. Sorry, I've stopped listening. I'm a bit distracted," she said. "I can't stop looking at my new ring." She held her hand up and turned her back to the sun, so that the sunlight hit the diamond, making it sparkle and dance. "I've got to ring Betsy," she said suddenly, patting the pockets in her jeans. "And my mum and dad. Where's my phone? Have I left it in the kitchen?"

"Possibly, I don't know," said Liam. "Shall we go back and then you can ring them?"

"Yes, please," she said, beginning to worry that her phone may have fallen out of her pocket. "I hope I haven't dropped it in the sand."

"I'm pretty sure that I saw it in the kitchen this morning," said Liam. He took hold of her hand as they began the walk back to the car.

"Are you happy?" asked Liam, a few minutes later, as he parked the car outside his house and turned off the engine.

"Yes, unbelievably happy," said Charlotte, tears beginning to prick the back of her eyes again. "I didn't see this coming at all. Not in a million years."

"Who do you want to tell first?"

"My mum and dad," she said. "If I ring Betsy first, I'll be on the phone for ages, so I'll ring her next. Oh my God, my mum's going to freak. She loves you so much."

"I know she does." Liam laughed. "Everyone does."

"Did you ask them if you could marry me?" said Charlotte, suddenly serious. She wasn't sure how she felt about the old tradition of asking permission for a daughter's hand in marriage, but she knew that her dad was old-fashioned and he would have wanted to be asked. It was just a courtesy.

"No," said Liam. "I didn't think you'd want me to. It's a bit old-school, isn't it?"

"Yes, I suppose so," said Charlotte, hoping that her dad would be understanding and wouldn't be too disappointed. She knew that he loved Liam as much as her mum did, so they would both be over the moon when they heard about their engagement. "Come on, let's go in, I want to find my phone. Shall we invite them over next weekend, if you've not got anything on at the hotel?"

"Sure," said Liam, getting out of the car. "And my parents too?"

"Yes, that would be nice, wouldn't it? Do they know anything about this?"

"No, I'll ring them after you've spoken to yours," said Liam. "My mum will want to speak to you, no doubt." He walked up the short path to the house, opened the door, and then stood to one side to allow Charlotte to go inside before him. She walked straight through the living room, towards the kitchen at the back of the house, excited to find her phone and start spreading the happy news. She would ring her parents, then her sister Betsy and then Hannah, and of course she needed to tell Linda. Or it might be better to go round to Linda's after she had spoken to Betsy and then call Hannah later. Now might not be a good time for Hannah; Ethan would probably be having lunch and she wanted her one hundred percent full attention.

Charlotte's thoughts were whizzing around her mind, fueled by adrenalin-filled joy.

"Surprise!!"

She jumped out of her skin when she opened the door to the kitchen. The room was full of people. Dozens of them, cheering and shouting. Someone let off some party poppers, making her jump again. Three large white helium balloons floated towards the ceiling, held down by gold ribbon. The words 'Congratulations on Your Engagement' moved backwards and forwards as the balloons drifted about in the breeze from the open back door. Bottles of Champagne and rose wine were lined up on the countertop, waiting to be shared, next to large silver platters of sandwiches, salads and miniature cakes.

"Mum! Dad! Oh my God," said Charlotte, as she burst into tears. "What? When did you all get here? Betsy! And Hannah. Oh my God." She couldn't take it all in. Her mum and Betsy rushed forwards, almost knocking her off her feet, as they hugged her and demanded to see the ring.

"How did you know about this? He's only just asked me. Liam, I can't believe that you planned all this without me knowing. How did you do it? I'm confused."

"Never mind all that, someone get me a drink," said Liam. He grabbed hold of Charlotte's left hand and held it high in the air. "She said yes."

Everyone cheered again, causing more tears, not only from Charlotte, but also from most of the other women in the room. Everyone she loved was in the same room and Charlotte couldn't be happier. Her mum and dad and sister Betsy; Linda; Hannah and Tom and baby Ethan; Liam's parents; his three brothers and their girlfriends and a group of their joint friends from in and around Warkworth were all there.

After passing Charlotte a glass of Champagne, which she was more than happy to accept, despite the waning hangover, Liam explained that he had spoken to her parents on the phone before he had bought the ring. He wanted to make sure that he had their blessing, even though he knew deep down that they would both give it readily and with pleasure. They had told him that they would be over the moon if he asked Charlotte to marry him. Then her mum and Betsy had very kindly helped him to organise the party and had arranged for everyone to arrive here today, while they were on their walk on the beach. Liam's family had all travelled up from London and stayed at the hotel last night and everyone else had stayed in Alnwick.

"I had to hide your phone this morning, before we went on our walk," he said. "Because I knew that you'd want to call everyone as soon as possible, before we got home, and that might spoil the surprise."

"You thought about everything, didn't you?" said Charlotte. "I can't believe that you arranged all this, and I had no clue what was going on." Liam kissed her on the cheek and took her hand as they made their way around the kitchen, greeting their guests.

"I told you that you had a good one," said Hannah, a few minutes later, after Liam had been dragged away by his friends. They had brought dozens of bottles of beer and pushed one into Liam's hand, which he took gratefully.

"I know," said Charlotte. "He's all right, isn't he?"

"And you know what the best thing is about this long-awaited engagement?" asked Hannah.

"That you no longer have to listen to me weeping and wailing about my love life down the phone?" said Charlotte.

"No," said Hannah. "You can weep and wail to me anytime. The best thing is that we now have a wedding to plan." Both of them shrieked and clinked their glasses of Champagne together.

"Betsy!" shouted Charlotte. She waved her arm to attract her sister's attention away from Liam's handsome single friend, Luke. "Come here a minute." When Hannah and Betsy were standing side by side, Charlotte topped up their glasses of Champagne. "Let's have a toast," she said. "To my two beautiful bridesmaids."

Hannah and Betsy both shrieked again and told her that they would love to be he
r bridesmaids and they couldn't wait to start planning the wedding.

***

The engagement party was a huge success. For Charlotte, the day passed much too quickly, in a blur of laughter, dancing, eating and drinking. She imagined that was how the wedding day would be, with her and Liam in the centre of all their friends and family, having the best day that they could possibly imagine. She was looking forward to it now more than ever and couldn't wait to start updating her Pinterest wedding board and researching possible wedding venues.

At the end of the party, when their friends had gone home and their families had returned to their hotel rooms, Charlotte and Liam stayed talking in the garden until the early hours of the morning. The rain clouds from the previous couple of days had been blown across to the North Sea, leaving a crisp clear dark sky, revealing thousands of stars, dotted about in the inky blackness as far as they could see. They lay on their backs, side by side on a woollen picnic rug in the centre of Liam's lawn, holding hands tightly and watching the sprinkling of stars. Charlotte had made sure that Liam was on her right-hand side, so that she could sneak surreptitious glances at her ring at regular intervals.

She had told him that she had always thought it was cheesy when grooms made the traditional wedding speech saying that they felt like they were the luckiest man in the world, but now she knew how they felt, because right now, she felt like the luckiest woman in the world. Liam whispered to her that he was the lucky one and squeezed her hand tightly.

"We've got so much to talk about," she said. "Like where we're going to live, when the wedding is going to be, where we're going to go on our honeymoon…"

He tried to silence her with a kiss, but she pushed him away. "And should I change my name? It says Charlotte Ashley on my Law Society Practising Certificate. I don't know whether to change it or not. I'd have to change the sign above the office if I did."

"I think you're getting a bit ahead of yourself now," said Liam. "And if you did change your name, we could stretch to the price of a new sign, couldn't we?" He laughed. "I'll buy you one as a wedding present."

"You will not!" said Charlotte. "If my wedding present doesn't come in a tiny little box, I don't want it."

"What if it has four wheels and a shiny new number plate?"

"In that case, I can make an exception. Seriously though, what about children? I know you want them, but how many? Just one? Or two? I don't think I want more than two. It is something that we need to agree on though."

"I think there's something that we need to agree on right now; we need to go to bed," said Liam. He jumped up and pulled Charlotte up by her hands and led her upstairs. "Can we talk tomorrow?"

She nodded, feeling suddenly tired.

After she had brushed her teeth and taken off her eye make-up, she climbed into bed next to her new fiancé.

"I've just thought of something," she said. "How did you know that I was going to say yes?"

But Liam was already asleep and as soon as Charlotte's head hit the pillow, she fell asleep too, with a peaceful smile on her face.

Chapter Twenty-Four

A few days after the engagement party, Linda and Storm boarded the eight-thirty train from Newcastle to Edinburgh and arrived at Waverly Station just after ten o'clock in the morning. After telling Linda all about the beautiful city and her university, Storm had suggested they had a day trip and she would show her the sights, which Linda was more than happy to do.

Yet again, yesterday, when Linda had told Charlotte about the trip, Charlotte had told her to be careful and to have 'her wits about her'. Linda assured her that she would. They had been sitting in the Bridge End Cafe sipping their coffees, and Linda, keeping a lid on her patience, had hoped that Charlotte would change the subject and would want to talk about wedding dresses, flowers, bridesmaids dresses, anything at all in fact, except for her day out with Storm. But she should have known better. Charlotte was a tenacious lawyer and she wanted to get all the facts in front of her before she was happy about the situation and therefore happy to let the subject drop.

"What I don't get," she had said, "Is why she wants to keep seeing you?"

"Other than the fact that she just enjoys my company, you mean?" said Linda, trying not to show how irritating she was finding the whole conversation.

"Oh you know what I mean," said Charlotte. "I know you're great company and you know that, and you're a great friend, but be honest, I don't think she's looking for another friend. She'll have tonnes of friends already. Everybody has tonnes of friends at that age, so that's not the reason, is it?"

"No, and I'm not treating her like a friend," said Linda. "Look, she was obviously still grieving for her mum when she went searching for her dad and I think it was a massive shock to her, to discover that he died before she could meet him. So I'm the one link between her and her dad and she clearly finds it comforting to be around me. That's what I think anyway." Linda shrugged. "It's tough being an orphan at my age, so I can only imagine that's it ten times worse when you're young."

"So she sees you as a parental figure," said Charlotte. It wasn't a question, more of a confirmation to Charlotte that she had finally got to the bottom of their unusual relationship. "I can see that." She could also see that whenever Linda spoke about Storm, her face lit up and she was visibly excited about their spontaneous trip to Scotland. Despite the fact that Linda had never had children, she was overflowing with maternal qualities. She was compassionate, loving, caring and tender-hearted and if this young woman needed some maternal love, then Linda was certainly the person to give it to her. When Charlotte had reached this conclusion and she was happy that her friend was safe, only then did she begin talking about the wedding.

As their train finally arrived at Waverly station and the passengers piled out onto the platform, Linda stopped to take a photograph of the beautiful nineteenth-century architecture. She held her phone high, to capture as much of the stunning glass ceiling as she could, oblivious to the impatient crowd of people behind her.

"Shall we do a selfie?" said Storm.

"I'm not sure that I know how to do one," said Linda. "Don't laugh, I haven't had this phone very long."

"I'm not laughing," said Storm. "Well, maybe a little snigger, that's all. My mum was hopeless with her phone too. Here, give it to me." She took Linda's phone from her hand and showed her how to turn the camera around, so that she could be in the photograph. Then she put her arm around Linda's shoulders and smiled at the camera while she took the shot "That's cute," she said, when they looked at the resulting photograph.

Linda's heart beat quickly in her chest when she examined Storm's captured expression and her wide smile on her phone. It was just like looking at Phil when he was that age. There was no doubt that she was her father's daughter. She had loved him then when he was young and handsome and not as angry as the man he later became.

As she sent the photograph to Charlotte, telling her that they had arrived safely, she remembered their conversation from the day before. She knew that Charlotte didn't understand Storm's need to spend time with Linda, or in fact Linda's need to spend time with Storm. But that didn't matter. As long as they were both having a good time, that was all that mattered. Like she had explained to Jessica when she had asked why she thought Storm wanted to see her again, if she could help her to come to terms with the loss of her parents at such a young age, then she was happy to do so. She tried not to overthink the situation. She was relying on her instincts to guide her and, right now, her instincts were telling her that spending time with Storm was doing them both good.

She was trying to forget about the missing money from Phil's wallet and when she did think about it, she dismissed any reservations that might be lurking in the back of her mind about Storm. She told herself that Storm wouldn't possibly have taken the money. Even though she had the opportunity while Linda had been in the garden, it would have been an extremely risky thing for her to do. Linda could have turned around and caught her in the act at any moment. She had decided that, no, Storm had nothing to do with it. When she got time, she would ring Dorothy and speak to her about it and ask her how sure she was about how much money was in the wallet. But it certainly wasn't a priority.

Today, all she wanted to do was to enjoy her day out. She had never been to Edinburgh before. In fact, she had never been to Scotland, so Storm was in charge of suggesting tourist activities for them.

After brunch and coffee in The Ivy (which Charlotte had suggested and Linda had paid for), they walked up Princes Street to the Castle, where they spent a leisurely couple of hours wandering around the medieval walls and learning about the castle's ancient history. They giggled at the royal bed chamber, where monarchs wouldn't have been left alone for a second, not even during their most intimate moments with their wives and husbands, and winced at the royal birthing room, where Mary Queen of Scots had given birth to the future King James VI, without any pain relief. In the Great Hall, where hundreds, if not thousands of banquets would have been held over the years, they read about what type of food might have been served at the ancient meals, but they soon grew bored of their written guides and, inevitably, their conversation was pulled back to Charlotte's wedding and what might be served at the wedding breakfast.

As they continued their stroll around the castle, Linda told Storm that when she had spoken to Charlotte yesterday, she persistently referred to it as 'my wedding' or 'the wedding' and Linda never considered correcting her and suggesting that she used the plural pronoun. It was almost as though a groom was superfluous. She remembered being the same when she had been planning her wedding, all those years ago. Storm asked her what her wedding to Phil had been like. She was genuinely interested in hearing what everyone wore and what colour flowers she had and what food they had eaten and what their first dance song was. Linda could remember the day as if it were yesterday.

"Was it the happiest day of your life?" asked Storm. "Everyone says it is, don't they?"

"Yes, absolutely," said Linda. "I loved every minute of it. I loved your dad so much in those days. He looked so handsome when I saw him waiting for me at the top of the aisle. Luckily, he wasn't interested in planning the wedding with me, so me and my mum made all the decisions, as is the case with most brides up and down the country, I'd imagine." She laughed, trying her best to portray a memory of an easy-going groom, who was happy to go along with anything that his blessed bride suggested. The truth of it was, of course, that Phil couldn't have given a toss about the minutiae of the wedding. He wanted to be told what to wear, what colour flower to have in his buttonhole and where he should be, and at what time. He had been happy for everything to be decided by Linda, not because he loved her and because he wanted her to have the wedding of her dreams. But because he was lazy.

"I thought about getting married in Edinburgh," said Storm, as they exited the castle and began their walk down the Royal Mile towards Holyrood House. "It would be such a lovely backdrop for the photographs, wouldn't it?"

"Yes, it's beautiful," said Linda. "I've never been anywhere like it. So, is there a particular Scottish man that you've got your eyes on?"

"Maybe," said Storm. "There is someone on my course that I like and we've been having flirty banter all summer over WhatsApp, but he hasn't asked to see me outside of the art room."

"He might just be a slow burner," said Linda.

"We'll see what happens next term. If he doesn't ask me out within a couple of weeks, he'll miss out. But whether I choose a man from Scotland or not, I'd like a winter wedding. Wouldn't it be lovely? The photographs would be amazing, me and him in the snow, with flakes falling around us, like confetti from Mother Nature."

"Yes, that would make a lovely picture," said Linda. "In theory. But you know how the country can grind to a halt at the slightest bit of snow. It would be awful if half of your guests couldn't make it."

"Yes, that's true," said Storm. "Okay, maybe I'll have to think again. I don't think I want to get married abroad though. The photos that you see of couples on the beach look lovely, but I saw a beach wedding once and the reality isn't what you see on Instagram."

"What do you mean?" said Linda, thinking that getting married on the beach would be a dream come true for most people.

"Well, it's a massive spectacle, isn't it? Everyone on the beach gathers around, so it isn't the intimate romantic affair that you might think it'd be, with the wedding party being surrounded by strangers in bikinis and random kids eating ice cream."

Linda's phone rang, interrupting their conversation. "It's Liam," she said, answering the call and putting him on loudspeaker. "Hi Liam, is everything okay?"

"Yes, good," he said. "I'm just phoning to let you know that I've been in to feed the cat. It's beginning to rain here, so do you want to keep the kitchen window closed, to keep her inside?"

"It doesn't really matter," said Linda. "She isn't a fan of the rain anyway, so she won't go out if it's too wet."

"Okay then," said Liam. "Well, I'll leave it closed then. It's safer while you're out, not that there's much crime around here, but you never know. I think your neighbour had the same idea as me."

"What do you mean?"

"Jessica from next door, she was walking down the side of your house, just as I got here. I think I gave her the shock of her life," Liam laughed. "She nearly wet herself when she saw me. I've never seen anyone look so pale."

"What was she doing?" asked Linda.

"She said she was checking on the house for you, because your kitchen window was open."

"That's kind," said Linda.

"Are you having a good time?" asked Liam.

"We're having the best time," said Linda. "Storm's the best tour guide ever. She knows Edinburgh like the back of her hand. We've been in the castle and we're just having a walk up the Royal Mile."

"Lovely," said Liam. "Well, I won't keep you, I just thought you might be worried about Nutmeg, but she's perfectly fine, which is more than can be said about your sofa," he said, laughing again. "She's covered it in cat hair. She's obviously been sleeping on one of your cushions and on the back too, haven't you? And now my jumper's full of cat hair too."

"You're cuddling her, aren't you?" said Linda, laughing. "I knew you were a cat person."

"No, not at all. What makes you think that?" said Liam, making the sound of loud kisses down the phone, pretending to be kissing the cat. Storm giggled.

"Hang on a minute, how did she get on the sofa? I thought I'd locked her in the kitchen," said Linda.

"Well you didn't," said Liam. "She was in the living room, stretched out on the sofa."

"But I'm sure I closed all the doors this morning," said Linda. "She's been moulting for weeks, so I don't allow her to have the run of the house while I'm out."

"It's not too bad," said Liam. "I'll give it a quick hoover for you while I'm here and then close her in the kitchen before I go."

"Thank you, but you really don't need to. I'm not so worried about the cat hairs, it's just that I could have sworn that I left all the doors closed. Nutmeg was in the kitchen when I left."

"Well, it was definitely open when I got here. Your bedroom door's open too."

"My bedroom door? Are you sure?"

"Yes, I'm right here, looking at it," said Liam.

Linda knew that she had closed all the doors. The cat would have been perfectly fine in the kitchen, but she had left the window open over the sink, so that she could go outside to the garden, if she wanted to. Something wasn't right about this situation. She looked at Storm, who was frowning at her. "I remember you telling me that you had locked the cat in the kitchen," she said. "Do you remember, on the train? You told me that you'd asked Liam to go in and check on her before he went to work."

"Yes, I do remember," said Linda. "Liam, could you do me a favour and check something for me?"

"Yes, of course," he said.

"There's a wall cupboard above the kettle, can you have a look in there?"

"Yes, got it."

"There's a large brown envelope at the back of the cupboard; it's got Phil's wallet in there. Please can you check how much money is in the wallet?"

"Yes, okay," said Liam. "Give me a minute while I put the cat down." Linda knew exactly how much was in the wallet now. When she had first counted the money, there was one hundred and sixty pounds in there. She had taken fifty pounds for her shopping and ten pounds this morning, so there should be one hundred pounds left. "I've found the wallet," said Liam after a few moments, "But there's no cash."

"No cash? Are you sure?" said Linda.

"Yes, of course. It's empty," said Liam.

"It's her!" said Linda. "I should have known it was her."

"Who?" asked Storm and Liam simultaneously.

"Jessica from next door. She's taken the money, I'm sure of it," said Linda. "She's small enough to crawl through the kitchen window, isn't she? I don't believe that she was checking on my house for me. She was breaking in."

Chapter Twenty-Five

Just as they were passing The Royal Mile Tavern, Linda decided that she was desperate for a glass of wine, which coincided well with the sudden inclement weather. As the heavens opened and the streets of Edinburgh got soaked, Linda and Storm managed to grab the last two bar stools in the busy tavern, where they sat down and waited to be served.

"I should have known it was her," said Linda. "There was something about her that I just didn't like." Despite what Charlotte may think, Linda knew a liar when she met one and Jessica was one, she was absolutely sure of it. When Jessica had spoken about her husband, Linda had the feeling that she wasn't telling the complete truth, but she had put it down to the fact that she had been elaborating slightly, for the sake of the story. She told herself that some people did that and it didn't mean anything. She was just a Drama Queen.

"Shall we have a whisky?" asked Storm. "Then you can tell me all about your horrible neighbour."

"I don't think I like whisky," said Linda.

"There's nobody on earth who doesn't like Scottish whisky," said the barman. He rested his forearms on the bar and winked at Storm, who winked back at him. "If you've had a whisky that you didn't like, then it wouldn't have been a Scottish one, I can assure you of that."

"I don't know where it was originally from," said Linda. "I used to buy it sometimes from the supermarket. It was probably their own brand, I don't know."

"Oh, good gracious," said the barman. "Promise me that you'll never touch that stuff ever again, as long as you live. Promise me!"

Linda raised her hand, as though swearing allegiance to the Crown and promised that she would never drink supermarket whisky again. The barman pointed out the shelves behind him, packed with a range of dozens and dozens of local whiskys and then suggested one that they might want to try 'to start them off'. A minute later, he pushed two small glasses of deep amber liquid towards them. "Try that, ladies, and let me know what you think. I haven't given you any ice because, in my view, it impairs the flavour. If you don't like it, I'll take it away and not charge you a penny."

Storm had had whisky before in the Edinburgh bars, plenty of times on nights out with her student friends, and she knew that she loved it. She waited for Linda to take a sip of hers, watching her face intently.

"Well, what do you think?" asked Storm.

"It's actually nice," said Linda. "I'm pleasantly surprised. I could get used to that." She thanked the barman and he promised to top up their glasses whenever they gave him a wave.

"So what are you going to do about Jessica?" asked Storm.

"I'm not sure," said Linda. "I don't suppose I've got any proof that she's done anything wrong. I know there's money missing from the wallet and I know that Liam saw her on my garden path, but I don't think that's enough. Isn't that what they call circumstantial evidence?" Storm shrugged and said that she wasn't sure. "If she needs money that desperately, then she and her dirty conscience can keep it. But I won't be in such a hurry to let her into my house again."

"And make sure you lock all your windows and doors when you go out in future," said Storm.

As they sat at the bar, sipping their whisky and watching customers coming and going, some escaping from the rain into the shelter of the bar, and others leaving, determined not to allow the rain to dampen their enjoyment of the city, Linda told Storm about the envelope that Dorothy had given to her, and which she had left on the kitchen table when Jessica had been in the house. "Dorothy told me that your dad's wallet was in the envelope and that there was two hundred and thirty pounds in it. I didn't check, but the next time I went shopping, I thought I'd take some cash, so I got the envelope out of the cupboard and found there was only one hundred and sixty pounds there."

"So you think she might have taken that too?" asked Storm.

"I didn't think that initially," said Linda. "I thought Dorothy might have been mistaken, but I am absolutely certain that there was cash in the wallet this morning, and now it's all gone. It seems a coincidence, doesn't it?"

"Yes, it does. And you're one hundred percent sure there was money there this morning?" asked Storm.

"Yes, I took a ten-pound note from the wallet, in case we got a taxi and I needed to give the driver a tip," said Linda. "Then I put it back, with the rest of the money inside it, into the kitchen cupboard above the kettle. And Liam said that she looked shocked when he saw her, didn't he? I know we can't prove it, but I'm sure she climbed in through the window and took the money."

"So, let's say that there was two hundred and thirty pound in there when you first got the envelope," said Storm. "When do you think she took it?"

"It was a few weeks ago," said Linda, not wanting to say that it was the same day that Storm had visited her for lunch. She knew that Storm would be devastated if she realised that she, too, had been under suspicion, although Linda had always hoped that she was wrong. "She came over for a drink. I think she wanted to vent to someone about her husband. The envelope was on the table. We sat outside for most of the time, but then I went to the toilet and I suppose she could have taken it then."

"She'd have to be quick," said Storm.

"Yes, I suppose she would, but she'd hear the toilet flushing, wouldn't she? That would give her a few seconds before I came out of the bathroom." Linda took a mouthful of whisky. "You know, this gets better with every sip."

"Yes, that's the problem," said Storm. She drained her glass and asked the barman for two more.

"There's something else," said Linda.

"What's that?"

"I've lost a gold necklace and bracelet that Charlotte and Liam bought me. But when I say lost, I mean I think it's been taken."

"Really? Are you sure?"

"Well, I'm not a hundred percent sure about this. But I've never really had any jewellery before, and obviously Charlotte and Liam are my best friends, so I looked after them and made sure that I put them away in their boxes every time I wore them."

"Where did you keep them?" asked Storm.

"They were in the top drawer in the chest in my bedroom. They were hidden underneath some underwear, but now the boxes are gone. I've searched the house and can't find them anywhere."

"Oh Linda," said Storm.

"I know. It's odd, isn't it?" said Linda.

Storm was about to say that the top drawer of a chest is where most people keep valuables and that would be the first place where a burglar would look, but Linda looked so distraught that she kept her thoughts to herself.

Linda's phone rang just as the barman placed their second glass of whisky onto the bar. It was Charlotte.

"Hi Charlotte," she said.

"Hi. I've just spoken to Liam and he told me that some money has gone from Phil's wallet, from your house, is that right?"

"Yes, and did he tell you that he saw Jessica in the garden?"

"Yes, he did," said Charlotte. "Do you think she's taken it?"

"I'm sure she has. Nobody else has been in the house since I last saw it there this morning," said Linda, hoping to emphasise the point to Charlotte that it couldn't possibly have been Storm, because she was here with her in Edinburgh.

"Yes, I know what you mean," said Charlotte, clearly understanding what her friend was telling her. "Do you want me to quiz her about it?"

"I don't see the point really. You know more about the criminal fraternity than me, but she'll only deny it, won't she? We can't prove anything. But you know what, the next time she has an appointment with you, she better not ask me to wait in for a parcel for her. I don't want anything to do with her from now on."

"When did she ask you to wait in for a parcel?" asked Charlotte.

"A couple of weeks ago when she had an appointment to see you. The delivery slot for the parcel clashed with her appointment, so she asked me to wait at her house for it," said Linda.

"But I haven't seen her for ages. I've sent her a few emails and I called her once last week, but I haven't seen her in person lately."

"Are you sure?" asked Linda.

"Yes, of course, I'm sure."

"Why would she say that, if it wasn't true?"

"Because she's a liar," said Charlotte.

"Well, yes, but why did she say she was going to see you? She could have just said that she needed to get some shopping, or something like that."

"I suppose it was so you felt like you couldn't say no. Having an appointment with me was something that you'd help her out with. Getting shopping is something that can be postponed."

"What a bloody idiot I've been," said Linda.

"Don't be so harsh on yourself. You were just doing a favour for a neighbour; anyone would have done the same," said Charlotte.

"But you don't understand," said Linda. "That's the day that my jewellery went missing." She explained to

Charlotte that she had wanted to wear her necklace and bracelet when she had gone out for dinner with her and Liam to the seafood restaurant, but she couldn't find them. After she had got back from the hairdresser's, the day that she went into the bank in Alnwick and had bumped into Storm, she was planning what she would wear for their night out the following day. She had chosen a dress and her shoes and she had hung the dress on the outside of the wardrobe door and it was when she opened her drawer to get out the jewellery, that she realised the boxes were missing.

She told Charlotte that she hadn't wanted to tell her before now, in case she thought she had been reckless and had lost them, but she was always careful with them and she knew that she had put them back safely in the drawer and she was pretty sure that she had seen them the day before.

Now all the pieces were beginning to fall into place. She was sure that Jessica had asked her to stay in her house to wait for the parcel to be delivered while she climbed in through Linda's kitchen window to search the house for what she could find. She knew that, more often than not, the kitchen window was left open for Nutmeg to be able to climb in and out. She had even asked Linda to text her when her parcel arrived, which would have given her time to get out of the house safely before Linda went back home, although she would probably have heard the courier arrive, so there was very little chance of her being caught. She had planned the whole thing.

"What a scheming bitch," said Charlotte. "Was anything else missing?"

"Not that day, no, but on another day, I'm pretty sure that a twenty-pound note disappeared from my purse. It was the first day that I went to meet Storm." As she said her name,

Linda reached over to Storm and patted her knee. "When I came back, Jessica was in the front garden, so I invited her in for a drink, and then you rang me. You were in Manchester for the weekend, do you remember?"

"Yes," said Charlotte.

"Well, my phone was in the hall, so I asked Jessica to put the kettle on while I spoke to you, but after the call, she said she didn't want another drink and she seemed in a sudden hurry to go home. I thought it was strange at the time."

"So your purse was in the kitchen?" asked Charlotte.

"Yes, it was in the cupboard over the kettle, where I keep the jar of coffee, where Phil's wallet is now. She would have seen it when she went to get the coffee."

"What was it doing there?"

"I always leave it there," said Linda. "If anyone breaks in and takes my bag, then they won't get my purse as well."

"Well, that's good crime prevention," said Charlotte. "Except on this occasion. Right, well, I'll leave you to enjoy your day out with Storm and we're going to sort this out, don't worry, and I'm sorry for giving you a lecture yesterday, you know, about the thing."

"Don't worry about it," said Linda. She knew that Charlotte had been careful not to say Storm's name in case she overheard anything. "I know you're always looking out for me and I love you for it."

"Are you okay?" asked Storm, as soon as Linda put her phone back in her pocket. She jumped off her bar stool and pulled Linda into a tight hug.

"I'm absolutely fine," said Linda. "I'm in Edinburgh with my new stepdaughter and I'm enjoying my first taste of a proper whisky, so there's nothing to worry about. I'm not going to let anything spoil our day."

"Well said, step-mum," said Storm, sitting back down on her stool. Linda hadn't consciously used the term stepdaughter; it had just come out. But for Storm to reinforce the fact that they were now family, by calling her step-mum, brought tears to her eyes. Storm laughed when she saw Linda becoming emotional and jumped down from her stool for a second time and hugged her again. "I'm so glad I found you," she said. "I think I'd much rather have you in my life than my dad. It's funny how fate works, isn't it?"

"Do you ladies want another?" said the barman. Then, "Oh, good grief, have I interrupted a moment here?"

Linda laughed and told him that she was crying happy tears. She told him that the beautiful young lady by her side was her long-lost stepdaughter and they had only just found each other. The barman smiled at them both and said that that was definitely a cause for celebration, but she turned down his offer of a refill, saying that three whiskys and a head full of emotion might not be a good mix.

She paid the bill and they carried on their walk up the Royal Mile, stopping at every shop. At some, they simply peered in at the window, admiring the kilts and Scottish souvenirs, and at others, they went inside. By the time they reached Holyrood House, they were weighed down with shopping bags filled with tartan scarves, sheepskin slippers, cashmere shawls and sugar-laden tablet, which Linda learned was the Scottish equivalent of fudge.

By the time they reached the end of the street, Linda had reached her decision. She had decided that she would give Storm the money that she had inherited from Phil. It was only fair that she shared it with her and she didn't care what

Charlotte said about it. Storm was entitled to her father's money, particularly the part that had been left to Phil from his father, even though she had never met either of the men. The Royal Mile Tavern hadn't seemed the appropriate place to impart such personal news, so Linda hadn't said anything, but as soon as she had the opportunity, she would be more than happy to take Storm's financial pressures off her young shoulders.

Throughout the day, every time Storm offered to pay for something, Linda insisted that the day out was her treat. But she knew that financial independence was important and that Storm would love to have enough money to at least buy Linda coffee and cake somewhere. So as soon as they found a cafe and sat down, she was going to tell her the good news.

Chapter Twenty-Six

Linda and Storm found a cafe on Abbeymount, at the end of The Royal Mile, close to Holyrood Palace, which had a free table in the window. Storm asked Linda to sit down and look after all the bags while she ordered the drinks.

"It's my turn," she said. "Please don't argue. I want to buy it this time." Linda hadn't argued with her, knowing that within minutes, Storm would have more than enough money in her bank account. "Would you like something to eat?"

"A sandwich would be lovely," said Linda. "I feel like I need something to eat to soak up the whisky. It's gone straight to my head."

"Lightweight," laughed Storm. "If you're going to be a regular visitor to Scotland, you'll have to get used to it. It's rude not to drink it."

Linda smiled to herself, as she watched Storm walk towards the counter to order their sandwiches and drinks. She would love to visit Scotland again and she would love to see Storm's university and some of her artwork. Storm had shown her pictures on her phone of some of the paintings she had done and they looked magnificent, but she would love to see them in real life, preferably hung on a wall and lit with one of those tiny overhead lights that you see above paintings in galleries. Storm told her that the paintings were a hundred times better in reality, although when Linda suggested that they were good enough to be sold in galleries, she said that she wasn't quite there yet.

Earlier, as they had strolled around the shops, and Storm pointed out various bars and cafes that she visited with her student friends, she told Linda that she would be very welcome to visit anytime. Linda said that she would definitely visit when she got back from her cruise at the end of November. Storm said that the Christmas markets would be on then and Edinburgh would be at its glittery best.

"If we're lucky, it will snow," she had said. Her eyes lit up, like a child's on Christmas morning who had just been told that Father Christmas had been.

Linda told her that she wasn't a fan of snow. She was frightened of the temperature dropping suddenly and then it would ice over and she would inevitably fall and make a right fool of herself. But Storm had laughed and told her that there were so many people about, that the snow didn't have a chance of sticking to the ground in the busy areas around the market and she would be fine.

"Last year, it snowed nonstop for three whole days," she said. "It was beautiful. We went sledging in the park near the university and made snowmen and then we came into town and got drunk on mulled wine at the market stalls."

Linda said that she would definitely visit and would look forward to it, snow or no snow.

As Storm waited to be served, a middle-aged woman and what looked like her adult daughter came into the cafe and sat down at the table behind theirs. The woman took off her coat, hung it onto the back of one of the chairs, and then joined the queue while her daughter saved their seats. The woman hadn't needed to ask her daughter what she wanted. She probably had the same thing every time they went out. Linda smiled to herself and hoped that one day, she would be in the same position with Storm. She was looking forward to the day when she knew her so well that she wouldn't need to ask her what she wanted when they went into a cafe. She would know whether she would choose a brownie or an almond slice, a cappuccino or a hot chocolate and whether she liked full-fat milk or oat milk.

She was looking forward to the future. A future in which she was a stepmother. She had long ago come to terms with the fact that she would never be a real mother - a biological mother - but she knew that there were millions of women like her and just because she didn't have a child of her own, didn't mean that she couldn't love Storm like she would have loved her own daughter.

Storm might grow to love her too. She would never be a replacement for her mother, but as long as they both enjoyed each other's company, that was all that mattered.

Storm returned to the table with a tray laden with food and drinks. "I'm hopeless at decision-making," she said. "So I got a little bit of everything so that we can share." She had bought a chicken salad sandwich on nutty granary bread; a smoked salmon and cream cheese wrap; a packet of cheese and onion crisps, and two hazelnut brownies. She put the food in the middle of the table, together with two small plates and two knives and forks. "They said they'll bring the cappuccinos over when they're ready. I got two brownies, because if you said you wanted to share mine, I think I'd cry. I've got to have my own, I'm sorry."

Linda laughed. She was learning about her already. Every time they had had a coffee, Storm had had a cappuccino, and she clearly loved brownies. "Thank you. I can't believe that we're eating again, after that huge brunch, but I've worked up an appetite with all the walking and sight-seeing."

Linda waited until their coffees had been delivered and they had divided the sandwich and the wrap before she began to speak. She wanted to make sure that they didn't have any interruptions. "You know that I told you that Dorothy had given me your dad's wallet with some money in it?" Storm nodded, her mouth full of food. "Well, there was a little bit of money in his bank account too, and I think it's only fair that I share it with you, so would you give me your bank details please and I can send it over to you?"

"Oh no, you don't have to do that," said Storm, with a dismissive wave of her hand. "He was your husband, so surely any money that he left is your money. You did share money, didn't you?"

"Yes we did, but because we'd been separated for a number of months, I don't really see it as mine. I want you to have it. It isn't much, but I'd really like to send it to you."

"Are you sure?"

"Yes, absolutely," said Linda.

"Okay," said Storm. "Thank you."

Storm put down her sandwich and tapped on the banking app on her phone. She then read out the account number and sort code of the account that she would like the money to be transferred to. Linda tapped away on her banking app for a moment and then asked Storm to check her balance, just to check that the money had gone into the right account. Storm opened the app again, while Linda watched her face carefully for any reaction. At first, she didn't say anything. She merely frowned and closed the app and then re-opened it. "I think there's been an error," she said. "That's not the right balance." She studied her phone carefully. The smile on Linda's face was adding to her confusion.

"Everything alright?" asked Linda. "Has the money gone in?"

"I don't understand," said Storm. "It says you've just transferred fifty thousand pounds. I'll send it straight back to you, don't worry. You've obviously hit the zero button too many times." Storm laughed, assuming that Linda had made a genuine error.

"No, no," said Linda, "There's no mistake. I meant to send you fifty thousand." She reached across the table and took Storm's hand in both of hers. "I want you to have your dad's money. It's rightfully yours. He left it to me because, well I don't know why, if I'm honest. Maybe he didn't know how to contact you, but I don't need it, so I want you to have it. You're his daughter and if he didn't provide for you during his lifetime, then he can bloody well provide for you after his death."

"But fifty thousand pounds?" said Storm. Her eyes filled with tears, which spilled onto her pretty cheeks.

Linda let go of her hand and passed her a napkin. "Yes, like I said, it's yours. Phil should have left it to you in the first place."

"Thank you so much," said Storm. "I'm in shock, I think. I can't tell you what a difference that amount of money will make."

"I hope that it will help you while you finish your degree," said Linda.

"Yes, it will. Oh my God, I can't believe it. I can pay off my student debt and pay for all of next year's course fees and all my rent upfront. Thank you." She stood up and the two women hugged while Storm cried again.

"I know it's a shock," said Linda, when they separated and sat back down. "It was a shock to me when I found out that he had named me in his will. But I want you to know that, although I'm grateful that he did that, after all, we were married for a very long time, I really don't need the money. My house is paid for, I've got a good inheritance from my dad and I'll also get some of your dad's pension as well as my own, so don't worry about taking it, okay?"

"Yes, okay, thank you," said Storm. "Thank you so much."

Linda nodded and paused while she took a sip of her coffee. "Good, because there's more."

"What do you mean?" said Storm.

"I can only transfer fifty thousand pounds a day, so that's your first instalment. I'll transfer another fifty thousand a day for the next four days, so you'll have two hundred and fifty thousand in total."

"No!" shrieked Storm, bursting into tears again. She covered her face with her hands and Linda allowed her to sob for a few minutes, while she stroked her back.

"Are those happy tears?" she asked when Storm began to calm down and finally looked up.

"Yes and no," she said. "I'm so incredibly happy and really really grateful, but it's so sad that my mum's not here to enjoy the money with me. She was always skint and she didn't get to travel as much as she wanted to, so I would have loved to have taken her away on a holiday."

"Where would she have gone?" asked Linda.

"Somewhere with gorgeous scenery," said Storm. "She went to Lake Garda in Italy once, when she was young, and said that it was the most beautiful place she'd ever seen, so I'd probably have taken her back there. She always said she wanted to have a go at painting landscapes, so wherever we went, I know that she would have found the beauty in it."

"And where would you like to go?" asked Linda.

"Well Lake Garda sounds amazing, with its beautiful lake and mountains, so I'd love to go there, and Austria or Sweden, somewhere like that. Somewhere with snow."

"Well, you'll have to make sure that you go to those places," said Linda. "When you get to my age, I want you to be able to look back on your memories of all the beautiful places that you've been to. Spend the money on travel."

"I will," said Storm. "Think of all the painting I can do while I'm there."

"I need a painting for my living room," said Linda. "So the sooner you go, the better."

Storm's eyes filled with tears again. "This is life-changing," she said. "I can't believe that you've been so kind. You hardly know me."

"That doesn't matter at all," said Linda. "I don't need to know you that well to know that you are the right recipient of this money. Your dad didn't give your mum a penny for you throughout your life, did he?"

"Not that I know of, no."

"So, now it's payment time. Listen, if your mum had some financial help with raising you, she might have been able to get a mortgage a buy a little house, and then when she died, you would have inherited that. It's not her fault that she could only afford to rent somewhere. Raising kids is expensive. However you look at it, the money is yours."

"Thank you," said Storm, wiping her eyes.

"You're welcome. Okay, now no more tears," said Linda.

When they had finished their sandwich and wrap, Linda checked the time on her watch. "Shall we go into Holyrood Palace, or do you want to hit the shops, now that your bank balance is a bit healthier?"

"We can always do Holyrood next time, can't we?" said Storm. "Shopping sounds good. There's a couple of things I need."

"Do you need paint and brushes and stuff like that?" asked Linda. "Or does the university provide them?"

"No, you need to use your own. I could probably do with a couple of new ones, but I also need some decent walking boots and some thick socks. I like to go hiking with my friends and my old boots have seen better days."

"I'll let you lead the way then," said Linda. "I'm completely lost." They wrapped up their brownies to eat later and set off back towards Princes Street.

Chapter Twenty-Seven

"I can't believe that you didn't question Jessica when you saw her coming out of Linda's house," said Charlotte. She was in The Masons Arms with Liam later that day, at their favourite table in the corner, waiting for their burgers and chips to be brought to them.

"I didn't see her coming out of Linda's house," said Liam. "I would have grabbed her if I did and asked her what she was doing. She was on the garden path."

"Yes, but she'd come from the back of the house, having just broken in." Charlotte had been thinking of the series of events all day and she was confident that she would have dealt with it differently. She knew that evidence was key and finding money on Jessica would make it easier to prove that she had committed some kind of crime. Being caught in the act was always preferable.

"Yes, but I didn't know that at the time, did I? I don't know any female burglars, so I assumed that what she told me about closing Linda's window was true. She was being a good neighbour, that's what I thought."

"Closing the window or checking the window?" asked Charlotte. She leaned across the table and gave him an intimidating stare.

"What?"

"Was the window open when you saw it, or had she closed it?" she said slowly.

Liam thought for a moment, while he took a mouthful of his beer. "I can't remember."

Charlotte laughed and sat back. "You're a rubbish witness. The defendant would get off with it. She would walk off, scot-free, thanks to your unreliable testimony."

Liam laughed. "Bloody hell, I'd hate to be in a witness box when you were cross-examining. I'd feel as though I was guilty of something and I'd end up confessing to a crime that I hadn't committed."

The waiter arrived at their table with their food and Charlotte asked him to bring them another glass of wine for her and another beer for Liam.

"So, what do you think we should do?" asked Charlotte. "I want to go round and interrogate her and then search the house, but she's a Warkworth House Hotel tenant, so I probably shouldn't do that."

Liam nodded. "I know what you mean. But I think we should do it anyway."

"But what if she makes a complaint? You can't just barge into someone's house when you're the landlord, can you?" said Charlotte.

"No, but who is she going to complain to? My uncle? First of all, she doesn't know that he exists and secondly, he wouldn't care. If she decided to leave, there would be plenty of other tenants waiting to move into that house, so it won't be empty for two minutes."

"Yes, I suppose you're right," said Charlotte.

"I manage all the properties that the hotel owns anyway. My uncle hasn't got a clue who the tenants are and he's quite happy to keep it that way." Liam took a bite of his burger.

"That burger's amazing. Spot on, as usual," he said, turning to the bar staff and giving them a thumbs-up sign. One of the young men behind the bar gave him a thumbs-up sign back, while the other one carried their drinks to their table.

"Thank you," said Charlotte, as he put the drinks on the table. "So, shall we go round to see her, do you think?" she whispered, when the barman had walked away, as though anyone within earshot would have an inkling of who they were talking about.

"Absolutely," said Liam. "Although I don't know what to say when we get there, so you might have to do the talking. I'd be more likely to push her out of the way and rush around emptying drawers and snatching the money and jewellery back."

"Yes, you can't do that," said Charlotte. "That's what criminals do. It's called burglary and you could end up doing some time at His Majesty's pleasure for that kind of thing."

"Which is exactly why I need to be led by the best lawyer in Warkworth," said Liam. He held up his beer glass and Charlotte clinked her wine glass against it.

"That's me," said Charlotte. "Bloody hell, it's her."

"What?"

"Don't look! Jessica has just walked in. She's standing at the bar with a man."

"Her husband?" asked Liam.

"I don't know, I've never met him. She hasn't told me that they're back together, but anything she does wouldn't surprise me. Look at her, standing at the bar, sweet and fucking innocent. No, don't look!"

"You just said look at her," said Liam.

"I didn't mean it literally." Charlotte scowled. "When I said look at her, I didn't mean look at her. She's probably wearing Linda's necklace and bracelet right now." She glared at Jessica and then suddenly flashed a smile and waved. "She saw me," she whispered.

"I'm not surprised," said Liam. "She could probably feel the heat from your animosity bearing into her soul."

"She'd feel the heat from the back of my hand if I had a choice."

Liam burst out laughing. "I love it when you're feisty. I bet you didn't put up with any shit from bullies at school did you?"

"Of course not," she said, laughing. "Don't you know me by now?"

To a bystander like Jessica and her male companion, Liam and Charlotte were eating their meal and chatting and laughing about something light-hearted and comical. Charlotte made sure that she kept her eyes fixed on Liam, so that Jessica wouldn't think they were talking about her and she told Liam not to turn around under any circumstances. Not even for a second.

A few minutes later, Liam swallowed the last mouthful of his burger, wiped his mouth on his napkin and told Charlotte that he was going to go round to Jessica's house to get the jewellery back. The keys to all four of the houses owned by the Warkworth House Hotel were kept in the safe in his office, back at the hotel, but it wouldn't take him a minute to go and get them. He had to pass the hotel to get to Jessica's house, so it was just a small detour to collect the key.

Charlotte told him that she wasn't sure. It was risky. The man had muscles. He was a bruiser. A gym-goer. As they deliberated, Liam told Charlotte that he should go right now, as every passing minute is a precious minute that he needs to search the house and Charlotte told him that she wanted to get the jewellery back - because of the principle, not only because it was Linda's and she loved her - but she was worried. This could go wrong. She envisaged Liam spending the night in a police cell.

She watched Jessica and her man walk away from the bar and find a table at the other side of the pub, around the corner. Because the pub was L-shaped, they were no longer in view.

"Why don't you casually go to the toilets, say hello to her on your way passed and ask her if she has ordered some food?" said Liam. "Then we'll know how long they're going to be here."

"I can't do that," said Charlotte. "She'll think I'm just doing it to be nosy, so I can have a look at the bloke she's with."

"Well there's no harm in that, is there?"

Charlotte told him that she couldn't do it and if he was going to go to the house, he needed to go right now before she changed her mind and pinned him to the chair.

Liam jumped up and went to the bar. "That burger was amazing. Tell the chef, will you? Is it Josh on tonight?" The barman said that it was. "I can tell. He's the best. I don't know why, but he makes them better than anyone else. If that couple ordered them, you should tell them that they are in for a treat."

"Oh, they ordered the fish and chips," said the young barman.

"Maybe next time, talk them into having the burgers." The barman laughed and said that he would.

As Liam returned to the table, Charlotte was shaking her head. "That was bad," she said. "That was really bad."

"No time for that right now. You can criticise my acting skills another time. They've ordered food, that's all I wanted to find out, so they'll be here for at least an hour, possibly longer if they stay for more drinks or order a dessert."

"Okay, well what are you still doing here? Go! Go! Go!"

Liam bent down and kissed her. "Text me when they leave."

"What do you mean? I'm not staying here on my own," she protested.

"You'll have to. I need to know when they're potentially on their way back."

So Charlotte capitulated and pulled her phone out of her bag. While Liam was gone, at least she could catch up with Instagram. Although she appeared to be a relaxed customer, nonchalantly scrolling social media while she awaited her boyfriend's return, her insides were wound like a tight coil, her heart was beating much faster than it should and her palms had begun to sweat. She wasn't in the best position for a stake-out and she was terrified that she would miss them leaving and Liam would be caught in the house by Bruiser Boyfriend. She told herself to calm down. Jessica's table was out of view, but luckily she was sitting close to the door and as there was only one way out, she would be able to see when they left. She could do this.

Another couple came into the pub.

A man and his old sheepdog left.

Time ticked by, infuriatingly slowly.

After what seemed to be half an hour, but was in fact only ten minutes, Charlotte watched Josh appear from the kitchen, holding two large plates of fish and chips. He disappeared around the other side of the bar, presumably delivering them to Jessica's table. She sent a text to Liam, telling him that the food had been delivered. He replied with a smiley face emoji.

Charlotte finished her glass of wine and decided against ordering a third glass. Her nerves would welcome one, but she needed to keep her wits about her. Just as she was watching an Instagram reel of a bunch of cute dogs leaping into a lake somewhere in Canada, Jessica's gentleman friend appeared at the bar and ordered two more drinks. Charlotte kept her head down, doing her best impression of a competent spy on an extremely important mission. One which she was determined she was not going to cock up.

She was desperate for the toilet and was contemplating whether she would be able to walk past Jessica's table without attracting suspicion, after all, Jessica had no idea what was actually going on, and going to the toilet after a couple of glasses of wine was a normal everyday thing to do, when she received a text from Liam.

I've found the jewellery. Not even hidden. In the bathroom, next to the sink x

Great, get out quick! He has just ordered two more drinks, so I assume they have finished eating x replied Charlotte.

I want to find the money x said Liam.

No! You can't prove that it's Linda's money, even if you found some, so just leave it. Get out! X

Liam didn't reply. For the next few minutes, Charlotte had her phone open, waiting for a message to appear on her screen. When she could wait no longer, she left the pub, rushed outside and rang his phone. He picked up immediately.

"Tango Mike Foxtrot receiving. Are they still there? Over." he said.

"Stop pissing about," demanded Charlotte. "Yes, they are still there, but I can't wait any longer. I'm walking down Bridge Street. My heart can't take the stress. You know that Dr. Singh told me that I needed to keep stress to a minimum. You're killing me here."

Liam laughed. "Yes, dear," he said. "You're so cute when you exaggerate."

"And you're so annoying, you arsehole," she laughed. "Are you out of there yet?"

"Yes, I'm done, I'll meet you at the corner of Bridge Street near the bridge."

"I can see you now," said Charlotte. Liam waved to her from the end of the street and she quickened her pace, to reach him as soon as she could. "I can't believe we've just done that," she said as she reached him and wrapped her arms around his neck, holding him tight. "Fuck! Fuck! Fuck!" she said suddenly.

"What?" asked Liam, jumping back and holding her at arms' length.

"She's going to think she's been burgled and she's going to call the police and your fingerprints will be all over the place. Oh my God, what have we done?"

"Do you really think she'd do that? Criminals don't tend to involve the police too much, do they? And anyway, if they send that dickhead policeman that Linda dealt with, is he going to be on the ball enough to arrange forensics?"

"I don't know," said Charlotte. "But we need to cover all bases. You'll have to go back in and wipe down the surfaces."

"Stop panicking," said Liam. "I didn't touch anything but even so, I don't think she'll report it. How could she report the theft of something that wasn't hers in the first place? She won't do it."

"Really?" said Charlotte, desperately in need of reassurance that everything was going to be okay. "I'm not sure. Have you got any wine at yours?"

"Of course, I have."

"Take me home then. I need some more."

Chapter 28
Two Months Later

Despite the fact that it was still dark and the alarm wasn't due to go off for another two hours, Linda was wide awake. She lay in the quiet stillness of the early morning for a few minutes before she decided to get out of bed. Ordinarily, she would have turned over in bed, pulled the duvet up to her chin, and tried to sleep for another couple of hours, but today was far too exciting and she didn't want to miss a single minute of it. So sleep was abandoned.

Today was the day that had been circled in red pen on her calendar since January, the day that she and Charlotte were travelling to Portsmouth for the start of their holiday on their Mediterranean cruise. Their ship was due to leave port at four o'clock tomorrow afternoon, although they could get on board any time after ten o'clock. Linda planned to be there on the dot at ten and she had already told Charlotte that tonight, in their hotel in Portsmouth, they would be getting an early night, because it was very likely that she would be up at the crack of dawn in the morning.

To say she was excited would be the biggest under-statement. She tried to live each day in the moment, enjoying every day as a gift and savouring it, but throughout the last few weeks, she couldn't help silently praying each night for time to slip by slightly quicker than usual, to bring her to this momentous day sooner.

When she had booked the cruise, she had contemplated going in the summer, but the more research she did about the scorching temperatures of the Spanish and Italian cities, the more she knew that she had made the right choice to go later in the year. She wasn't interested in sunbathing. She did enough of that in her own back garden. She wanted to see all the beautiful cities in Europe, to wander around their narrow cobbled streets and peruse the delights of their shops and beautiful cathedrals, the extravagant harbours and promenades and she had chosen to go in November so that she could do all of that comfortably in the cooler temperatures.

She had bumped into Ava in the supermarket last week and had told her about her upcoming holiday, only because Ava had spotted her with a book in her hand, reading the blurb on the back, which said that it was the 'perfect holiday read'. After the initial niceties of how have you been, very well thank you, how are you, Ava had asked her whether she was going anywhere nice. She had probably presumed that Linda would tell her that she was going somewhere in the UK, somewhere not too far away. A place where someone like Linda would go, maybe Whitby or Scarborough. Somewhere easily accessible and English.

But Linda was very happy to tell her where she was going and with whom. For once, she didn't care that Ava was the village gossip. She could run and shout it from the rooftops, if she so desired. Linda wanted everyone to know that she was going on a cruise. And not one of your cheap party boat ones either, like she would have been forced to endure if Phil had taken her, not that he ever would have. No, hers was a posh one where the guests had to dress for dinner; where arriving for breakfast in bikinis or shorts was not acceptable. One where standards were high and the guests were expected to abide by the rules. In return, they were called Madam or Sir by the obsequious staff, who were more than happy to cater to their slightest whim.

Of course, Ava had been on several cruises and she spent more time than was necessary explaining to Linda how everything worked, what to expect and what she would be advised to see at each of the ports, when the ship docked. Linda bit down on her tongue. She wanted to tell her that she would find out for herself and she wanted every experience to be new, not second-hand. But seasoned travellers shared holiday experiences with each other, didn't they? It was perfectly normal to chat about the places they had been and things they had done. She told herself not to be so territorial about it. So she nodded and smiled and thanked Ava for her kind advice.

When Ava asked her what cruise company it was, Linda took great delight in telling her. Anyone who knew anything about cruising would know that Linda had not scrimped on the price and had chosen one of the most expensive and luxurious ships and Linda made sure that she knew that she would be occupying a cabin with a balcony. Ava had never been able to hide her emotions. Her face betrayed her feelings and Linda instantly knew what she was thinking. Puzzlement, envy, resentment, displeasure and yearning all expressed themselves clearly, before she forced them away and replaced them with a polite smile. "How lovely," she had said. "I hope you have an amazing time. We should have a catch-up when you get back." Linda said that they should and told her that she must be getting on, as she had lots to do.

She had no intention of catching up with Ava, other than when forced to do so in the tinned food aisle of the supermarket. She smiled to herself as she walked away, imagining herself to be one of those 'ladies who lunch', the ones who give air kisses to all and sundry while insisting that they 'should do lunch sometime'. She had always wanted to be one of those women, cossetted and cared for by a kind and wealthy husband, with nothing more important to think about than the fulfillment of a social diary.

Now, as she waited for the kettle to boil, she checked Storm's Instagram profile to see whether she had posted anything new in the twelve hours since she had last checked. Storm was currently in Stockholm, where she was spending a few nights before flying on to Berlin, as part of her tour of Europe. She had deferred her final year at university and was travelling with a friend, Stefanie, who was on her course. She claimed that she was visiting art galleries and museums and learning about local artists, past and present, in each of the places that she visited, which she had insisted would lead to a better mark in her final year assessment. That may be true, but Linda knew that she was also taking plenty of time to enjoy herself. The plethora of photographs of espresso martinis and glasses of sparkling strawberry-decorated Prosecco in crowded bars told her that they were both having a great time.

Today, there was a new photograph of her in a dimly lit street, walking away from the camera. She was wearing knee-length boots and a thick dark winter coat. The huge hood was pulled over her head and the tote bag that Linda had bought her for her journey was casually hanging from her left arm. Flutters of snow were gently falling. Underneath the photograph, Storm had written the caption, "Winter has officially arrived in Stockholm. The city always looks beautiful in the evening but tonight, when the snow appeared, it was breathtaking. I hope it sticks around. I love it! #ilovesnow."

Linda smiled as she looked at the photograph. She knew how much Storm loved snow and how much she would have enjoyed her walk in it last night. The photograph was beautiful.

Their journey had begun in Paris. They had rented a small apartment that they found on Airbnb close to the city centre and, although it hadn't had a view of the Eiffel Tower or the River Seine, Storm told Linda that it was directly above the best bakery she had ever visited. Every morning, the delicious sugary smells wafted into their apartment and filled the air, forcing her to scramble into her over-sized t-shirt and leggings and run downstairs, where she would order two warm pain au chocolat and two strong coffees. Then she and Stefanie would sit on their beds, eating their breakfast and planning the activities for the day.

After a week, they moved on and had already been to Amsterdam, Hamburg and Copenhagen. They had now been in Stockholm for two days and were staying in a hotel in the middle of the city, so that they could walk everywhere.

Storm was having the time of her life. She was documenting her adventures in a blog on her new website called The Artistic Traveller, which Charlotte had advised should be made into a book when she got home. Between them, she and Stefanie were taking some amazing photographs, which she would be able to sell as limited edition prints when she got back.

Linda loved scrolling through her photographs and reading her posts. It had become part of her morning routine. They had spoken on the phone a dozen times in the past month and each time, Linda felt them getting closer. She was pleased that she was fulfilling her dream, but she also couldn't wait for her to get back. Despite the fact that a few months ago she had no idea that she existed, she had quickly become a part of Linda's life and she was missing her.

If she had her way, Storm would move into the house next door, which had been empty since Jessica had moved out. Linda would love to be able to see her every day, but she kept her thoughts to herself. She was determined not to put any pressure on her and in any event, she knew that she would be going back to Edinburgh to finish her degree next year. After that, the world was her oyster, as they said. If she chose to relocate to somewhere in Europe, then she would go with Linda's love and blessing and Linda would visit her as often as possible. With her as yet unused passport, the world was Linda's oyster too.

She poured boiling water onto her teabag and added a splash of milk. Then, taking her tea with her, she wandered into the living room to double-check that her passport, her purse and her jewellery were all safe. Following the incident of Jessica stealing the money from her, she had chosen a new hiding place. Her purse and any spare cash were no longer hidden in the cupboard above the kettle, which Charlotte and Storm had both told her was too obvious and would be one of the first places that any burglar would look. She now hid them behind her books on the third row down on her tall bookcase. She knew that nowhere, except a locked safe, was one hundred percent safe but she felt better that she had chosen a slightly more inconspicuous place.

She removed her copy of Memoirs of a Geisha and took out her valuable possessions. They were safe and sound, where she left them. She smiled to herself as she knew that she didn't need to put them back, as they would be going with her to Portsmouth today. She walked back to her bedroom and put the purse and the passport in her travel bag. She left the two boxes containing her necklace and bracelet in the middle of the bed. She would be wearing them later and had no intention of taking them off for the next two weeks.

She couldn't believe that Liam and Charlotte had managed to get them back for her. Liam, in particular, had taken a massive risk in going into Jessica's house while she was having dinner with a man who apparently was built like a full-back from the English rugby team. His crooked nose was evidence that he didn't mind getting into an altercation or two. But luckily, although he had stayed overnight at Jessica's house, he left early the following morning, and as soon as Linda heard his car engine and was sure that he had left, she phoned Liam to let him know. Within ten minutes, he was at Jessica's door with her eviction notice.

Linda could hear Jessica's raised voice through her open window, but Liam had calmly and quietly told her that if she didn't vacate the property by the end of tomorrow, he would be ringing the police and reporting the theft of Linda's jewellery and cash.

"I knew it!" Jessica had shouted. "I knew someone had been in and taken it. Did you take the fucking money too?"

The cheek of it, Linda thought. She hadn't heard Liam's reply but he told her afterwards that he had said that he didn't know what she was talking about. Linda hadn't got all of her money back, but Liam had found sixty pounds thrown haphazardly into the cutlery drawer, which he had taken and returned to Linda. She had kissed him and told him that this was the second time he had saved her and he was her hero. The first time, he had stood up to Phil when Linda was moving out and had made the experience a lot easier than it would have been if he hadn't been there.

Last week, Linda and Charlotte had been having a glass of wine at Charlotte's house and Linda reminded her, again, what a gem Liam was and how she was very much looking forward to the wedding, which had been booked for 22nd April next year. Charlotte said that she knew how lucky she was.

Then, unexpectedly, Linda said that she wished that she had her own special someone and that it would be nice to take a plus-one to her wedding, although she was enjoying having the freedom to be able to make decisions without answering to someone and without having constant criticism. Charlotte told her that she needed to get out of her mind that not all relationships are like hers and Phil's. She had been unlucky that night when she met him, but now it was time for her luck to change and she could meet someone new. She wanted to add that she believed that a person made their own luck and that Linda had sealed her own fate when she decided to stay with Phil, rather than walking away from him years ago. But Linda already knew that and reminding her would only open old wounds and cause pain. In her next relationship, Charlotte would be there, to make sure that she was treated like the queen that she was. She deserved the best.

Without wanting to appear too enthusiastic, Charlotte suggested that Linda might want to try internet dating. "Never in a million years," said Linda, shaking her head emphatically. "I want to look into a man's soul, to see what kind of person he is, before I agree to go on a date. You can't get that through a screen."

"Well, there's slim pickings around here," Charlotte had said. "You need to cast your net wide in order to catch the best fish. That's why they call it the world wide web. The clue's in the name."

That's when Linda told her about the man that had been 'checking her out' in the pub, that day when she had first met Storm. He had definitely shown that he was interested in her. He had been flirting, although very surreptitiously, and had raised his glass to her before he took a drink. She hadn't known what to make of it at the time, so she had looked away and concentrated on talking to Storm. But then she had seen him in the bookshop a couple of weeks ago when she went in to get some more books for her holiday. He did a double-take and she smiled at him.

"I didn't mean to," she said. "But it was though my face took over and just did it instinctively. That was it, he saw it as a green light and came straight over to me."

"You're joking," said Charlotte. "Why didn't you tell me about this? You can't keep secrets like this to yourself."

"Saying hello to a man in a shop is hardly newsworthy," said Linda.

"So what happened? Did he chat you up? Did he ask for your number?"

"Should he have done?" asked Linda.

Charlotte frowned. She wasn't sure what was going on. She had never seen this coquettish side of Linda. She said that she was excited to hear more about this handsome stranger who would rescue the lonely old widow from years of unfulfillment.

"You cheeky bugger," said Linda, laughing. "I'm not an old widow! He was definitely older than me. Still very handsome though."

Linda described a tall man with grey curling hair. His imposing stance told her that he had his fair share of self-esteem and confidence with women. She said that his name was Jeff Anderson and that he told her he was originally from Dundee, but he had lived in Northumberland for the past five years, ever since he and his wife had divorced. They chatted for quite a while, but Linda eventually told him that she had to go shopping, as she was going on holiday soon, so they said their goodbyes.

"Jeff Anderson? Tall man, about sixty, grey hair?" asked Charlotte.

"Yes," said Linda.

"Slight Scottish accent, but very well spoken, like he'd been to Gordonstoun?"

"Yes," said Linda.

"Well dressed gentleman?"

"Yes, yes, yes," said Linda, smiling at Charlotte's excited face.

"That's my bloody landlord!" she squealed. "He's a lovely man. He owns my office building and the one next door, which he rents out as a holiday cottage."

Charlotte said she was annoyed with herself for not thinking of him sooner. She could have introduced Linda to him. They would be perfect together. She jumped up and ran into the kitchen and reappeared holding the bottle of wine. As she topped up their glasses, she told Linda that she needed to have a think. She would arrange something. She could find out when he was next due to do a visit to the office, or she could call him about something that she needed him to look at, a pretend leaky tap or something, and Linda could be there at the same time, looking beautiful and available, of course. As Charlotte chatted on, Linda appeared nonchalant and told her that he seemed like a nice man but she wasn't too bothered about another relationship, while secretly her heartbeat quickened with excitement.

The following day, Charlotte telephoned Jeff, telling him that she thought there were mice upstairs in one of the rooms and could he please come over and have a look. She hadn't seen any droppings, but she thought she had heard something and she was frightened that they might be in the loft. As she knew he would, he told her that it was no trouble and he would come over immediately. She told him that she had clients to see, but if possible could he come over around noon. So he did. Five minutes later, Linda walked into the office wearing a casual black linen dress and beige shoes. Her make-up was perfect! The light brown eyeshadow, plenty of black mascara and bronzer, and her new hair colour made her look stunning. Charlotte had lent her a black Miu Miu handbag to complete the look.

When Jeff came downstairs, telling Charlotte that she was safe, he couldn't find any evidence of mice, Linda was waiting in the reception area. She managed to look surprised and told him that she was a close friend of Charlotte and that they were about to have lunch. Charlotte told her that she would be another ten minutes; if she didn't mind, she needed to make an urgent phone call, and she left Jeff and the ever so slightly flustered Linda alone.

By the time Charlotte reappeared, Jeff had asked Linda out to dinner. He had given her his business card and had asked Linda to phone him whenever she had minute and let him know when she was free. Linda wanted to tell him that there was no need to phone him, she was free tonight. And tomorrow night. And the next night. But over lunch, Charlotte warned her of the perils of appearing too keen. Men like to chase, she had said. Even if they know that their catch is certain, they still like to feel as though there is some kind of pursuit. Play the game and she can have the prize.

Linda had telephoned him that night, Monday, and told him that she was free on Saturday. "Don't let him think that you're waiting at home with an empty diary," said Charlotte. "You're an exciting social butterfly and he will be lucky to pin you down." Linda's diary was empty, except for her meeting with the book club, which she would have been willing to forego. But she took Charlotte's advice and waited until Saturday.

On their first date, he collected her in his Range Rover and drove her to the beautiful seafood restaurant in Alnmouth, where she had been with Charlotte and Liam. He was so friendly and amiable that her nerves settled quickly and she began to enjoy herself. After the meal, when she got up to use the toilet, she was pleased that she could tell him that she knew where they were, thank you, and that she had been here before with friends. If he wanted to think of her as a social butterfly, who frequented the best restaurants on a regular basis, then so be it.

When she returned to the table, he had already paid the bill and completely dismissed her offer to pay next time. For a second, she was disappointed, as she desperately wanted to see him again, but he told her that he was an old-fashioned type of bloke and if he was taking a lady on a date, then he would like to pay. She smiled and asked him if there was going to be a second date and he said that he sincerely hoped so.

He drove her back home and kept the car engine running, which she took as a sign that he had no assumptions that he would be invited in. Linda had no intention of inviting him in. Not yet anyway. She leaned over and kissed him on the cheek and thanked him for a lovely evening, but when she didn't quickly pull away, he put his hand on the back of her head and kissed her on the mouth. Linda never knew that kisses could feel that good and didn't want it to stop. But she had to play the game, Charlotte had reminded her before she went out, and she mustn't appear too keen.

But he was keen too and invited her to have Sunday lunch with him the following day. Since then, they had spoken on the phone every day and she was very much looking forward to seeing him more when she got back from her holiday. She wanted to introduce him to Charlotte and Liam and, of course, to Storm when she got back from her travels. She had told Jeff that she had a stepdaughter and had explained that she was a result of her husband having an affair. They had been walking on the beach on Sunday afternoon after a huge roast beef lunch in The Masons Arms. Jeff had stopped walking and had pulled Linda towards him in a comforting hug. He kissed her tenderly and told her that her husband had been a fool and if he had taken the time to see what was in front of him, he wouldn't ever have let her go. She hadn't yet told him that Phil had been abusive and that she was happy to be let go. Relieved in fact. That conversation was one to be had when they knew each other a little better.

But right now, she needed to get ready. She had a cruise to go on.

THE END

Author's Note

When I finished writing Just Breathe, I had no intention of writing a sequel. In my view, the story ended happily and the reader was left to use their imagination as to what happened next. At the end of the book, Charlotte and Liam had just got back together and Linda had filed for divorce and had started to look for her own house. I was honestly surprised when people began asking for a sequel - family members, friends at my book club, people on Facebook, people on Instagram and even a couple of reviews on Amazon mentioned it - so I began to consider it.

Many months before I put pen to paper (or rather fingertips to keyboard), I let the ideas fester and tried to imagine what the characters might get up to.

Linda, obviously, needed to blossom away from the confines of Phil. She needed to do more of the things that she loved and hadn't been able to do when under his control - read more, travel more, just live more. Charlotte, on the other hand, having already lived her younger life to the full, needed to slow down and appreciate the beauty of her surroundings. Her life in Warkworth was the exact opposite of her old life in London. Would she be able to cope with that, or would she yearn for the excitement of a city? I came to the conclusion that she would want to slow down and smell the roses, as they say.

But that would be boring, wouldn't it? I needed to drop a few bombs. I hope that I managed to do that and I hope that you weren't disappointed with the direction that both women decided to take. But what about the other characters in the book? Maybe there should be a story about them?

If you would like to know where Linda's various quotes are from, here they are:

Chapter one
"When one burns one's bridges, what a very nice fire it makes."
Dylan Thomas

Chapter Five
"Uneasy lies the head that wears a crown."
Henry IV, Part II, William Shakespeare

Chapter Seven
"Don't worry about tomorrow, for tomorrow will bring worries of its own. Today's trouble is enough for today."
Gospel of Matthew, New Testament Bible

Chapter Twelve
"Oh beware my lord of jealousy! It is the green-eyed monster which doth mock the meat it feeds on."
Othello, William Shakespeare

Chapter Twenty
"Rain, midnight rain, nothing but the wild rain on this bleak hut, and solitude, and me."
Edward Thomas

In chapter twenty-seven, I wanted to use the phrase scot-free and wasn't sure whether it should have a hyphen, or did scot have one t or two. So I googled it and various websites appeared, telling me the origin of the phrase. I love stuff like that. To me, it's fascinating the way that language evolves over time, so I read all of them. They are different that I've still no idea which one of them is true, so I thought I'd share them with you and you can make up your own mind.

Phrases.org.uk – "Dred Scott was a black slave born in Virginia, USA in 1799. In several celebrated court cases, right up to the USA Surpreme Court in 1857, he attempted to gain his freedom. These cases all failed but Scott was later made a free man by his so-called owners, the Blow family."

After reading this, I decided that I needed to think of another phrase, as I didn't want to use one that was associated with the slave trade. But then I saw the other websites..

Theguardian.com/notesandqueries - "SKOT was an early Icelandic and Old Norse word for "payment" or "tax". It came into Middle English as "bescot", referring specifically to a customary tax paid to a lord, bailiff, or sheriff, and into Old French as "escot", and ultimately into modern English as "scot". Thus "scot-free" literally means "exempt from tax"; it has since been broadened to indicate "exempt from punishment" - as in "the prisoner got off scot-free"."

Knowyourphrase.com – "The origin of the phrase 'scot-free' is believed to be from somewhere in the 12ᵗʰ century. You might ask: 'What is a scot?' According to Robert Hendrickson's *The Facts on File Encyclopedia of Word and Phrase Origins,* a scot 'was a municipal tax in 12ᵗʰ-century England'. Hence, is someone were to avoid paying their taxes, they were getting away scot-free. In other words, they were getting away tax-free. Eventually, this phrase went on to describe, not just the avoidance of taxes, but people who avoided any sort of punishment or precarious situation; they get away freely, without harm."

.

Printed in Great Britain
by Amazon